RACHEL LOUISE DOVE is a wife
Yorkshire. She has always loved writing and has had previous
success as a self-published author. Rachel is the winner of the
Mills & Boon & *Prima Magazine* Flirty Fiction competition and
won The Writers Bureau Writer of the Year Award in 2016. She
is a qualified adult education tutor specialising in child develop-
ment and autism. In 2018 she founded the Rachel Dove Bursary,
giving one working-class writer each year a fully funded place on
the Romantic Novelists' Association New Writers' Scheme.

Also by Rachel Dove

The Forever House

RACHEL DOVE

ONE PLACE. MANY STORIES

HQ
An imprint of HarperCollins*Publishers* Ltd
1 London Bridge Street
London SE1 9GF

www.harpercollins.co.uk

HarperCollins*Publishers*
1st Floor, Watermarque Building, Ringsend Road
Dublin 4, Ireland

This paperback edition 2022

1
First published in Great Britain by
HQ, an imprint of HarperCollins*Publishers* Ltd 2022

ISBN: 9780008480974

For all the scribblers and dreamers

Prologue

'Well, Mum, here goes nothing. Wish me luck, okay? I love you.'

Isaac sent a kiss up to the heavens and clicked on the record button on his computer. Resting his elbows on his computer desk next to his keyboard, he took a deep breath and sat back into his high-backed gaming chair.

'Hi, guys,' he said to the screen, ruffling his short brown hair as he tried to steady his nerves. 'I know that my subscribers are used to me doing gaming videos, and sharing my animations, but today I kinda wanted to talk about something else.'

Leaning forward, he reached just out of shot, picking up a photo set in a dark wood frame from the desk, which housed his monitor, phone, and keyboard. A pile of schoolbooks sat off on the other side of the desk on a dresser, a pen pot overflowing with pens and pencils next to it. His room was neat, well, neat for an eleven-year-old boy anyway. The walls were freshly painted, his dad having had the whole house painted cream before they moved in just six weeks ago. It was different to the poster-plastered room he'd left behind in London, more spacious but less personal. A blank canvas, which Isaac felt summed up their lives now in Yorkshire.

London was his home; or had been for his whole life before

this. It was quieter here, greener. When he was back from school and his dad was home from work, it felt too quiet. He'd walked around sometimes, to kill the boredom, and the village was nice, but quiet. He hadn't seen any kids hanging around. He thought of the friends he'd had back home, right on his doorstep. Yet another thing that was proving to be an adjustment.

He looked from the screen to the object in his hands. A photo frame, three happy people staring out at him from behind the smudged glass. He turned it towards the camera, holding it up and pointing to the man in the trio. A handsome, smiling man.

'This is my dad, Calvin. He's a graphic designer. He designs for huge companies, and housing developments. He's working on the new eco shopping centre project in town at the moment, so you might see him around. He's really clever. He taught me everything I know about computers.' The smile on his face dimmed a little as he moved his finger to the woman in the photo; in his dad's arms. 'That's my mum. She died a couple of years ago. We've just moved house. We came to Yorkshire from London a few weeks ago. Dad said it was for work, but I think it was because Mum died.'

Isaac bit at his lip, a nervous gesture that he had been doing far too much lately. He was getting a sore patch on the inside of his lip, but he couldn't quite stop doing it. It helped his brain stop feeling like it was swirling around like a whirlwind inside his skull. He took a deep breath and, putting the picture back, tried and failed to look at the camera. *I hope this works out. Dad is going to kill me if not. Then he'll REALLY be alone.* He had to be brave. Or, like his mate Kai said, "grow some kahunas". He pushed his worry aside and faced the lens once more.

'That's why I'm making this video. Because Dad's sad, and I don't know how else to help him really. Mum made him happy, and he misses her. My mum's not here anymore, but I think he needs someone. It's just me and him now. He pretends that he's okay, but I know he's not.' He paused as he heard his name being called. 'That's him,' he said, urgently now. 'He's made dinner.' He frowned, his face furrowing as he thought of what was to come. 'He's a rubbish cook too. God knows what he's made tonight.' He heard a clatter of pans, and a yelp before more clattering ensued. 'He's burned himself twice this week and set fire to the kitchen trying to cook a roast dinner last Sunday.' He laughed at the memory, his whole face lighting up. 'We ordered pizza instead. It was well lush, but we can't live on pizza forever.'

'Isaac, off the game! Dinner!'

His dad's voice filtered up the stairs to his room, and Isaac leaned in close to the camera. 'I've got to go. He doesn't know I'm doing this, but we need help. I want to find a girlfriend for Dad, and I'm not old enough to go on dating sites, so I made this video instead.' He grabbed the photo, pushing the picture of his dad's smiling face towards the camera.

'If you can cook, and want a boyfriend with a lovely kid—' he beamed at the camera then, giving his audience his best angelic look '—then reply to this video. He's a great guy, and I'm tired of seeing him sad. I'll be doing more videos, but if you like what you see, get in touch. Please. You must be nice, like children, and have a job of your own. My friend Robbie from back home said that some women dig gold for a boyfriend, and I don't think we want one like that. Send a photo too, because Robbie said that some people lie online, and I don't want my dad to get hurt.'

He could hear footsteps on the stairs now, and he turned his head towards the door. Taking a piece of paper from his desk, he held it up to the camera. On it was a hashtag and an email address.

#cupidcrusadeforcalvin

Albrightfamilyseeknewmember@gmail.com

'Reply to this email if you want to get in touch! If you know my dad, please don't snitch. My dad will ground me forever. Isaac out. Bye.'

Isaac checked that his video was being processed, then he hit send. He just managed to jab at the screen-off button on the monitor before his bedroom door creaked open.

'Isaac? Didn't you hear me, buddy?'

Calvin stood in the doorway, a food-splattered white apron tied haphazardly over his casual blue denim jeans and black T-shirt.

Isaac turned to his dad, snapping a photo of him standing in the doorway with his mobile phone.

'Nice look, Dad. What's that down your front?'

Calvin half fell for the deflection, looking down sheepishly at the red and brownish stains down his "kiss the cook" apron. It was one of his leaving presents from the firm he'd worked for in London. They'd made him a "single dad survival kit". The gesture had brought a lump to his throat that had made it hard to swallow. It was both touching and scary, all wrapped up in a big wicker basket. *Was that really what he was now? They'd made little comments before, but now his colleagues had seemingly written him off. Did they think he was mad? He did have people in London. They both did. Seemingly, the fact it was just going to be the two of them meant that he was just a label, not a man. Even after two years, they still didn't quite understand.*

He didn't like any of the new labels he seemed to have acquired over the last couple of years. AD. After Diane. Widower. Single dad. Lone parent. Even the bill from the council with the one-person discount on it depressed him. It all reminded him that his life, the one he'd been living anyway, had been cut short when his wife's was. It had taken him a while to realise he was still breathing, at the time. He'd felt like the first full breath he took was the day after the funeral; the juggernaut of organising it had gotten in the way of thinking, grieving. He'd needed the numbness, but it lingered in him still. The labels didn't help. They all served to make him feel finished, washed up somehow. He didn't want to feel like that. He was still young (well, youngish, as Isaac had pointed out).

He had his own teeth and hair, and judging from Instagram, that was somewhat rare these days. Men took a lot more interest in their looks nowadays, and he'd been happily domesticated. He was out of the loop. He felt like people dressed a lot differently to when he was at uni. Women scared him sometimes. Still, he had a career, he loved his family and he slowed down to avoid squirrels in the road. He not only put out the bins, but he recycled as well. He was a dab hand with a cordless drill, and he washed his own pants. Women had rated those qualities in a man at one point in time, not whether they could enter the *Love Island* Villa and crack on successfully. All the same, he didn't quite feel like he had parted with fun forever, even though he wasn't twenty-one anymore. He still had a personality, right? He was still FUN, a cool dad even. *Lone ranger* was far cooler than *lone parent*.

That was the thing about growing up. Your life never turned out in quite the way you thought it would. One small piece changing could alter the rest of a person's life in every way possible. He hated how alone and boxed off he felt. He still had a life, one worth living.

The leaving party the firm had thrown him when he'd announced he and Isaac were upping sticks was a kind, if slightly insensitive, gesture. He'd been taken out for a long lunch with the boss on his last Friday and, when they returned, the place had been decorated. There were drinks and food, a lovely cake, and everyone showed up to see him off. Cal had been embarrassed, as ever not wanting a fuss. They were a good bunch of people; they'd known Diane too. She'd popped into the office lots of times over the years; meeting him for lunch and swinging by with donuts for the team when she knew they were up against it with a deadline.

They looked at him differently after her death. Sometimes they stopped talking when he entered the room, and when the basketful of single dad goodies had been "wheeled out", Cal knew he had made the right decision. He and Isaac needed to be in a new place, one where he wasn't Diane's widower, and one where Isaac wasn't always thought of as the boy who'd lost his mum. They needed to start anew.

On the day of the basket, he'd held it together until Isaac was in bed and then he'd cried. Proper bawling. He knew they meant well, but they saw him differently now. His wife's death was always in their thoughts when they worked with him. And they worked together so closely as a team that there was no escape. It wasn't something they could relate to either. Not many could, and he wondered where all those people were. People died every day. Where were the ones left behind? Did they feel invisible now, like he did? Did they just shut their grief off, like he'd tried to do for so long?

'Dad?' Isaac was frowning at him now, and he knew he'd gone off into his own head again. He hated doing that in front of Isaac. He snapped himself out of his pity party for one and smiled at his son.

'Dinner kind of got away from me. Did you take a photo just then?'

'No,' Isaac said innocently, putting his phone face down onto the desk. 'What did you cook?'

'Sausage surprise.' Cal ran a hand through his hair.

Isaac groaned. Loudly.

'Daaa-aaaad … again?'

Calvin shrugged. 'Yeah, well, I forgot to put the sausages in too, so it's more of a baked bean surprise.'

Isaac grimaced, and Calvin's face fell.

'Sorry. I'm sure it will be nice.' He crossed the room to hug his dad. They both stopped at the last minute, laughing as they looked at the stains adorning the apron. Calvin took it off, rolling it up carefully and tucking it under his arm.

'I tell you what, let's go for drive-thru instead. Deal?'

Isaac's relief was palpable. 'Sounds good. If I eat any more beans, I might end up farting in class.'

Calvin laughed, ruffling his son's hair with his hand. When he pulled away, he noticed a bean sat in his parting. He pulled it off his head, flicking it into the wastepaper bin by the door.

'Farting in class is never cool. I must admit, I have been feeling a bit flatulent at the office lately.' He went to say something else but thought better of it. 'Come on then, let's get ready. I might even spring for ice-cream if you promise not to laugh at my cooking again.'

Isaac screwed up his face. 'Sorry, no guarantees. I reserve the right to poke fun, or vomit. Or maybe both.'

'And pass wind, apparently,' Calvin joked, and Isaac pushed his palm against his mouth and made a loud noise. Calvin followed suit, and the pair of them dissolved into making silly noises and laughing with each other. Once the laughter had died down, and Isaac was still breathless, Calvin went to leave.

'Right, in the car in ten, okay, buddy?'

'Okay,' Isaac replied, already diving under the bed to retrieve his discarded trainers. 'Hurry up!'

'I will.' Calvin smiled and closed the door behind him, then sagged behind the wood. That was the first time they'd laughed together, carefree, for a while now. It made his heart sing, but it didn't last long. He still felt like he was a big fat failure. Downstairs, the pan he'd left to slowly congeal was one of his better efforts, and that didn't say much for his culinary skills of late.

He'd never been much of a cook. Diane had always been the chef of the house, ever since their university days. He'd still have been living on Super Noodles and burnt toast if it hadn't been for her. Now they'd left London, he was really trying to get better. He had lists. Lists of things he wanted to get sorted. He just needed to start ticking things off. He needed to start making this place a home for him and his boy. Grabbing a jumper from his bedroom, he looked around as if for the first time. It was pretty bare and unloved. He just slept in here really, got changed for work. Maybe if he actually did some of the jobs on the list, he'd feel better too. Perhaps then he wouldn't feel so reluctant to get out of bed in the morning and start the day.

Most nights he ended up falling asleep on the couch with the cat, eventually making his way up to the empty, lonely bedroom. It had been two years since Diane had passed, and while the grief was manageable, the loneliness wasn't. He knew that Isaac felt it too, but he didn't know how to talk about it with him. His own father had been rather stoic when his mother passed. He'd adopted a kind of "suck it up" mentality, but he didn't want that for Isaac. He didn't want to be that kind of father; he never had been before. They'd always had the best relationship. Maybe Diane had been the glue; maybe that was why they'd come unstuck of late.

Coming back to his hometown was supposed to be a fresh start, but even that was starting to feel like a misstep. He didn't even have any family here. Above ground anyway. He wasn't sure why he even felt like this was home anymore, but packing up his life in London, taking a new job up North, had felt like they were moving towards something. As he pulled out a sweater from his dresser drawer, and threw his dirty clothes into the hamper, he remembered something. How happy he'd been here as a kid. How homesick he'd felt heading off to university. Of course, he'd had something to be homesick for back then. *Someone.*

Shrugging off the memory, he pulled on the sweater, hearing the front door go and Isaac heading to the car. Grabbing a pair of joggers, he shoved his feet into his comfortable tattered slippers, and headed out to get dinner with his son. He needed to pull it together, and he needed to do it fast. This was home now, and he wanted them to be happy here. Like he was, once upon a time.

When he thought of his own childhood, growing up in the sleepy town of Hebblestone, set amongst the hills of Yorkshire, he had fond memories. Of his parents, who had passed before their time, of school days and bike rides at the weekends. Football on a Saturday. A normal life, full of friends and fun. Or so it seemed to him anyway. When he had left for university, he'd felt as though he'd been ripped in half. Funny how some things come full circle. And how some things just didn't. Some stories were cut tragically short. Some of the most memorable moments in a person's life were simply a footnote in their life stories.

He felt like he and Isaac were writing a new story now, but something was missing. *I thought we might find it here. Start at the beginning and all that.* He'd toyed with the idea of putting a pin in the map, starting fresh somewhere completely new, but he'd quickly dismissed it. He'd felt the call of home, as daft as that sounded to his own ears.

He wondered how much of the younger him had been hidden away in the man he was now. Maybe it was one of the reasons he'd decided to uproot both their lives in London and come back. He didn't really know for sure, but the more he walked London, the more shadows he saw. Ghosts of the past. Not haunting him but reminding him of happier times perhaps. When he had been happier. His life with Diane had been amazing, but he'd blinked and it was over. Truly over. Not broken up over, not left hating some ex-wife who'd broken his heart. Diane was gone, and he was left.

He and Isaac had been tiptoeing around their house in London for so long, not wanting to change anything that Diane loved; not wanting to throw a ratty cushion away because she'd chosen it. The house held ghosts, echoes of the life that would never be there again, and in the end, he'd had to get out too. His friends were her friends; university bonding them for so many years. Through studies and fresher parties to mortgage and job chasing, marriages and kids. Now he was the widower, and he knew that his friends, their friends, had done their best, but it just wasn't the same. He knew it, and so did they. He had to leave.

In the aftermath of those dark days, more and more he had thought back to when he was happy. Before he left home, licking his wounds from an unspoken and unrequited love he never thought he would get over. Till the minute he met Diane on campus and his foolish heart had taken the leap once more. He didn't regret a thing, but being here, as odd as it was, felt right. Right-ish. It was early days, as his old dad would say, and he was willing to buy into his father's wisdom. He did wonder what his father would have made of the move – and what his mother would have thought. They'd wished him the best when he left, and supported his every step, but they were gone now too, and it was another loss he still felt acutely. He'd laid flowers with Isaac the day they'd arrived in town. He'd pointed out his childhood home to Isaac that same day. It had felt like taking the DeLorean for a spin.

The honk of the car horn outside broke him out of his reverie, and he headed down the stairs to his waiting son. As long as they were together, everything else would fall into place. He hoped. After everything they had been through, having hope in itself was both a huge surprise to him, and a sign that maybe there was life in the old dog yet. A fresh start, back where he started, was worth a shot.

He grabbed his coat from the hook near the front door, dropping the latch as he headed out to spend time with Isaac. Make some new memories, ghost-free. As he got into the car, his son moaning that he was starving, he thought of the lists. He'd start tomorrow. He was settled in at work; Isaac was enjoying his new school. It was time. He brushed the thought aside as they drove away, knowing deep down the list would probably stay unbegun.

Chapter 1

The groom, looking resplendent in a hand-stitched Italian ivory suit, complete with gold waistcoat and elegant gilded cravat, was misty-eyed as he heard the impressive ornate wood doors open at the back of the beautifully arranged church. The pews, matching him with ivory flowers and golden bows festooned on the end of each aisle, were full of expectant guests, their eyes on the same spot. As he turned, catching sight of his bride, the tears began unabated, as a collective 'aaah' rang out amongst the couple's nearest and dearest.

Wearing an original heart neckline ivory dress, from the collection at Boothroyd Bridal, York, and followed by her niece Tilly, a flower girl dressed in a gold floaty dress, and bridesmaids in the form of four of the bride's nursing colleagues, all eyes were on the beautiful bride. As she walked down the aisle, the groom shed a single tear, viewing the woman he was about to pledge his life to, forever …

'Jesus Christ, Emily, it's a wedding announcement, not a bloody Harlequin romance. He's probably already shagged half the bridesmaids!'

Emily rolled her green eyes and shoved her mate and long-time colleague Beth away from her cynical perch, which was currently over her shoulder, peering at and mocking the words she was typing onto her computer screen.

11

'Sod off, Beth! You wouldn't know a Harlequin romance if it hit you in the face, so stop bashing it. And where did you come from? You're like the bloody grim reaper, popping up and scaring the crap out of me every five minutes!' She thrust an elbow out at her annoying friend and heard a satisfying screech as she connected with soft flesh. No one else in their screen-divided beige office batted an eyelid at them.

'Ahh!' Beth reeled back as Emily turned on her swivel chair behind her. Beth held a hand at her right rather voluptuous boob, giving it a rub as if she were trying to get a genie to come forth and grant all her wishes. 'Leave Kendra out of it!'

'You are so strange,' Emily retorted as Beth sat down at her desk, which was directly behind Emily's. 'And don't name your tits. I told you, it's just weird.'

'Well, my Dave would disagree, wouldn't he, Kendra?'

'Kendra and Kendall are downright weird names for your breasts if you ask me. And you've ruined Kendal mint cake for me forever.'

Beth cackled like a witch, scooting her chair back under her desk.

'Good, it tastes like foot cream anyway. Are you really going to submit that sentimental clap-trap? Joanna will never go for it, you know; she never does.'

Emily turned back to her screen, puffing her dark brown fringe out of her face.

'I know, but she said if I upped my game for the next couple of months, she might consider me for the features section again. I can't write weddings forever. I know you love writing obituaries like the Queen of Darkness, but I don't want to be still doing this when I'm forty. And we still have to run the rest of the advertising section; I'm writing copy for sunbeds and second-hand cots half the time.'

'I know, forty and still not married. That just smacks of Miss Havisham. I can imagine you going full *27 Dresses* soon, what with all your work outfits.'

'Shurrup, I will be married by then. Besides, a modern woman doesn't need a man. Or a ring. It's not a prerequisite to being happy, you know.'

She heard Beth's squeaky chair swivel back into her direction, and she turned to see a pitying look on her colleague's perfectly made-up face.

'Oh really? Just realised that, did you? Did Tim finally set the date then?'

'Well … no, but we did talk about maybe looking at our diaries …'

Beth's unimpressed face said it all.

'Oh, shut up, Beth, we're engaged. People don't just get engaged for the fun of it, you know.'

'Telling me to shut up won't change the fact that your engagement has lasted longer than most marriages, including the loved-up saps you write about. That one at the Country Club last month was in the news section the other week. The groom's going to court for punching his dad. Apparently, the dad gave the bride more than a speech!' She cackled again, slapping her trouser-clad knee at her own joke. Emily pouted at her but said nothing. To be honest, she'd seen the bride in flagrante behind the staircase. She'd even herded the groom out of the way, distracting him by asking about some details she already had for the article. She did think (hope, pray and perform a rain dance) it might just be a case of one champagne too many. Obviously not.

'Oh, Emily, I was only joking, but come on. You don't need a big day, if money's the problem. Dave and I went to the registry office and down the Nag's Head after. We had a right party. We've lasted ten years, and I still don't want to murder him in his sleep. It's out there – you don't need all the bells and whistles.'

'I know that,' Emily said quietly, slowly deleting the romantic tone from her latest piece for the wedding section. It was a tad OTT for *The Hebblestone Herald*. Beth was right: Joanna would only roll her eyes and edit it to death anyway. 'It's not the fancy stuff I care about, it's the romance of it all. I want to get married, and hopefully only do it the once.'

'So why wait then? Why the hold-up?'

Beth obviously wasn't going to drop this. She checked her piece over one last time and emailed it to Joanna for her to check over. She had another two weddings booked in for the weekend, and she wanted to get a jump on the research for them. She had an appointment later that afternoon – a new gift shop had just opened on the high street, and they were offering bespoke invitations for events, including birthdays, christenings and, more importantly, weddings. She wanted to cover it for the paper, and hopefully give the owner a head-start with the business. Shops didn't always last long in their small town, so getting footfall going was important. Many of the locals ordered online for the invitations, but Emily thought it was pretty cool that a local business was offering the service. She might even get some samples for Timothy to look at. Maybe they could set a date, get some save-the-date cards.

She knew the thought was futile even as it entered her brain. Tim was lovely, but he was dragging his heels a little. She could push him, but when she thought of her wedding lately, all that came to mind was spreadsheets. Tim's spreadsheets, truth be told. The ones he kept at home, with their five-year plan strategically filled in. It was as depressing as their joint account. The one they'd opened at his bank with a view to putting money aside for the big day. It still had the same £200 in it that they'd opened the account with. The best intentions and all that.

Whatever savings she put away, she just stuck them in her own ISA. She knew Tim must do the same. She knew he had to *have* savings; he was careful with money. Sometimes so tight he could peel an orange in his pocket. They just never mentioned where the money was. Tim just banged on the five-year-plan drum once in a while. Normally when she wanted to book a mini-break, or talk about the wedding. He was just … frugal. She used to find it sexy: him being ambitious for their future, and their big plans. He had a plan for everything, but lately, it felt like his spreadsheets had become *too* important to him. Maybe her promotion would be the change. With the extra money, they could move things up a gear.

'I don't know, Beth, it's just … not something we talk about.'

We don't talk about a lot lately, truth be told. Last night, we spent two hours discussing the housing market, and the impact of interest-only mortgages on the economy. We don't even have a mortgage. We don't even live together. He has his place; I have mine. We shuttle back and forth from each other's houses like teenagers. Dawson's Creek *was cute, but not so much after you hit thirty.*

She kicked her overnight bag under her desk, booting it against the back of her desk space. 'We're saving for a house, and everything takes time and planning. They don't just throw mortgages for dream homes about anymore, you know. I need to finish my work, okay?'

God, I sound like a right cow now. What's happening to me? Why does it get my back up so much when someone mentions my future plans? I've got things in hand. Why leap into things, like Tim said? We're together; we have all the time in the world. It's this bloody promotion – it's making me feel inadequate.

She opened her inbox and started reading emails to distract herself. They just needed to talk, that was all. Talk about what was really important to them.

After the mortgage talk last night, she needed to try again anyway. She had to get Tim to see more than the figures on a spreadsheet. He was so laid-back he'd fall over in a stiff breeze. Another reason she liked him so much. They were comfortable together; he hated stress and rushing about. She'd never seen a man so comfortable with his lot. It was nice. She could rely on him. She just wanted them to push on to the next stage. Reignite the passion of the first days of their engagement.

15

Beth didn't say anything for the longest time, and when Emily looked back at her, she was studiously typing away at her computer. She turned back to her desk, and picking up her mobile phone from her desk, she typed out a text.

Can we talk tonight?

E x

It only took a second before it buzzed back with a reply.

Can't tonight, squash after work, remember? It's on the calendar. Mine, about ten?

She was about to hit reply, to say yes and ask him if he needed her to bring anything, but instead she found her fingers typing something else.

No problem, got a work project anyway. Will sleep at home tonight. See you tomorrow. E

She passively aggressively left the kiss off the end of the text, a sure-fire way of signalling to him the fact that something was off. She'd asked him to talk, and he'd not even asked what about. Maybe time to think would make him realise, or she could work out a better way to tackle him about it without turning into Rachel Riley with her whiteboard.

Okay, pretty tired anyway. See you tomorrow night. Love you.

Ah, not so sure-fire then. He was probably busy at work though. He was the manager of the biggest bank in town, and it was coming up to lunchtime. He was always telling her how busy the midday rush was, how overworked he was at the bank with all the important and, what seemed to her, the intensely boring tasks he did daily with his assistant Pippa. Perky Pippa.

She had started to tune him out when he talked about his day lately, and she'd seen his eyes glaze over on more than one occasion when she talked about her work. Which, to be fair, she did understand. She was bored of it herself. Bored of everything, if she had the lady balls to admit it to herself. She felt a little like she was a toad, stagnating in some deep, dark, mouldy, murky waters, not being bothered to move, or not knowing how to. It

16

was nice and comfy in the waters, and who knew what was out there, ready to strike.

And now she was comparing her life to a toad in a pond. And if she was bored now on the last Friday in April, which was pretty much the start of the wedding season around here – and her busiest months at work – then something wasn't right. She needed to pull her finger out and start making some bloody plans in her life so she could get that promotion. But the thought of everything she was facing only served to depress her further. She needed a break from her worrying; she needed to take action.

'I'm going out for lunch,' she declared wildly. She heard Beth's chair swivel in her direction.

'What?'

Emily grabbed her bag and, opening the contents of her sandwich box, chucked the lot in the wastepaper bin beside her.

'You heard me! The wedding fund can stand a tenner for lunch out. You coming?'

Beth picked up her jaw from the floor, her bright blue eyes widening as she took in Emily, all cardigan and determination.

'Bloody hell, yeah! Let's go! I pick the place though, deal? I'm not sitting outside Tesco eating a pre-packed egg sarnie. You might as well have kept that monstrosity.' She flicked her finger towards the lunch Tim had packed for Emily. It was a little bland, but he was trying to save money for the wedding, and their house, their future. Although it wasn't going into the joint account. What the hell *were* they saving for – just for it to sit in their own banks? After all, the cardigan she was wearing was from a charity shop. Not that there was anything wrong with charity shops, but it was two years old to her. Would a new bit of work clobber really break the bank?

They'd been having this discussion last weekend, when they'd been talking about her trying to get promoted. Tim did have a point, though. It wasn't her wardrobe that would clinch the promotion; it was the merit of her work. But she'd noticed that the full-time reporters often did dress up, although so did she when she attended functions. Charity shops came in handy there too; easy to bag a formal outfit worn once only, and every now and again, rotate them. It would be worth it, when she bought her wedding dress. That would be brand new, and never to be sold on. That would make all the sacrifices, all the curled egg sandwiches, utterly worth it.

Not today though. She felt the delicious flicker of rebellion in her stir. Just for a day.

'Deal,' she said with a flourish, and grabbing their things, the two women headed out. They had just got to the lift when Emily turned to her friend. 'Beth, are Tim and I okay? Long engagements aren't that weird, are they?'

Beth watched the lift change floors for a moment, her usual candour playing for time it seemed. Emily's heart sank a little further. As the lift doors opened, the reception of the newspaper offices before them, Beth linked arms with her friend and pulled her towards the front door.

'Come on, if we hurry up, we can hit the department store on the way back. I sense a new slinky top in your future.' Emily gauged her friend's face for some kind of answer, but just saw excitement at the thought of shopping. *She didn't answer because it's a stupid question,* she thought to herself. Of course, they were fine! They were happy doing their own thing. Everything good in life was worth working for and waiting for at that. She was fine. They were fine. They just needed to talk, to get things moving again. Every love story had a lull now and again. No one was sunsets and roses around the door all the time. Life got in the way of plans. She knew that well enough.

Experience also reminded her that waiting for something to happen wasn't always worth it either. It was that thought that her brain couldn't quite shake. She needed something to happen. She needed to shake things up.

Chapter 2

Emily was starting to feel better, tucking into her meal, which was luscious, and enjoying her large latte and chatting about clothes with Beth. She'd smashed and grabbed the local "cool shop" that Beth recommended, and she'd found some nice new clobber. She'd spent a fair bit, but Beth had given her a stern look when she'd wavered. 'Screw it,' she'd urged, and the card was in the machine. She was right – sod it. She deserved a splurge, and it wouldn't do her promotion prospects any harm either. She'd spotted a soft grey suit in a trendy cut, so that too was sitting in the bags at her feet, along with her other purchases. She was feeling better, optimistic even. Then the door to the cute little eatery they were dining in opened and her past walked in. Literally walked in.

'Holy shit,' she breathed, her fork stabbing her in the cheek as she turned her head away at lightning speed from the man who'd just walked in. 'Ouch!' She dropped her fork, and it fell with a clatter onto her plate, pinging a piece of lettuce leaf into Beth's open mouth.

'Eugh, Ems! That was grim. What's up?'

'Nothing, sorry. I got startled.'

'Startled enough to stab yourself in the head? What did you see?' Beth's head was on a swivel now, trying to look at the doorway. 'Tell me!' she half yelled. She could never bear to miss a thing.

'Please beeeee quiet,' she said between clenched teeth. 'It's nothing. I think an old school friend just walked in.'

Beth was staring at her now. 'And? Did you not get on or something?' She looked again at the small queue waiting at the counter, nodding to a woman just in front of the man Beth was cringing over. She was wearing a short woollen dress, socks and crocs. 'Is it the gator feet woman with the socks and Crocs? Cos, I've got to say, I get it.'

'No, no, nothing like that. It's not a her, it's a he.' Well, it was a bit like that. Emily was still trying to stop herself from passing out. She never thought she'd see him back here again. Any other day she'd be at her desk now, eating her slightly sad lunch. Of all the days.

'Ah, I see. Was he one of those idiots who twanged bra straps and thought he was too cool for school?'

'No, no. Nothing like that. He was just a friend. It's just a shock, that's all. He moved away a long time ago.' Her gaze flipped back to Calvin, who was still there. Not an illusion. *Jesus, what a day.* He looked good. Why did he have to look so good?

'Oh, the guy behind! Hey, he's a bit of all right you know. I'm surprised the women of this town let a hunk like that leave! How did that happen?'

Beth went on to chat about some of the things the "women of the town" had said to Dave over the years. It was a little scarce on the man front, granted, but times had changed. More people were coming to live here, but it was hardly a metropolis.

'So like I said to Dave, women don't need a man to complete them. Sorry to break it to you, Tom Cruise.' Beth's voice filtered back into her head, and she frowned at the turn in conversation.

'Tom Cruise?'

'Yeah! You know, in that film? She's a nice single mum, and he's a complete mess, and he really gets it wrong.'

Emily nodded away at her friend, looking over to where Calvin Albright was ordering a drink and a sandwich to take out. He was taller than she remembered. She'd always had to crane her neck a little bit when they were younger, but judging by the size of him now, she'd need a portable footstool to look him in the eye. Or a neck brace. He said something to the cashier, and she threw her head back in laughter as he tapped his card on the reader. She looked away, not wanting to watch all of a sudden.

'So, how did you know him then?' Beth asked, munching on a crust of fancy bread from her side plate. 'What's he called?'

'Calvin Albright. We went to school together. He was in a lot of my classes. Extra-curricular stuff, you know.'

'Aww, a geek like you?'

Emily crossed her eyes at her friend before continuing. 'Yes, he was. We both were. Before college. I wonder why he's here.'

'Er, fairly sure he's ordering a ham salad and a large coffee. He looks like he's on his lunch break. From Abercrombie and Fitch. I mean … damn that man can wear a suit. I can't believe you never told me about him. He's …' Beth was leaning over in her seat now, watching as he scrolled through his phone at the counter. The cashier was still making googly eyes at him, Emily noted, but his head stayed focused on the screen. She looked away, focusing intently on the remaining food on her plate. Her appetite had disappeared, replaced by what felt like a ball of wool in her gut. Meanwhile her mate was still trying to think of the perfect word for the man before them. 'Oh … I don't know. Fit seems a bit weak, and he's not burly like my Dave. He's a bit more Clark Kent.' She took a sip of her drink, waggling her eyebrows saucily at Emily. 'Dave's more Bruce Banner.' She returned to study Calvin as though he was a specimen in a jar, awaiting classification of species. 'Look how he fills that suit. He's Iron Man material.'

'Beth!' Emily was getting more uncomfortable by the second. She wanted nothing more than to stick her shopping bags over her face and run out of the door. She would have by now, if it hadn't meant walking right past him at the counter. 'Can you not? He'll hear you!'

'What, with his bionic hearing? I'm married, Em, not dead! I can still appreciate a fine-looking man when one walks by me. And, more to the point—' she scrunched her eyes up tight at her friend, who in comparison had eyes the size of saucers '—how come you never told me you knew a man who looked like that? You always told me you never did the dating thing till later.'

'I … I didn't – we were much younger then. He didn't look … That's not the point!' Emily rebutted, a little too loudly. 'I mean, what is he doing here? Back home?'

Beth pursed her lips tight. 'I don't know, but he's clocked you.'

Emily turned around and her eye line slammed straight into a pair of eyes that she hadn't seen for years but knew so well. It really was him. Her heart rate sped up with the knowledge, even though she was pretty sure her nerve endings had felt him walk through the door.

Recognition lit up his features, and his mouth formed a perfect O as he took her in. His eyebrows shot up and, after a moment's pause, he started to walk over. Emily realised she wasn't breathing and took in a shuddering gasp of air as he reached the table.

'Emily Hendrickson! I thought that was you!' Her name sounded so different in his mouth. Dark, husky.

'Calvin Albright, hello!'

The two of them kept grinning at each other awkwardly, Calvin shuffling from foot to foot.

'Bethany Jenkins!' Beth interjected from her seat after the seconds had limped by, threatening to turn into minutes. Emily and Calvin both stared at her. 'Sorry, I thought we were doing a thing. I need to visit the ladies'. Too much latte.' She shot an apologetic look at Emily, who silently begged her with her eyes to stay. Beth grabbed her bag and was already standing up before either of them could answer. Calvin nodded to the empty chair in front of him and Emily tried not to panic. *Beth and her bloody tiny bladder.*

'Do you mind? I have to get back to the office, but I have a minute.'

Emily nodded like an idiot in his direction, and he unbuttoned his suit jacket and slid effortlessly into the seat. She shoved the cardigan further down into the back of her seat, trying her best to flick her hair away from her face. Why was it the law of society that you had to look like crap when you saw someone significant? She felt like roadkill beside him. He looked so good. His once gangly frame was now more muscular, and his suit looked well-tailored and new. She felt herself shrink down in her seat.

'So, how've you been?' Calvin turned to Beth then. 'I'm sorry, I'm being rude. I'm Cal.'

Beth reached for the hand he held out and shook it enthusiastically. 'Pleased to meet you, Cal. You sound like a cowboy from one of those romance books.'

Cal laughed, which thankfully drowned out the sound of Beth's over-the-top girlish giggle. Emily was staring at the pair of them like she was watching an episode of *The Bachelor*.

'It's Calvin actually, more like the posh underpants than a horse rancher.'

Beth's guffaw in reply almost sent Emily into hiding under the table. Beth was not subtle, but luckily her bladder was outspoken too. She retreated to the toilets, leaving the two of them in her shocked wake.

Emily felt like her face had exploded with embarrassment. He gave Emily a sidewards glance, and she shot him a rueful smile.

'I am so sorry about her.'

'It's fine, don't worry. She seems nice. So, how have you been? It's really nice to see you.'

Ever the gent, Emily thought. That was the Calvin she remembered.

'Good thanks, I work at the paper.'

'Oh, you're writing. That's great!' Calvin brushed his hand over the back of hers, before putting it back onto the table. 'I knew you would. What are you now, the star reporter?'

'Almost.' She didn't want to tell him what she really did for some reason, as if it would be a let-down given all that she had wanted to achieve back when they were growing up together. She wasn't that goofy kid anymore. Well, not quite. He just looked so together, and she felt embarrassed that she wasn't where she wanted to be yet. He was like a reminder that time was passing. Passing her by even. 'I'm on my way.' She left it there, shooting a glance at him to gauge his reaction, but he looked nothing but pleased. 'How about you? You here for work?'

It was his turn to look away now, and Emily waited.

'Er, yes and no. I moved back recently. I've started with a local firm.' He laughed nervously, looking anywhere but at her. 'The rat race got a little too much, to be honest. I needed a change of pace.'

It was Emily's turn to make contact now. Her hand was covering his on the table before she'd even registered the movement. He looked at it but didn't pull away. It felt easy, like old times when they were such close friends. They were always touching each other back then. It was easy. They were so close. Their child-hoods had been intertwined forever. Em and Cal, the pair of them were as thick as thieves. They were always together. In each other's house, or at Hebblestone Castle. It wasn't every place that had its own historic castle ruins. It had been the backdrop for many of their best times. They knew everything about each other. Closer than close. She'd once atomic wedgied him so hard he'd had ball burn for two days from his boxers. Their bodies were long since acquainted, but she felt the heat from his hand now. It was a different kind of feeling. She couldn't place what it was. She pulled it away to brush a wisp of hair away from her eye, putting it firmly on her lap and pulling her face into what she hoped looked like a normal, happy expression. Her hand felt weird, warm in her lap.

'I can't believe I didn't know! We should meet up – properly

I mean. Catch up.' *Oh God, why did you say that? Shut up, Emily. Awkward social meetings are not on the five-year plan.*

He looked straight at her then, and their eyes locked once more. He looked so handsome, so grown up. Which was a ridiculous thing to be thinking at this moment, but she'd looked at this boy every day for years, and now she felt as if she was looking at the finished version. She'd wondered so many times over the years what he'd turned out like. He looked even better than she'd imagined. Calvin, all grown up and in the flesh. What a weird day. Beth appeared, and the moment was snatched away.

'Er, Ems … sorry to interrupt but we need to be getting back.' It took them both a hot minute to break away from each other. Their bodies never moved. 'Earth to Emily!'

'Wha? Oh, oh shit, yes. Calvin, I must get back to work. I'm sorry, but it's been so nice to see you again.'

Calvin took his hand away from the table slowly and nodded.

'Of course. I need to get back too, actually.' He reached into his suit jacket and pulled out a card, sliding it across the table to her. 'It was really nice to see you again. Do you have a card? We could have that catch-up.'

Emily looked across at Beth, but she was busying herself with grabbing muffins for the afternoon. She plucked the card from the table awkwardly, as if it was a sordid love letter, and grabbed one from her bag to give to him.

'Sure, that'll be nice!' After another moment of wishing she'd never erred from her routine, she tried to leave with a little grace. 'Have a great afternoon, mate!'

She playfully punched him on the shoulder and, grabbing her bags and cardie, she practically dragged Beth out of the place, giving him a distracted wave on her way out of the door. As she looked back, she could see him heading back to the counter to collect his order. He looked back, till she couldn't see him anymore. His expression was unreadable, but he'd raised his hand in response. They just managed to round the corner before Beth squealed in protest.

'Oh my God, where's the fire? You'll squash the muffins!'

'Sorry. I needed to wee.' Emily linked arms with her, and speed-walked in the direction of the newspaper offices. 'We need to get back, anyway.'

Beth was having none of it. 'That was not you needing the toilet. First of all, you're like a bloody camel at work, and we just left one back there! What's the deal with Calvin? You were weird in there.' Her eyes narrowed. 'Is he … an ex?'

'NO!' Emily protested loudly. 'No, of course not. He was the old school friend I told you about. Our parents were best friends.'

'That's your old best friend?' Beth looked behind her, as if he would be standing there on a plinth, like a museum exhibit for her to scrutinise. 'Well, what's weird about that? It's a good thing, isn't it? And while you're pointing things out, how did you leave out the fact that he was hot?'

'I did not!'

Beth raised a sceptical brow. 'You didn't once mention it in all the stories you told me about him.' Emily could see the cogs turning and felt panic rise. Why did she have to be best friends with someone so bloody observant all the time? She remembered every little detail. She had always thought it was cute that her friend cared so much. Now, she would rather she was more like Tim. Obliviously happy, and with her beak in her own business. 'Oh … wait.' Her eyes shone with realisation and Emily groaned, dropping her head to her chest in defeat. 'I KNOW WHO HE IS! THE CASTLE BOY! THE PROM THING!'

'Not the prom thing,' Emily groaned. 'Please. I wish I'd never told you that!' She sidestepped a pigeon, walking towards her on the pavement with half a bagel in its mouth.

'I'm glad you tell me things! Especially the prom thing!' She clapped her hands together gleefully. 'Oh my God, I had a whole other picture in my head of Mr Prom Guy. Cute, but not hot.

Gawky, braces, that kind of thing. That—' she jabbed back in his direction with a determined finger '—was HOT.'

He was hot. Crazy hot. She'd nearly melted into a puddle the minute she'd seen him. It had shocked her, seeing him there. That was all. A bit like meeting one of your favourite TV stars in the supermarket. It just felt surreal … surprising. She WAS glad to see Calvin again. Sure, it had been awkward, but it was done with now. She'd probably not see him much anyway. She hadn't even known he was back, and that said something for Hebblestone.

'Well, everyone has different tastes, don't they? I never thought of him like that. He was my best friend since we were little. He looked different when we were kids. We all did. Our mothers were friends; we played in each other's paddling pools.'

'So did Bridget Jones and Mark Darcy, and look how that ended,' Beth shot back, deadpan. 'Hell, I'd play in his paddling pool now and I'm a happily married woman. You honestly never thought of him like that? Come on, give me the goss. You are allowed to have fancied people before Tim, you know.'

'I know that …'

'Well then! Come on, tell me. You must have thought about it.' She pinched her fingers together, squinting theatrically. 'Not even a little bit?'

Only every day since I was about fourteen. He was my person. I wanted to keep him forever.

'No, never. He was like my brother. We lived in each other's pockets; our families were great friends. Nothing ever happened like that. And before you get your hopes up for the single ladies of Hebblestone, he's married. He met her at university.' *Stupid university.*

'I didn't see a wedding ring.'

'You looked?'

'Of course I did! The man was carved from marble. I was looking for the sculptor tag!' Beth screeched, startling a passing couple.

'Sorry,' Emily said to them, pulling Beth into the reception of their workplace and trying to ignore the indignant stares from the pair.

Beth never skipped a beat. 'There was no wedding ring line, no sign of a dent or a tan mark. That man is not married now, mark my words.'

'So?'

'So! Well, I don't know. He's your friend. Maybe he's moved back for a reason. Aren't you a little bit intrigued?'

'Well, people do tend to have a reason for moving, yeah. He took a job; it happens.' They both smiled at the supply temp behind the reception desk and headed to their areas. 'We didn't talk about much, just work really. I probably won't even see him again. Can we just drop it?' She rearranged her blouse in the lift mirror. She could feel a little trickle of stress sweat run down her spine. She didn't want Beth poking at that wound. She had enough on, with the big chat with Tim looming.

'I think it's nice he's back. You've been in a bit of a rut lately. A catch-up with a buddy might not be the worst thing for you.' Beth stopped to chat to Jackie on the way to her desk and handed her a muffin.

Emily followed her and sat down at her desk. She looked at the business card that was still clutched tight in her hand.

Calvin Albright
Graphic Designer and Project Leader
Electric Melon Graphics

She ran her finger along the embossed lettering. Even his business card was better than hers. More accomplished-looking. He'd looked like an adult. Like he'd seen life. His edges had hardened, just a little. Like his now-chiselled jaw. She'd well and truly been left behind by her old friend. Did she really need to reconnect? She was still trying to be the woman she wanted to be; she didn't need to be delving back into her girlhood. *Why was he not wearing his ring though? No, Emily. No. It's none of your business.*

'No good can come of this, Emily Hendrickson,' she told herself in an authoritative voice. 'Leave it well alone.' She dropped the card into the wastepaper basket by her desk and started work. Half an hour and two muffins later, she fished the card out, pushing it into the back pocket of her purse, and chucked her cardigan in instead.

* * *

Calvin headed back to work in a daze, his head full of the past. Emily Hendrickson. He couldn't quite believe it. What were the chances of seeing her again? Well, actually there was every chance of course. Given that she still lived in their hometown. He felt foolish now to think about how stupid that notion was. It wasn't London, where you could live in the next street to someone and not see them for years. If ever. It wasn't like that here, he remembered, but it hadn't lessened the shock of seeing her sitting there. He'd reverted back to his bumbling self the moment their eyes had met, but as usual, Emily didn't seem to notice. She never had back then when they'd been the best of friends. Growing up, they'd been the Dawson and Joey of best friends. Except, he'd been Joey. The lovesick puppy to her Dawson, full of creative dreams for the future. Dreams that she'd achieved too.

He felt a surge of pride, thinking of her out there, doing what she'd dreamed of. She'd done it – she was a writer. He had always known she could do it; when they'd both said goodbye and headed off to their respective universities, him to Bristol and her to Leeds to study English literature and journalism. He'd done what he'd wanted to, of course, so it was undiluted pride he felt. He'd got the career he'd wanted, and he'd found love. Had a son. He realised belatedly that he'd not even asked Emily if she was attached or had children. He'd never even mentioned Isaac, which wasn't like him.

He told all and sundry about his son, being so damn proud of him. *It was just the shock – that was obviously it.* If he called her, there would be more time to chat. He could tell her then about Isaac.

He was sitting at his desk, fingers steepled together, as he looked out of his office window at the place he now called home once again. Of course, telling her about his son would lead to more questions. Like where he came from. Cal knew that Emily stopped believing in the stork delivering babies a long time ago, so the next logical question would obviously be who Isaac's mother was, and where she was. He had avoided the question as much as possible so far; his employers knew, of course, but that was only due to him ticking a box on a form. He was confident that Emily wouldn't send him a questionnaire, worse luck. He would have to have the conversation. He hadn't thought about that when he'd given her his card, and now it was all he could think about.

That was the problem with social interactions, and why he'd pretty much avoided them since Diane had passed. Even before, truth be told. He'd been quite happy to live in their own little family bubble, but now it was just the two of them, Cal knew that he needed to stop being such a hermit. He'd bought far too many sets of sweatpants online lately, and his Netflix account was near exhausted. He'd even started bringing work home, just to have something to do when Isaac was in bed and he was staring at blank walls. Another thing to hide from Emily when he called, perhaps.

If she answered, of course. They hadn't spoken in years, after all. He'd kind of ambushed her with the business card, maybe she'd just taken it to be polite. And she'd given him hers out of politeness. That was Emily too. He did it himself all the time; at work, at the school drop-off point. One of the mothers had knocked on his window and after a brief conversation, had practically shoved her card into his hand, talking about meeting up for coffee sometime. He hadn't called her of course. The thought of going out for coffee with a strange woman had him shrinking back into his tracksuit bottoms faster than a tortoise retreated into its shell. She'd seemed a tad predatory too, which he knew wasn't for him. The way she'd hoicked her boobs in his direction had scared him. What would she do over coffee? He'd shoved her business card into his desk drawer, and there it still sat.

Emily was an old friend, and he was glad to see her. He hoped she did want to talk, but he would understand if she didn't, and he wasn't going to dwell on it. He needed to get on with work if he was going to get out on time tonight, get home to cook tea for him and Isaac. He fired up his computer, and pushing his lunch meeting out of his mind, he cracked on with his big project. It was times like this that he wished his parents were still around. His mum would be the one person who could tell him if he was doing the right thing. Being back here helped him feel closer to them in a way, but he did wish he didn't feel like a teenager, playing house. He had corrected his sixteenth typo when he gave up. Reaching for the phone and her card, he dialled. No answer.

'Damn it,' he muttered. He tried to get back into work, but he was still staring at her card half an hour later. Maybe he was just reaching for something to cling to, but he couldn't help but feel the loss of his old friend once more. The irony of it was, the one person who could help pull him out of this funk was a stranger to him now in many ways. Still, nothing stayed the same. Even in Hebblestone. Time moved on, no matter what.

Chapter 3

'All right, cockney boy?'

'Original,' Isaac countered, glaring at his classmate Kai. 'Got any more to get out of your system?'

Kai thought for a moment, so much so that Isaac thought he looked constipated.

'Get arrtt of my pub!'

'Nice. You done?'

Kai nodded, a little grin across his chubby face. 'Yep, all done.'

'Good, can we move on then? I need your help with the video. It's not had many views yet, and the only comment was from you, pretending to be a cockney admirer.'

Kai sniggered, and Isaac shut him down with another hard glare. 'Okay, I'm sorry. It only went on a few days ago though. These viral things sometimes take a bit of time to catch on. How many hashtags do you have on it?'

'Not many – I hate hashtags. How is a hashtag going to get my dad a new girlfriend, really? I don't want him to go out with some kind of influencer who's going to dress him like a Ken doll. He'll hate that.'

Kai thought for a moment, looking around him at the people eating around them in the lunchroom. The tables around them were filled with people chatting, laughing, scoffing their faces with pizza slices and jacket potatoes. On the far table, some of the other year sevens were sticking pens into their bottles of pop, laughing and shrieking as the plumes of fizzy black liquid sprayed the group of girls sitting on the next table. One of them, a blonde girl with a pink headband in her hair, turned around and, after taking aim, threw an apple at one of the offending lads. She called his name seconds before she released her weapon, and the apple hit him right between the eyes, sending his own shower of blood across the table from his newly exploded nose.

'Jesus! Isobel just sparked Jonah out with a Granny Smith!'

Isaac turned to look at the commotion. Jonah was now groaning on the floor, his friends pulling him off the tiled surface, laughing their heads off. Isobel was already focused back on her lunch, looking as if butter wouldn't melt. The lunch staff headed over, one of them motioning for Isobel to follow them. She rolled her eyes, grabbed her bag, and headed out of the busy room.

'Err, hello? Earth to Isaac?'

'Huh?' Isobel disappeared from sight, followed by another member of staff who was helping Jonah to make his exit. A drip of blood punctuated their retreat like breadcrumbs in the forest. 'What?'

Kai flicked his head towards the exit. 'Isobel. You like her!'

Kai was not one to be quiet or hold back. Since the day Isaac had started school there, they'd gravitated to each other. Kai had trouble keeping friends sometimes as he was a little outspoken, in class and out, but Isaac didn't mind any of that. It was nice to be around someone who was free with their words, especially since at home now a lot of the things he wanted to say to his dad weren't very forthcoming. He knew his dad felt the same way. He could tell sometimes, when they were quiet on the couch, or in the car. He knew his mind was elsewhere. Missing someone who should have been right there with them.

Kai was a big ball of fun, and that was a welcome distraction

33

to Isaac. Plus, his mother had always taught him not to judge kids at school, and from some of the comments and looks Kai got from his classmates, their parents hadn't taught them the same lessons. Having ADHD just made Kai him, as far as he could see. He liked his friend, so he just ignored the others and their comments when he could. Stepped in when he couldn't. They'd rubbed along so far. He'd definitely made his short time in school a better experience than he'd expected. He knew his mother would have been proud too. Thinking of her again ruined his mood, but he smiled at Kai.

'Sorry, mate, I wasn't listening.'

'No, you were daydreaming about how much you fancy Isobel.'

'I don't fancy her!'

The snort from his mate told Isaac that he begged to differ.

'Ha ha! Nice try, mate, I can see you looking at her, drooling every lunchtime. Why don't you just go and talk to her?'

'Oh yeah.' Isaac blushed. 'And get a piece of fruit shoved somewhere painful. She's not exactly approachable, is she?'

Kai shrugged, shoving a piece of shortbread into his mouth while he pondered a plan of action. Isaac could tell he was planning something; his facial expressions made him pretty easy to read.

'It doesn't matter anyway,' Isaac continued, thinking back to the video. 'We need a plan to get the video viral, get Dad some dates.'

'Hey, how about if we got some celebrities on the case? There must be someone who would get on it with us?'

'I hardly think Harry Styles is going to pop into the local pub and flash my dad's photo around, Kai. I was thinking more of getting more shares, maybe looking for a dating service around here, or online. It's just tricky because you have to be over eighteen for the sites. He would kill me if I signed up to one of those.'

'Why not Harry Styles? He fed someone's fish that time, didn't he? Maybe he does odd jobs on the side?'

'I don't think so, Kai. I think we need some real help. I really want to help him. He bought some more sweatpants the other day. He never bought those before apart from for the gym, and he's stopped running. He just sits on the couch most nights, watching home makeover shows and sighing. I think he's lonely.'

The bell went, and Kai patted his new buddy on the arm.

'It'll be all right, mate, don't worry. I'll think about it, okay? Let's get to class. Mr Skinner will be on the warpath if we're late again. He's still annoyed about what I did last lesson.'

Isaac got up, throwing the rest of his lunch into the bin. He wished life was easier sometimes. Parents were hard work to look after. It was fast becoming a full-time job. He and his dad both needed to get a life, big time. His dad needed an Isobel of his own to moon over.

Chapter 4

Emily chucked her keys into the bowl by her flat door and dumped her handbag on the floor. She reached into the carrier bag in her other hand, pulled out the bottle of wine she'd bought on the way home and then shoved the pint of ice cream into the freezer for later. She had big-night-in plans; the whole evening to herself. She was also proving a point to her distracted fiancé that she could get along just fine without him, and that he needed to pull his socks up. Of course, he hadn't texted or called since their lukewarm conversation, and she was pretty sure that she wouldn't hear from him either.

She was well aware that relationships could be a lot less loving than hers. She could trust Tim. He was strong, steadfast. He was kind. If the worst thing about him was the fact he left notes, well, she didn't have any right to have doubts, did she? Beth had told her enough stories about Dave leaving puddles on the toilet floor when tipsy and his epic farting prowess. She knew she was lucky. She just didn't quite *feel* it at the minute, and she was taking it out on Tim; focusing on a few silly notes. They were irritating, though. She'd once got up to go to the toilet at his place, and he'd left a note on the mirror. It was to remind her to get his dry cleaning on the way to work. He'd had some big meeting the following day planned and wanted his sharpest suit for the occasion.

She still remembered that note. The lettering, his uniform neat script. It read:

EMILY
DRY CLEANING
TUESDAY DEADLINE

Nothing sinister. It was a couple of words, no doubt written at the last minute before he went to bed. It was the tone of it. Just an instruction. Like a formal memo. A task and a deadline, as if she was on the payroll. It had upset her, and she'd cried in the toilet before slipping back under the covers next to him. For some reason, his words had chilled the heart of his wordsmith fiancée, and that didn't really go away.

She'd been noticing things ever since. That night, when she'd lain next to him, listening to him breathe, she'd never felt so alone, so far departed from the girl she once was. The fiery young Yorkshire lass who was going to take a pen and a Dictaphone and change the world, one sentence at a time. The unspeakable sadness she'd felt reading that note. She'd left it scrunched up in the bottom of the bathroom bin, under used floss and contact lens capsules. She met the deadline, but that was the start of the realisation that she wasn't quite as happy as she'd thought.

Beth had laughed her arse off when she'd told her about #notegate. She'd still been seething when she got to her desk the day after and the saga of the little note fell out of her. Minus the sadness bit. Beth thought it meant the death of romance on his part, but some of the other girls hadn't made much of it; he was just being practical. She'd seen their point and then felt ashamed that she'd kicked off over a few Post-its after they compared Tim to their past horrors. She kept coming back to the same thing. *Tim is nice. He cares.* After all, she was marrying him. The little stuff didn't write off the happy ever after, did it? Prince Charming definitely left the toilet seat up on occasion. Didn't he?

She should have been firmer with Tim, explained how she was feeling. She must make the effort. She'd not exactly been showering him with attention. Work had been full on; things had slid a little between them. She couldn't pin all that on him even if she wanted to. She'd worked a lot of late nights the past few summers, leaving him alone. He had always been so under-standing about it. Work was work to him. It was logical. Like their five-year plan, right down to the family they'd planned to have. Right at the start of it, when it all seemed possible. She was a dreamer, and he was a planner. Yin and Yang – things were bound to get bumpy along the road. When they got over these hurdles, it would come together. She was sure of it.

Still, she could only imagine how he'd be when they had kids. She always wanted to be the kind of mum who left little notes in her kids' lunchboxes, but Dad's little messages would probably be a bit less cute and inspirational; more positive mental attitude. They used to love joking about it, picturing smart little versions of themselves running around. Planning where they would go, how they would marry. Over time, the excitement waned. It became less and less, till – finally – it just stopped. Lately the talk stayed on the same subjects. The day-to-day grind. The price of petrol.

She'd stopped trying to imagine them having kids full stop lately, to be fair. She was having enough time visualising the wedding these days. It just seemed like a far-off pipe dream, like buying a bookshop in the Cornish sunshine in her retirement years, or writing that novel she'd always started to write but never finished. Something that might happen someday, somehow. Her wedding felt like one of her discarded manuscripts. Unfinished, forgotten.

This was all wedding frustration, she realised as she pottered around her flat. Everyone around her seemed to be getting further in life. Mortgages to buy "starter homes" and people getting married. She couldn't get away from that, and it was a bit of a busman's holiday planning her own. But that was it, she wasn't planning a wedding, and it was that "someday" that needled her daily lately. The fact that weddings were her job wasn't exactly his fault, was it? He dealt with the practical side of love daily. Mortgages, joint accounts, family breakdowns.

Could that be it? Their jobs? They were both working long hours too. It had to take a toll. She knew she felt exhausted come the end of the week. That was when someday seemed so very far away.

Speaking of someday, she thought of the chance encounter she'd had at lunch. She hadn't even begun to process that heart-stopping event, on top of her swirling emotions about her relationship. Reaching into her bag on the floor, she fished out the business card and went to open the wine. The card sat on the countertop in her neat little kitchen, watching her pouring a big fat glass of the glorious pink stuff she loved. Nothing like a hot bath, a glass of rosé and a good romance novel to relax a girl after a weird and frustrating day at work.

Taking a deep sip of the cold wine, she looked at the phone on the corner of the countertop and tapped her finger along the surface of the card. Was it too early to call? Should she even call, really? What would they even talk about? The fact that she was angling for a promotion that never seemed to come, or the fact that she was engaged to someone she was having problems with? She'd never even mentioned it, and she'd had the opportunity. It was only a brief conversation, though. Not enough time to talk about everything. She'd only told him about work. She felt inadequate enough telling him that, after seeing him looking so well … grown up. Like an adultier adult.

Could she just slip it into the conversation somehow, straight off the bat? She felt guilty towards Tim for the omission, especially today after she wanted so badly to straighten things out in her head, and with Tim. She didn't normally not tell people. Everyone just knew. It wasn't news anymore in Hebblestone. It was a bit of a shock though seeing him there, she kept telling herself, and with Beth acting like a lunatic on the fringes, it wasn't the best timing. Besides which, he had a wife, and that felt a little awkward too. It's not like they'd ever met. She'd never wanted to meet her. She felt like they were in very different places in life too, and her own girlish plans seemed foolish now. Plans that weren't budging an inch to boot. She felt the curl of frustration wrap around her once more, and kicked the kitchen bin to make herself feel better.

So to call or not to call? *Hmm, it was a real head scratcher.* If she saw him again in town, it would be awkward if she hadn't called him. And he hadn't called her either. Doubly awkward. *Right day to branch out of your routine, Ems. Well done.*

She took another sip of her wine and spritzed her plants as she pondered what that scenario would look like. Or what if she did call, or he did, and then she and Tim bumped into him and his wife? Wouldn't that be more awkward? She plucked off a yellowing leaf from a spider plant, flicking it into the bin with a sigh.

He seemed so accomplished, so happy. He was obviously doing well, but she'd sensed that something had made him come home. The rat race comment had struck a chord with her. He'd always wanted to get out there and take the world on. What had changed?

Maybe he'd been working too hard. Tough at the top and all that. He was never the most carefree person. He'd always had a nervous kind of zingy energy about him back then. She wanted to know more about his life. It wasn't that unusual to catch up with someone either. In today's social media age, everyone was pretty much woven together, like it or not. And Hebblestone wasn't the biggest place; they were going to cross paths again at some point.

One quick phone call couldn't hurt, surely? She took another glug for courage and after taking the phone and the card through to the lounge, she flumped down onto her cushion-filled sofa and continued to stare at it.

Calvin Albright
Graphic Designer

She stroked her finger over the embossed name she knew so well. Calvin Albright, back in town. Who would have thought it?

Well, she had returned, hadn't she? Not that she'd expected to. She'd wanted to go out there and burn bright, make her mark, all of that. The thing was, by the time she'd finished her degree, she had grown tired of living where she was. It was just as easy to go home and stay local for a while.

Then she'd met Tim, and things had just evolved. Or evolved a little, and then stagnated. She wasn't doing what her other friends were doing exactly, but was that such a bad thing? Who knew what the right thing was nowadays anyway? Some people lived off-grid, needing nothing but themselves; they didn't care about a five-year plan, did they?

Maybe she could just chill out for a bit? Her old friend was back in town, and that was a good thing. Maybe having him around might bring a bit of the old Emily back too. The passionate one, the girl who wanted to chase stories. She'd always pictured herself dashing about like Anneka Rice, hanging out of choppers and scooping the news. Well, maybe not quite, but not being an eternal wedding guest either. She looked once more at the card. Calvin had changed though. He was a man now. A real man too. She'd proved her teenage self right, and that was a little unsettling too.

Jesus, she was a pure mess of emotions. Reaching for another glass of wine, she flicked on the TV and searched for something to distract her. As she went to check her email, she noticed a missed call. He'd already called her.

Chapter 5

Calvin was checking his phone fruitlessly when Isaac bounded up to the car.

'Hey, Dad!' Isaac chucked his bag into the back seat, pulling off his clip-on tie and throwing it to meet his bag. 'Ah, the sweet relief from the shackles of conformity.'

Cal chuckled, ruffling his son's hair. Isaac shook him off, scowling and putting his brown hair back into place in the usual cool, rather shaggy look he sported. He hid behind his hair sometimes, and he wasn't ready for cutting it yet. It was his armour against being the new kid when all eyes were on him. Calvin remembered his own teenage self, and how gawky he'd felt. 'Gerroff, Dad!' Isaac tried to be cross, but Calvin glimpsed a little side smile. Mission accomplished. He still had his ways of breaking the tension between them. Most of the time. 'Man, my hair's well bad now, bro!'

'Good day?'

'Not bad, I suppose. I see your shackle is still on.' Isaac nodded to his dad's tie and Cal chuckled again, pulling it off and also throwing it into the back seat.

'That better?'

'Much.' Isaac beamed. 'What's for tea?'

Cal opened his mouth to answer when there was a knock at the car window. Cal jumped, pressing the button to wind his window down to admit a rather glamorous-looking woman. Isaac rolled his eyes as she put her head right into the space and practically licked his dad. Her perfume filled the car; an overbearing, rather sickly scent that tickled Isaac's nostrils like pepper from a pot. Glancing across at his dad, he could see that the smell hadn't gone unnoticed by him either. He looked like he was trying not to sneeze.

'Hello, Mr Albright! It's Suki's mum, Heather! I just wanted to say hello, touch base as it were!' She giggled girlishly, and Isaac groaned. Cal nudged him with his elbow, a small movement that Heather hopefully didn't see.

'Hi, Heather, that's nice, thank you. Have you got classes with Suki, Isaac?' He turned to his son.

'Er, maybe …' Isaac tried to place a Suki, but the only Suki he remembered was a cat his nan had once had. It had been a flea-bitten white thing at that. 'Blonde hair, right?'

Heather's smile dimmed just a little as she blushed right through to her dyed roots. 'Er, no, she's a little darker in hair than I am. She gets it from her father, but that's a horror story for another day.' She leaned in further, beaming maniacally at Isaac. 'You remember Suki? She's in your French class I think.'

'I don't do French,' Isaac replied.

'Yes, French!' Heather grinned. 'So, I was thinking, maybe we should set up a study date or two? At mine?'

'I'm a bit young to date,' Isaac chipped in glumly.

Cal's lip twitched and he took a moment to recover before answering. 'Ah well, we have got a lot on at the moment.'

'Aww,' the woman simpered, still sticking her head through the window like an overfriendly giraffe at a drive-in safari park. 'Too busy to focus on education for the youth of today? That can't be right! I can bring wine! And nibbles! M & S, of course.'

'Of course,' Isaac mumbled, and Cal shot him a friendly but warning look.

'Ah, no, of course not, but we do okay on our own. Don't we, Isaac.' He gave the woman what he hoped looked like his most endearing smile. 'Can I get back to you? I'm actually in a bit of a rush this evening.'

The woman's smile dimmed, but she recovered well. Well, she gurned for half a minute, in a way that made both men realise that she was very accustomed to getting her own way.

'Well, don't leave it too long!' She made it sound like an offer that was going, going, gone. Isaac looked like he just wished it was gone. Calvin had to agree. He'd had a sudden image pop into his head of this woman standing in their kitchen, dressed in a nightgown that would no doubt be M & S or swankier, making pancakes and fawning over his son like some simpering fool. *Not on my watch*, he resolved.

'I won't. I'm sure we'll see you on the school run.' Cal closed the window and put the car into drive, making the point that he was about to pull away. The woman flashed him another huge smile, and reluctantly retreated from the car window.

'Er yes, another time then. I'll hold you to it!' She smiled again, nodding swiftly to each of them in turn.

'You're not going to make me study with her daughter, are you?' Isaac asked as they headed towards home.

'No, I don't think so. Not much point studying something you don't take as a subject, for a start. Do you really not know who her daughter is?'

Isaac couldn't shake his head fast enough. 'Nope, and I don't think she'd be someone I'd want to hang out with. I'm quite happy never to meet her if I'm honest. You don't want to meet up with the mum, do you?'

Cal burst into laughter, indicating left and turning into their street.

'No fear on that score; she was a little scary for me. Speaking

44

of friends though …' He used the opportunity to slip in his meeting to his son. 'I did bump into an old friend today. I used to know her when I lived here before.'

'Really?' Isaac's ears were pricked up like a dog's now. Calvin wondered what he was thinking. Once upon a time, he would have just asked him. 'Who is she?'

Calvin looked at his son and, for once in his life, he couldn't feel an easy lie coming off his tongue. All kids were lied to by their parents, of course, but Diane was better at it. Far better than he ever was. Yes, the tooth fairy does skip tooth collection in messy bedrooms. Yes, Santa was real, and he was watching. He found this awkward though, even though he didn't have any dark history with Emily. It was all good, if a little filled with angst on his part. Well, quite a lot of angst, and a bit of incidental journal writing. Hell, he used to doodle in class watching her, which was how he found out he wasn't half bad at art, as well as at computers. It had boded well for his future career. It didn't help him to answer his question now though.

'She was the girl next door,' he said simply, hoping that would be enough. 'Anyway, I was thinking about maybe inviting her out some time.' If he managed to speak to her. 'To catch up. What do you think?'

'To the house?'

'Er … no.' They had just pulled onto the drive, and the two of them looked at their home. It looked a bit drab in the light of day. Like they hadn't quite moved in yet or something. 'Not the house. I was thinking a bite to eat maybe, a coffee. Nothing serious.'

'Sounds like a good idea, Dad,' Isaac sounded breezy in his reply, and Calvin glanced across at him for any signs of distress. He'd dragged the kid across the country; any plans since he'd agreed to do that were fifty-fifty as far as Cal was concerned. He didn't want his kid to ever feel like an afterthought. 'Wear something nice though, eh?'

Cal opened his mouth to speak.

'And suits don't count,' he added for good measure. 'You need new clothes for out of work, Dad. You've started to look a bit too … comfy.'

Calvin's mouth slammed shut. As Isaac got out of the car, he heard his dad call out to him. 'Isaac, get back in the car. I think we need to hit the shopping centre.'

Isaac hid his grin and did his best bored teenager zombie walk back to the car.

'Thanks, bud.' Cal pulled out of the drive, and headed towards the motorway. 'Do I really look that bad?'

Isaac looked across at his dad and smiled. 'Aww, Dad, of course not. You just look a bit sad sometimes, you know? And the sweatpants have got to go.'

'My sweatpants are cool. I heard that someone from *Love Island* even wore the same ones.'

Isaac groaned. 'Err, Dad! No. Just no. You need … you know, dad clothes. Nothing cringe though.'

'Oh, I shudder at the thought.' They laughed together. 'What do you mean, I look sad?'

Isaac's nose screwed up before he answered. Calvin felt a surge of sorrow towards his son. Guilt too. He had kind of given up a bit. Well, a lot. After Diane died, he just didn't see the point most days. He was definitely more with it now, but this only made him notice how absent he *had* been.

'Well, you know since Mum … I just think a new set of clothes might not hurt.' He was brushing it off, Cal could see, but he wanted Isaac to understand that he *was* okay. And more importantly, despite his occasional ditherings, and crap cooking, he was still his dad. First and foremost.

'I'm okay, Zac, I'm just figuring it out I suppose. It's new to both of us, moving and everything. I don't want you to worry though.' Cal pulled into the left-hand lane, when the signs for the shopping centre in the next city rolled up at the side of the motorway. 'You like it here, don't you?'

Isaac thought of their quiet nights in the house, and missing Mum so much his chest ached. He thought of his new school, and his friends. And of Isobel. They weren't quite happy in his eyes, but he just knew that things were going to change.

'Yes, I like it here. No Suki study dates though, okay?'

Calvin's worry lines dissolved into laughter, and they fist-bumped each other as Calvin went to take the turn.

'Deal. Now help me get some decent clothes.'

'Dad, I thought you'd never ask.'

'Cheeky.'

* * *

Emily was a bath, half a book and three large glasses of wine in when she finally picked up the phone and dialled Cal's number. He picked up on the second ring, which was about the same second that Emily had a minor panic attack and temporarily lost the power of speech.

'Hello?'

'...'

'Hello?'

'... *barely audible squeak*'

'Hello? Who is this? Buddy, are you on the land line?'

'Hi,' she managed to coax out. *What the hell is happening to you, Emily? This is Cal. Little Calvin Albright from your street. You ate mud pies with this man. You had sleepovers right up until college. Your mum was best friends with his mum. It's not Jamie Dornan at the end of the line – it's Cal.*

'Hi,' Calvin replied warily. 'Who is this?'

'Hendrickson.' *Welcome back, tongue.* 'Emily Hendrickson.'

'Oh.' The voice went quiet for a rather unhealthy and worrying amount of time. 'Hello, this is Albright, Calvin Albright.'

Emily gripped the phone while she got her breath back. She heard him calling her name through her top. She grabbed at the phone and stuck it back to her ear. *Get a grip!*

'Hi! Yep, I'm here. Sorry about that, dropped the phone.'

'Hope it's shaken, and not stirred.' She heard Calvin do something akin to a groan, and then he spoke again. 'Sorry about that, a bad joke. I'm glad you called me back. I was wondering if you wanted to meet up for that coffee? I was thinking Saturday?'

He was still him on the phone. He'd suggested meeting up, and had taken the onus off her awkward self. She realised with a jolt that it was nice to have him back in her life and it made her heart glad. It was what she didn't know she'd even needed. Something to shake things up.

He'd been such a good friend to her for so long, maybe he could be again. She felt energised just talking to him, as if a flicker of the old get-up-and-go Emily was ignited.

'I'd love to, but I actually have to work from ten, so it would have to be quite early. I'm reporting on a wedding. It's an all-day thing normally. How about Sunday?' She thought about the wedding she was covering this weekend, *all day and all night long, truth be told.* She always covered the receptions too, as part of the piece. It was her job to go to these special slices of life, and report back on the little details that made the day special. Not a lot of the events of the night made the press, of course, and the rest was rather more rose-tinted when it became paper and ink. A lot of things from awkward dad-dancing to fist fights were never shown the light of day in the paper. Luckily, her photographer was a genius too, and they made it work.

'Sunday's good, but it would be another early one. Nine?'

Emily had to be up anyway, despite her longing for a long lie-in. 'I'll be wired from the night before, nine's good with me.'

'Great. Work sounds interesting, big story is it?'

'One as old as time,' Emily sidestepped neatly. 'It's nothing exciting really, just par for the course with work.'

'Can we meet at the park, near the clubhouse?'

'That sounds perfect. Meet you there?'

'Er, I could pick you up? I don't mind.'

She was about to say yes but then she remembered that she was due at her parents' for dinner that day.

'Er no, that's okay. I'll need the car.'

'Oh, okay, no problem. So, nine on Sunday, okay?'

'Yeah, that's great. Looking forward to it.'

'Me too,' Calvin said, and she could tell he was still smiling from the way he spoke. His daft grin was still there, it seemed. She felt a little wave of nostalgia wash over her. 'It was really good to see you the other day, by the way. I'm sorry if I was a little weird.'

Emily thought back to their encounter. Him striding over in his suit, all polished and easy charm. Her sinking deeper into her chair, feeling like she was sitting there in school uniform and pigtails in comparison.

'Weird?' she supplied, wondering what the holy hell he was talking about. 'No, not at all.'

'Ah good,' he said, seemingly relieved. Emily was just beginning to wonder what he was alluding to, and whether he had a dose of the nerves she had, and he spoke again.

'Er … I'll let you go then. You're probably busy. Friday night, you must have plans …'

Emily looked around her tidy flat, at the television screen and the melting tub of ice cream sitting on the coffee table and shook her head.

'Oh, you know, just hanging at home tonight. Just me, Ben & Jerry.'

'Oh,' he said softly. 'Me too. Well, you know what I mean.' The silence hung in the air between them. They both spoke in unison, but the intention was clear.

'If you're not—'

'Well, do you fancy—'

Chapter 6

It was almost eight o'clock when Emily's cab pulled up to the bar. It was one of the trendier places around, all wooden bars and muted cosy lighting. Emily sometimes came here with Beth, Friday night drinks after work.

She'd just read a text from Dad, reminding her about lunch the day after, even though she never missed it. She smiled, thinking of him sending it, the same text every week. She wondered what he'd think if he knew where she was, and what he and Mum would think about Calvin coming back. They had loved him like a son till university happened. Then, once they heard Calvin was getting married, Emily never heard them ask about him after that. He dropped out of their conversations altogether.

Time just moved on, she supposed. Which also begged the question about why he was back. Emily hadn't asked Calvin much about his life because sometimes it was easier to wonder than have things confirmed. We don't always want to know that someone we once cared for is a total douche now, or sometimes we do, come to think of it. Something about meeting your heroes clanged in her head. She'd always imagined him off living his life, with his wife, maybe a family. It just hurt too much at the time to think of him being so happy, when a big part of his life was missing.

Me. His friend. The girl he used to draw in his notepads when he thought she wasn't looking. Time moved on, and so did people. She did, after all. She was following her own plans, forging her own life. She'd changed too.

It was different for her though. Seeing Calvin was more than feeling inadequate beside him. It reminded her of other things too. Moments between them. The boy who drew, and the girl who wrote. She'd written down what she wanted once, poured out her dreams, and it hadn't come true. The sting of that had never quite left her.

She always wondered why it caused pain to so many people, when the world is nothing but change and rolling with the punches. *I guess we have moments in time we cherish more than others. Those moments might not always feature the people in your life now.*

'Are you getting out, love, or you changed your mind?' The friendly cab driver was looking right at her through the screen, and she came to with a start at the sound of his voice.

'You ever wonder why people take the paths that they do, and end up with the people that they do? How do you know you're on the right path?'

He looked nonplussed for a second, his brow furrowing. 'Boyfriend?'

'Fiancé.'

'Cheating, eh?'

'No. Nothing like that. He's nice.'

'Nice, eh?' He twisted his neck a little further to look her in the eye. 'Who's got the cold feet?'

Emily almost laughed. It had been that long since they'd done anything wedding-like, her feet felt like they were encased in ice. She jabbed her thumb at herself instead.

'You have to have a wedding on the horizon to get cold feet I think. I don't think it's that.' She worried for a moment that maybe it was like that for Tim. Was that why he was dragging his feet?

'I just don't know what I'm doing.' *Did you seriously just tell your cabbie that?* That third glass of wine was making its presence known, loosening her tongue. 'I want things to work out.'

The driver looked like he was about to press the ejector seat in his cab, but he rubbed the scruff of his beard instead, pulling off a photo that was stuck in his front sun visor.

'Darling, this is the wife. It's been twenty-seven years, and I love the bones of the woman. Does she get on my wick end sometimes? Of course. She was sent by the gods to both make me happy and wish I was never born.' The driver was beaming out from the photo, arms wrapped around a rather stern-looking woman. She was holding a handheld vacuum cleaner with a Christmas bow on it, so the context of the photo was a metaphor for the memory it seemed, and no doubt the marriage at times. 'Life's for living, love, so tell your chap how you're feeling. He loves you, he'll understand. Like the wife says to her mates down the bingo, just strap on the big girl boots you lot have these days and give 'em hell. Life's too short, believe me.'

'Yeah.' She nodded, slowly at first but speeding up as his positive attitude rubbed off on her squiffy brain. 'Yeah, you're right! Thanks. I'll just talk to him.'

'That's it, my girl. Oh, and you owe me £12.50.' He tapped the meter.

Emily passed him a twenty. 'Keep the change, and thanks for the pep talk.'

The driver grinned, taking the note, and giving her a friendly wink. 'Anytime. Have a good night.'

'Thanks. Love to the wife!'

She watched the car drive away, feeling oddly exposed post therapy session as she stood on the pavement outside the perimeter of the outdoor drinking area. She could see people sitting outside, eating, drinking cocktails, discussing their days. Some were still dressed in work clothes, others obviously on a date. Looking down at her outfit, she realised that she might have made a bit too much of an effort just to meet an old school friend. She had her best heels on for God's sake, the ones she didn't get to wear when she went out with Tim. Normally because he used restaurant coupons, and they ended up eating early to save even more money using the early dinner specials. Seeing Tim there in his "casual" suit, wallet full of vouchers and timings of the best deals of the evening in town, somehow took the shine off date-night after a while. It was all a bit too prepared, too "arranged" for her liking.

It would be nice to just decide to go out off the cuff, dress up nice and head off into town to see where the night could take them. She and Tim had never really done that, she thought with a pang. Maybe they should. A coupon-free spontaneous date night.

She pushed her thoughts away, resolved to remember all this when she was standing in front of Tim and, slowly, she started to walk towards the bar.

* * *

Calvin tapped one hand against the polished wood of the well-lit bar, feeling both like a teenager and an old man. The bar was filled with office workers and couples. In jeans and white shirt, open at the collar, he investigated the mirror behind the bar and wondered if he was a moustache short of a Tom Selleck looka-like. He had the height, the jaw, the hair. The dress sense of an older gentleman trying a little too hard, maybe? *Oh God, man,* he thought to himself, glaring at his own reflection in the mirror and grabbing his glass to take another deep gulp. Isaac definitely had a point about the dad bod. He was definitely out of the loop when it came to socialising.

He reached for his drink to settle his nerves. When he swung his arm back to down the amber nectar, he heard his name being called at the same time and, turning, felt his elbow connect with something hard.

53

'Hi … heeeeeeyyy!'

Turning in horror, he saw Emily sprawled backwards over the bar stool as people around him stared. The whole bar noise lowered to an uncomfortable level, but Calvin didn't even notice it as he jumped off his stool and was at her side.

'Oh my God, I am so sorry! I'm such a dick. I didn't see you at all, obviously. I am a bit of a bull in a china shop.' He reached for her hands to pull her out of her backwards crab, moving the stool back and settling her onto her feet. *Wow, her legs didn't stop growing. She looks even taller in heels.*

'I remember,' Emily replied, a glimmer of a smile playing across her lips. She rubbed at her thigh where it had connected with the stool, then smoothed herself down. 'How do I look?'

She turned to one side, noticing for the first time that they had gained some rather obvious attention. Calvin blushed furiously. She looked gorgeous. She was wearing a black dress that shone where the light hit it, red heels and a little denim jacket. Casual, and elegant. It suited her. 'You look … lovely. Sorry, people are looking at you now. Do you want to go somewhere else?' He wanted to rewind time, but there was little chance of that.

'No, don't be daft. I'll sort it.' Emily shook her head. 'Whoops,' she said to the woman nearest to her, loud enough for everyone to hear, 'he's such a klutz. Aren't you, darling?' She leaned forward, dropping a tiny kiss on his lips before he could even gather a thought. Or even half a thought. Her skin barely touched his, but the tingle was real. He found he could only resist the urge not to touch his lips by licking at them instead. He felt like someone had lit him on fire from the inside.

Emily's eyes widened a little as she watched him, her neck glowing with the same colour spreading on her cheeks, and he felt something stir deep in his gut. His hand found the small of her back, and the heat seared his palm as he pulled her closer. Her lips were so close again. If he just leaned in … just one more tiny touch … As though she was hearing everything his brain was commanding his body to do, she leaned in.

'Nice move, stud,' she whispered under her breath, close enough to his ear for her hot breath to blow onto his neck. He shuddered a little, nodding at her once from his stupor. She smelled like her. She still had the same girl next door smell, he marvelled as her lips parted. 'I think they bought it. We can stay now.' She laughed, and turned back to the woman, who smiled at the pair of them and headed off to join her party.

'Thanks,' he said smoothly, clearing his throat when his voice gave out. What the hell was that? He felt like he'd stepped through a wormhole back into the Nineties and short pants. His nostrils were still full of Emily as he laughed. 'I think you're right.' They weren't the only one. He'd bought that kiss too. Hell, if it was on a shelf, he'd have stocked up.

Nodding once to the onlookers, dismissing them entirely, he put his arm around Emily and guided her into the stool next to his. When she was seated, he turned and pulled his closer to hers.

'Thanks for that. I think half the bar thought we were having a domestic. I'm so sorry though. Are you really okay? It looked painful.'

'I think I might have a bruise or two.'

Nice, you've bloody scarred the woman. 'Oh God, I'm sorry. Want me to take a look?'

'At my arse?' Her left brow shot to her hairline. 'I'll pass thanks. I think the bar charge for shows like that.'

'Oh yes! Sorry, of course. Well, can I get you anything? Ice, a rubber ring perhaps?' He was busy thinking where he could get an arse sling on a Friday night when her laughter stopped him.

'I'm fine, Calvin,' she said, dipping her head till she caught his eye. He could feel his shoulders relaxing as he locked on to her smiling face. 'It was just an accident. You always were clumsy. I just needed to be reminded. I'll bring my crash helmet next time.'

He relaxed utterly then, laughing.

'I've missed you,' she blurted out, her hand reaching out to swipe playfully at his shoulder. 'I'm glad we're back in touch.'

'I've missed you too, Ems. So, are you saying there'll be a next time already? Even after that? You're not going to lose my number for years again?'

He meant it as a joke, a hopeful little dig for information, especially after his colossal tittery. As soon as the words left his mouth, Emily went from smiling and nodding to dropping her hand. *Shit.*

'Oh God, I'm sorry. I didn't mean it like that.' *I did mean it. Just a little.*

Emily took the napkin from his grasp slowly and turned on her stool to look at her reflection in the back of the bar.

'It's okay. I know you didn't.' She didn't know that, but she hardly thought he had brought her here just to have a go. 'You have a point though.'

It was Calvin's turn to wince then, and she took a deep breath and held out her hand.

'Let's start again. Hi, Emily! Calvin Albright, right? Long time no see! Do you fancy a drink?' She flashed a smile at him, and his heart banged against something long covered in dust.

She's bloody gorgeous. I knew she would be, of course. She was always beautiful to me. But now, she's a woman. A stunning woman. She kissed me.

I'm utterly fucked here. I can't articulate myself at the best of times, and she's just made my whole throat forget how to work. Not to mention the fact that her beautiful body is bruising because I elbowed her like a total knob the minute she arrived.

She always did make me very aware of my own body. Too aware sometimes, which adds to my natural clumsy nature. Isaac was always laughing at him for it. He was the exact opposite. Isaac was just who he wanted to be, and he didn't seem to care what others thought of him. *He's braver than me. Had to be, I guess. My turn now. Pull it together. You're not a teenager anymore.*

Surreptitiously wiping his rather sweaty palm on his trousers, he put his hand into her grip and looked her straight in the eye. *She looks just the same, just more … real. I cannot believe she's sitting right in front of me. Why does this not feel weird?* He searched his psyche for a glimmer of guilt, but there was nothing dark lingering in his thoughts. Wasn't this why they'd come back? To find the old him again? Sitting here, it made sense.

His face breaking out into a wide smile, he said the opposite of what he wanted to say. Those words he pushed firmly to the back of his mind. 'Emily Hendrickson, I can't believe it's you. Let me get you a drink. What's your poison?'

They'd shaken hands twice, but now their hands just hung there in the space between them still clasped together, both silent and communicating to the other. Cal was the first to break the silence.

'I didn't get the chance before, but you look beautiful, Emily. I'm glad you came.'

Their eyes met, and Calvin wondered if his were as bright as hers in the bar lighting. It made the sudden blush on her cheeks even more obvious. *Still the same Ems, she never did know just how lovely she was. Is.*

'Thank you. Can I have a white wine please?'

Calvin nodded, turning on his stool towards the barman, who was serving a couple a little further along the bar. He didn't let go of her hand till he had to reach for his wallet.

He ordered a whisky and a white wine, asking for dry when the barman queried, knowing it was her preferred wine from memory. Emily didn't comment, and his heart skipped a little beat at the little nugget of ease between them. He wasn't feeling quite such a mess now, having a task to focus on. He needed to find his feet. He used to be able to be around her. He could do it again. It felt like repeating an old pattern though, and the thought irked him a little. Being Emily's unwavering, goofy best friend hadn't always been easy.

Chapter 7

'Still a whisky fan then?'

He paid the barman and turned back towards her. She couldn't help but look down at their knees, but he didn't move in as close this time. Much to her surprised chagrin.

'Definitely, although I don't drink a lot these days.' He took a deep swig. 'This is my second though, so I'm one in front.'

She laughed, thinking of the wine she'd had before leaving.

'Oh, I don't drink like I used to in the old days, but I could still match you pint for pint.'

He raised a brow at her, and she felt a flutter in her stomach as he looked at her.

'You know, you aren't so gangly anymore.'

He laughed, throwing his head back a little, and moving in a bit closer in his seat. Their knees connected again, and Emily had to keep her face straight. *Calm down, Jane bloody Austen. It's a knee, not a come-on. Get a grip!*

'I have been told. I just seemed to fill out at university. It did help that I hit the gym a bit too.'

Emily nodded dumbly, taking him in and reconciling the boy he was with the man. It was jarring but comforting too. Like finding a comfy old blanket in the back of the wardrobe on a sad day. Or, more accurately, finding out that not only did your childhood friend and secret crush come home, but he also came home HOT. He was always good-looking, but in a boy-next-door way. He was her boy next door. She found herself wondering what was under his shirt now. And whether it went well with the Pony song. She blamed the wine. And the kiss. She hadn't meant to do it, it was impulse, but the jolt she'd felt when her lips brushed his wasn't easy to forget. She pulled herself away from all thoughts of his lips.

'It really helped with your co-ordination, yeah.' She rubbed at the bottom of her back, where it had connected with the bar edge.

'Oh God, does it still hurt?'

'No, no I'm fine, honestly.' She went to put her hands over his to stop his nervous hand gestures, and he slipped them into hers. 'Let's just forget it happened.'

Calvin's face relaxed, the relief evident on his features.

'Okay, okay. If you're sure.' He squeezed her hands, then slowly let them go. He swallowed hard, and Emily looked at what he had seen. Her engagement ring.

'You're … you're engaged!'

Emily clasped her hands together, feeling very sheepish given what thoughts had been parading through her mind since she'd kissed him.

'Oh … yes! Yes, I am.'

Calvin nodded, his smile looking a little crooked on his face. 'Congratulations! I didn't have a clue.' He looked a little confused for a moment. It passed, and he focused back on her. He looked different now, subdued. 'So, who's the lucky guy?' He turned and took another swig of whisky.

'He's called Tim. He's a bank manager.'

Calvin blinked rapidly at her.

'What?'

'What?' Calvin repeated.

'Never mind what, Brighty.' This was another nickname she'd

59

given him. One she saved for when she was getting a bit ticked off. 'You know what. You did that blinky thing you do when you don't want to upset someone.'

He groaned loudly, waving her off with his hand. She took the opportunity to check out his hand and was shocked when she didn't see a ring. Beth was right. She cursed her hawk-eyed mate silently, adding a quick thank you for making her think of looking in the first place. Dave would be screwed if he ever cheated on Beth, not that he ever would. He was devoted, and utterly smitten. Which was a good job, because Beth was like the SAS. She would sniff adultery a mile off and let him have it, both barrels.

'I don't blink!' Calvin refuted, blinking rapidly.

'Ha!' She declared proudly. 'Did it again!' She copied him, blinking rapidly and laughing her head off. Calvin was not impressed, but she could see the mirth in his expression.

'I don't do that. I never did!'

Emily almost choked on the wine she was sipping. She managed not to laugh before she swallowed.

'You so did! You just did it. When you think you're going to upset someone with something you want to say, you go all blinky.' She fluttered her eyelashes at him rapidly as she demonstrated his tell once more.

'I once again deny your accusations emphatically,' he quipped, staring at her without blinking until she laughed again. 'So, when's the wedding?'

'Oh, not for a while yet. What with work and everything …' She trailed off, reaching for her glass. 'Anyway, how are you? Are you settling back in okay?'

* * *

Calvin's pocket started to vibrate before he could answer. The bar was playing low background music from hidden speakers, and the rest of the clientele were enjoying the evening, chatting and laughing. He pulled his phone out of his pocket and looked at the screen. Isaac. He would have sent anyone else on the planet to voicemail right now, but he clicked the green icon on the screen and mouthed his apologies to Emily. She nodded, pulling out her purse and signalling the barman for another round.

He got to his feet and stood a little way away, keeping one eye on Emily and the stool next to him. He'd noticed a man looking at her as they were talking, and now the same man was eyeing up the stool as if was a portal to another world. *Creep.* He put his phone to his ear.

'Hey, buddy, everything okay with Laura?'

He'd hired a local sitter, one who came with a good reputation for being a straight-A university student and who was hoping to be a teacher. She was strict and Isaac liked her. One good thing to come out of the legions of mothers at the school gates. Tips on good babysitters with their own transportation and ability to occupy a pre-teen for the odd night. Away from the Xbox preferably.

'Yeah. Thanks for telling on me by the way. She made me do ALL my homework and tidy my room.'

Calvin laughed. 'Well, a night away from the screens won't hurt, bud. What's wrong?'

The man, dressed in a rather expensive work suit, was now slowly making his way over to Calvin's stool.

'I just wondered how your night was going. With your friend.'

'That's why you called me? I've been gone, what, an hour? We've barely started talking yet, especially after the bar stool incident.'

'The what?'

'Nothing. Listen, you be good for Laura okay? And do what she says. I won't be too late.'

'Okay, well have fun, Dad. Night.'

Calvin made his way back to his stool, taking big, even strides to deter his competitor, who slunk off in another direction as though this was his intention the whole time.

'Night.'

'Oh, and Dad?'

'Yeah?' Calvin took his seat, noticing that there was a fresh whisky waiting for him. Emily was putting her phone back into her handbag.

'Don't tell any jokes, okay. Especially not the bad ones.'

'Okay, deal.'

He heard Isaac laugh down the line.

'Thank God,' he said, and the line went dead. Calvin shook his head, a big daft grin on his face.

'Sorry about that.' He raised his glass and Emily followed his lead.

'To your big day.' He plastered on a smile. 'You'll make a stunning bride.' The smile accompanying that sentence was as genuine as it was wide. More of a gurn.

Emily clinked her glass with his, taking a deep gulp of her wine.

'What about you?' she asked, giving him her full attention. 'How did things work out?'

Calvin didn't know where to start. Her question was so open, so tactful. She hadn't come to the wedding. Not that he'd expected her to. They'd lost touch well before that, but he had thought she might. All day he had half expected her to walk in, share his and Diane's special day, talk to him. People grew up, he'd reasoned, and then life went on. They'd moved on and their paths didn't cross again. He wanted to put it a better way, in the bare honest way they'd always shared. He wanted to tell her about everything that had happened, but it wasn't the time. So he stuck to the script instead. The one he had had to trot out at school meetings, work meetings, whenever he had to discuss his personal life to other people. He kept it simple. To the point.

'That was actually my son on the phone. Isaac. He's twelve. He's at our old school, funnily enough. He likes it. He's with a sitter.' That fact about their shared school always made him smile, and looking at Emily, he could see her taking it in. It was amazing

62

that in their hometown she hadn't heard anything about him. Still, he'd heard nothing about her either.

'Wow.' She didn't look at him, and her smile was crooked on her face. 'What's your wife doing tonight. Working?'

Oh God. She really didn't know.

'My wife, Diane, died two years ago, so it's just Isaac and I now.'

He took a swig of his drink to replace the moisture in his suddenly dry mouth. He was looking intently into the bar mirror when he felt her arms go around him. He wrapped his free hand around her, putting his glass back on the bar and wrapping his body around hers. She wound her arms around his back, and he pulled her closer.

Chapter 8

'I'm so sorry, Cal, I had no idea.'

All she could see was his stricken face, reflected back at her in the mirror behind the bar. The lights made his eyes sparkle, and she wondered if he was holding in tears. His arms were tight around her, and she nuzzled into him. He still smelled the same. She couldn't resist taking a surreptitious whiff of him even as she digested his bombshell.

'It's okay. We're fine. I am surprised you didn't know, though. Your parents came down for the funeral.'

'They did?' Shock made her grip on him tighten, and he tightened his in response. *Mum and Dad bloody well knew! They never said a word. I'm going to kill them both.* 'That was nice of them. I'm glad they did.' *Dead to me. Both of them.*

She pulled away, feeling like a prize idiot now. Jesus, she'd been feeling jealous at his seemingly perfect life, and he'd been through so much. Maybe being an adultier adult wasn't as much as she'd thought it for him. Her heart broke for her friend.

'You really didn't know?'

She looked at him sheepishly. If she had known, she would have reached out.

'Of course not. How can you even ask me that? I would have

called you.' *I would have been on the motorway in five seconds flat. He's still my person. I would never have let him go through all that alone. The past wouldn't have come into it.* The thoughts ran through her with an electrifying jolt. She clocked a twig of relief on his features and realised with a pang that he might have thought that she had known about his loss, and had still stayed away. She really hoped that wasn't true, but she found herself unwilling to ask. Not now, anyway. It didn't matter, given his obvious pain and grief. Her heart went out to him, but her parents' actions confused her. 'My parents never said a thing.'

'They didn't?'

His face confirmed it for her. He did think she knew. She felt a little crushed at the thought of that adding to his pain. She felt like a bitch by proxy. What were her mum and dad playing at?

'Well, I guess they didn't want to gossip,' he said, ever the gent. 'Listen, Isaac and I are fine. I have a great job, the house is great, Isaac's doing great at school and everything's just … well, great!'

'That great eh?' She raised a single brow at him as they sat back on their respective stools and took another drink.

'Yep,' he said, a little too shrilly. 'And you're getting married to Tim!'

'Yes!' she replied, matching him shrill for shrill. 'So, is he okay?'

Calvin frowned, blinking hard, his brows knitting together as he tapped his index finger on his top lip.

'Well, I can't say without meeting the bloke, but Tim's a bit of a crap name, isn't it?'

Emily rolled her eyes. 'I meant Isaac, Blinky.'

His eyes widened, and her lips tightened, trapping a giggle.

'Oh, Isaac! He's fine. The babysitter is making him do chores and homework.'

'Ah, okay. Do you have any pictures?'

Calvin produced his phone again, bringing up a screen where Calvin and a young boy both stood in the dark, lit up by their laser guns and flashing neon armour.

'Laser World, a few weeks back. He won, but I have demanded a rematch.'

Emily looked closely; she could see that Isaac looked a lot like Calvin. They both looked so happy in the photo.

'It looks like a great day. He's adorable.'

He smiled at the screen before putting it away.

'Adorable, annoying, expensive, moody. He's a good kid.'

'I can't believe you're a father, and to a grown boy!'

'I know, when the hell did we grow up, eh?'

'Oh.' Emily shook her head. 'I'm not sure I've quite gotten there yet.' She ran her fingers around the ring on her finger.

'Oh?' His eyes were on hers again. 'Want to talk about it?'

That was a difficult question to answer. If she'd been talking to her childhood friend back then, before it all went wrong, she would have told him her woes. Asked his advice even. They used to do that so easily, even though she did feel the odd pang now and then when he was interested in a girl. Well, not so much a pang as a twelve-inch knife through her heart chambers. She couldn't tell him now though, about Tim and her doubts about where she was going in life. Especially not after the revelation that he'd lost his wife. She'd never attended the wedding; the invite had been swiftly thrown in the trash can. She could hardly moan to him about her relationship. She told him something she could tell him instead. Over time, she'd stopped talking to anyone about it really. It felt like something she couldn't achieve. She found herself wanting to know what he thought.

'Oh it's nothing, just work stuff really. I'm trying for a promotion, and it's taking longer than I thought to get to where I want to be.'

Over another drink, she told him about work. About how she wrote the wedding section articles and wanted to be a fully-fledged writer. She wanted to write real features, books eventually. She even told him about her stories being published, and he was beyond thrilled for her.

'So you want to write books too? Have you subbed anywhere? I loved your stories.'

The bar was livening up now, and they had found themselves shouting to hear each other above the din. Walking down to a quieter bar they both remembered, Scruffy's, they'd fallen into an easy step together as they made their way along the lamp-post-lit streets of their hometown.

'I'd love to. Hopefully once I get more established at the paper. I have written a few pieces, but nothing feels quite finished yet. My boss is not one for flowery prose; she pretty much shoots down all my ideas. I've sent a few things out, but nothing has come of that so far. Par for the course, I know.' She knew how hard it could be. She'd never balked at the challenge before now, but her steely resolve was starting to buckle.

They were crossing the street, Scruffy's in front of them. A place that held great memories. The old landlord would serve local teens on the quiet, so it was one of their favourite hang-outs growing up.

'I'll warn you now, I haven't been here for a while, but they haven't redecorated anything by the look of it. You ready for the sticky floors and ripped beer mats?'

Calvin grinned at her, and his sexy smile almost floored her. She felt like her world was tipping sideways.

She took a step and stumbled into a pothole, her heel snapping as she tried to regain her footing. *Damn you, heels!* She was bracing herself to hit the deck when she felt Cal's arms grab her. She ended up wrapped in his strong embrace, her now bare foot sitting in a puddle. She looked up at him from her wonky position, and he was looking right back at her.

'I've got you.'

He almost whispered it, but those three words had such an effect on her whole body she felt as though he had spoken it to her very soul. She was glad he had a tight hold on her because she was tiddly, her foot was drenched, and she was fit to swoon like a *Bridgerton* admirer.

'Are you okay?' He straightened them both up gently, not taking his eyes from her face as they got off the road. 'Anything hurt?' He turned to scowl at the road as they came to a stop on the pavement in front of Scruffy's neon-lit window. 'Bloody potholes.' He ran back to pick up her shoe from where it had been discarded. The heel was hanging by a thread.

'Damn it,' she heard him say, and he snapped the rest of the heel off, dumping it into the bin on his way back to her. She reached out for it, but he kneeled by her feet instead. He patted his shoulder.

'Here, lean on me. Lift your foot up.'

Oh my God, how embarrassing. My bare, puddle-soaked foot. Knowing my luck, there's probably a discarded fag butt from the street tucked between my toes. She slowly pulled out her foot, squinting at it and hoping that she would be looking more Cinderella and less Shrek in the trotter department.

He placed her broken-heeled shoe, which was now more of a flat, back onto her foot. Her foot was thankfully clean, one errant twig brushed off lightly with his finger.

'It's the best I can do I'm afraid without chopping the other heel off. Do you want me to get you a taxi?'

Her heart sank at the thought of the night ending. She'd been enjoying herself so much. She wasn't ready for the moment to end.

'Although,' he said, taking her arm into his on the broken heel side and helping her towards the pub, 'we are here now. We could just stay a little while, get a taxi from here later? I promise to protect you from the sticky carpets.'

'We can't very well miss out Scruffy's on the first night we're here together,' she agreed, trying her best to look good whilst walking like Long John Silver with a touch of wood rot. He moved his arm from where he had been holding her up, tucking her into his side as they slowly walked the few steps to the pub. 'It wouldn't feel right, would it?'

Looking at him under the lights from the pub, she knew that

nothing about this night felt wrong. She felt better with him around. She always did. Her lovely friend.

'No, definitely not.' He opened the door, the noise of the pub cutting the silence of the night.

As they walked in, she found herself thinking of the night they'd last been together. The night it had all started to change, and not for the better.

Chapter 9

'Oh, Emily, you look so beautiful.'

Standing at the top of the staircase, Emily looked herself up and down in the mirror. She wouldn't call herself beautiful exactly; she wasn't that. She did look good though. The pale blue satin of the dress fitted her well, making the most of her gangly, boyish frame. At least she'd got the boobs now, finally, and in this dress, it changed her. With her hair freshly washed and styled into dark brown curls down her back, she saw a glimpse of the woman she would become. She smiled at her reflection, wondering what the future would hold. She couldn't wait to get started.

'Thanks, Mum. Is he here yet?'

'Give him chance, love,' her mother said from the bottom of the stairs. 'It's not even seven yet! Come on, let's have a photo in the lounge.'

They were almost at the lounge door when the doorbell rang. Emily's mum Carole practically shoulder-barged her out of the way to get to the front door first. As soon as she opened the door, she snapped her camera. The flash went off, and there was a nervous squeak from the front path.

'Mum!' Emily's cheeks exploded into a tomato-like hue as she tried to get the door from her mother's grasp. 'Calvin, are you okay?'

Eighteen-year-old Calvin was standing at the front door, blinking rapidly, a bouquet of flowers and a small posy in his arms.

'Yep, all good. My retinas are a bit worse for wear, but luckily it's dark where we're going.' *The ladies moved aside, and he stepped over the threshold. The hallway felt a little claustrophobic with his tall frame, and her mother ushered them into the lounge.*

'Sorry, Calvin love. You look lovely! Doesn't he look nice, Emily?'
Emily stood before Calvin as her mother wittered on excitedly.

'Yes, he does,' *she said in a soft voice.* I love you, Mum, but please, just bugger off. *She felt mean for even thinking it, but it was awkward enough. Calvin was staring right at her, his eyes looking her up and down and resting on her face.*

'Cup of tea, Calvin? Glass of bubbly?'

'That'd be great, thanks, Mrs Hendrickson.'

'Oh, Calvin, Carole, please! I've been telling you for years, less of the formality. You're like family!'

Calvin blushed. 'Yeah sorry Mrs— er … Carole.'

'Such a polite young man.' *Carole cut off his apology with a pinch of his cheeks. Her mum finally went to the kitchen, and they were left alone.*

'You look stunning, Emily.' *He held out the small posy of fresh-cut flowers.* 'The bouquet's for your mum. I know this college prom thing is not the same as an American prom, so I thought a corsage might be a bit daft …

She took the simple little flower arrangement and thought it the best thing she'd ever received. She bent her head to the flowers, breathing in the delicate scent.

'Thank you,' *she said, his beautiful blue eyes pinning her to the spot.* 'They're perfect.'

'Woo!' *They could hear Carole popping the cork with gusto in the kitchen, and the two of them laughed awkwardly.* 'Two minutes, you two lovebirds! Bubbly's on the way!'

Emily's smile died on her face, her eyes darting to search his face for a reaction to her mother's clanger. He looked just as horrified as she felt. He had gone puce in the face, and he was shuffling from one foot to the other. *Is he petrified at the mere prospect?* She felt her heart sink a little at the thought, but she brushed it away. Either way, she would know. Mere hours from now, she would know.

What was it her dad would say if he were here? *'Let the chips fall where they are, my dear.'* Thank God he was at work, or he would be bloody hopping on the spot right now. Her dad never had missed a trick, seemingly since the minute she was born. He'd given her a pep talk before he'd left for his night shift at the hospital. He would be waking her up in the morning, no doubt the minute he walked in. Before her mother woke up demanding coffee. He was almost as anxious about tonight as Emily was.

'Sorry about her,' she said, rolling her eyes dramatically for lack of something else to do with her face.

'It's okay.' He smiled, and her worries faded into the background. He reached out his fingers, and she weaved hers through his. 'Come on, let's get a drink, darling,' he joked.

He whimpered a little when the unexpected thrill of his words tightened her fingers around his, hard, but he never said a thing. A half second later, she felt him squeeze hers right back.

Her mother looked like she had already had a glass of fizz or two. She was dancing around the kitchen with the dog jumping around with her. The radio on the kitchen worktop was playing her oldies radio (it was dance music half the time, Mum's little joke) and there were two glasses of fizz sitting on the countertop, next to Mum's camera.

'Come on in, grab a glass! I'll get a photo!' Carole lunged for the camera, managing to knock both glasses down the right trouser leg of Calvin's dapper suit.

'Mum, no!'

'Yiy-yiy!' Calvin yipped loudly as he jumped two feet in the air, his trousers staining a deeper shade of their original colour. Champagne dripped from his previously pristine and rather shiny shoes onto the kitchen linoleum.

Her mother was no help either. She was running around like a headless chicken, screaming, 'Dennis! Dennis! Get the hairdryer!'

'Dad's at work, Mum! Get a grip!' Emily was trying to avoid anything splashing on her outfit, her mother swinging her arms wildly. So wildly it was as if she'd set Calvin on fire, not just drenched him in alcohol.

The rest of the time, before they left for the prom, was utter chaos, involving crotches and trouser legs, hairdryers on full blast and Emily scowling at her mother the whole time. By the time they managed to get the heck out of there and to the venue, Emily was thoroughly stressed out. Too stressed out to even enjoy the ride to the college grounds. Calvin was as genial and polite as he always was to her mother, almost apologising to her for being in the way of the spillage; he was that honourable about it.

Over his shoulder, Emily had made faces at her mother, leaving her in no doubt that her daughter was decidedly not impressed with her antics. Her dad would surely have something to say too. Cries of her being an overenthusiastic saboteur probably. Before she had a minute to compose herself, refocus on the night and everything it meant, they were outside college. Calvin looked across the seat at her, holding out his hand for her to take hold.

'Come on,' he said briskly, a little shadow of something she couldn't name dancing across his features. 'This is our night, Ems. Let's forget about everything and have some fun, eh?' The instant her skin touched his, she felt better. Of course they'd be all right. They were Calvin and Emily. They were always good when they were together. BFFs. She brushed off the panic of the last hour, and focused on the night ahead. She had everything she wanted, almost. She was on track, and ready to take life by the horns.

* * *

'I'm so sorry. Again. My mother is a nightmare sometimes. Even with you.'

73

They were sitting in a quiet corner now, chairs smushed together behind a white-tableclothed round table. The dance was in full swing, and the pair of them were tucking into the food that Calvin had braved the buffet table for.

'Stop saying sorry to me,' Calvin begged, a prawn vol-au-vent halfway to his mouth. *He ate the whole thing in two bites and reached for another from the huge plate he'd brought for them to share.* 'It was an accident. Your mum apologised already. Loads. I'm fine!'

'Yeah, well I'm mortified.' *She picked up a cocktail stick filled with cheese and pineapple cubes, taking a half-hearted nibble.* 'She's so embarrassing.'

'Oh I don't know, she's pretty cool. And your dad. My folks tend to like it a bit quiet at home.'

'Young mums eh?' *Emily shrugged, and Calvin nodded. His parents had had him later in life, so the lively household of the Hendricksons had been a source of some entertainment to him over the years.*

'Don't knock it, that's all I'm saying. It's pretty cool that they're so involved in your life.'

'Up my arsehole you mean. My mum can't spell the word boundary, *never mind understand what it means. She's always in my business, asking stupid quest—* Oh look at Kirsty Barnett over there! Jed's only gone out for a smoke and she's sniffing around that dude that Maz brought with her. There's going to be blood on the dance floor, I bet you.'

'He's not gone out for a smoke. I caught him kissing Adele Wainwright in the lads' toilets ten minutes ago.'

'Eugh! Gross.'

'They're not that bad, pretty clean as it goes.'

'Not the toilets! Adele! She's seen more pricks than a second-hand dartboard.'

'Wow, the claws are out tonight.'

Emily sighed. She knew he was right, and she wasn't that girl either.

74

'I know, I know. It's just the booze talking.' And the nerves.

Calvin raised a brow, and her heart leapt at the devastatingly gorgeous boy before her.

'Two drinks is hardly your limit, and one was that alcopop we had on the way over. You okay?'

His gaze fell on her hands, which were clasped together in her lap. He put one hand around both of them. 'Come on, Ems, you've been weird all night. I – I actually want to talk to you too. The thing is, Ems, I— Oh, for God's sake!'

His mates were coming over now, talking to each other in a rapid fashion and eyeing the pair of them as if they were the talk of the night. Emily looked around her in confusion, but all she could see was the usual. People dancing, laughing. Little groups of people messing about, the jocks on the next table between them and the bar area snickering about something, just out of sight behind their table. Typical meatheads for this school, all testosterone and over-inflated egos. Stereotypes aren't nice, but it did sum up these goons.

'Listen, I just need to go sort this lot out.' Calvin nodded his head towards the descending rabble, his eyes darting towards the jocks. 'They'll only end up fighting if I don't; but listen, just stay here and wait. Please?' His eyes were beseeching, and she focused on his face.

'Cal, what's wrong?'

She reached up and touched his face, and he broke into a broad grin.

'Everything's fine. I just really need to talk to you, and I really want you to listen. Okay?'

'Okay,' she agreed, and he took her hand off his face, dropping a kiss onto her palm. He gave her one last look, their faces up close. Emily yearned to take the leap. To say something, to ask him to leave with her. They could go to the castle; no one would be there. They could sit there together, watching the world like they always did. She could just show him what she was feeling, right now. She could move an inch and a half closer, touch her lips to his. She could bloody well kiss his face off, right here, in this darkened corner, *under the flashing lights. 'Is this about university, Cal? I mean, I know we're going to different places, but I real—'*

'It's not about uni. Well, it is I suppose, in a way.'

'Calvin, come on, dude!' His cronies were getting louder, and closer. Emily's friends were all off in quiet corners with their dates, and here Emily was, trying to get her words out to Calvin, his eyes darting from hers to his mates. He looked stressed. A light sheen of sweat was showing on his skin under the sparkly lights.

'I'm coming!' He half bellowed over his shoulder. Turning back to her, looking positively panicked now, he sighed heavily. She felt the hair around her face move with the wind of his exasperation. He smelled of chewing gum, and bubbles, and Calvin.

'For God's sake!' He shouted this to no one in particular before stomping off towards his mates. Emily watched him drag them back, away from her. His movements were animated, all gesturing arms and expressive facial expressions. His mates were a little more subdued now to say the least. The music changed. Cyndi Lauper began singing about girls wanting more fun, and Emily wondered what the hell was going on. The music was whipping up the dancing couples now, the party ramping up a notch as the alcohol buzzes kicked in, and the cheesy hits loosened their singing warbles. She scanned the room, spotting one of her friends – Hannah – queueing to get a drink.

Emily stood up, picking her dress up with one hand to navigate around the table legs. She saw Calvin's head turn in her direction, and he said something to his friends and took a step towards her. She smiled, waiting for him to come back over and explain why he was like a cat on a hot tin roof tonight. She needed him to just sit down and let HER talk. She needed to get this out of her. She couldn't go home and face her dad in the morning if she didn't follow through with their plan. She'd been waiting for far too long. Years too long, and now they had just a few short weeks together before university came along. They both wanted to get there early, get themselves settled into their dorms, start exploring their new surroundings. It would be too late then. They'd get busy, and the distance would widen between them in the way she feared.

She stopped walking over to Hannah, standing right where she was and watching him walk back to her. His mates were all acting strangely, looking at her and him as if they'd never seen a conversation between a man and a woman before. What were they drinking tonight? Emily made a mental note to stay clear of whatever it was. Calvin was halfway to her now, the music still playing, everyone for the most part oblivious to the simmering tension and excitement that Emily felt with every step Calvin took. She looked him in the eye, and her whole face broke out into a huge beaming smile. Calvin's face mirrored hers, and the closer they got to each other, the more intense the look. The bigger the smile. She thought her whole face might split apart; she was that happy. Did he feel what she did? Oh she hoped he did, so much.

Something caught her eye, a flash and a flurry of blurred movement from the jock corner. She looked across to see what the fast-moving thing was, her head snapping back to Cal's just in time to see his smile disappear as something hit him, and he disappeared.

'Cal!' She was up on her feet the second he went out of view. The music stopped, the crowd parting. The jocks' laughter was deafening in the otherwise silent hall.

'Oh man, that was frickin' awesome!'

'Who did it hit?'

'Those guys are the worst!'

'Poor Calvin.'

Emily grabbed her dress and ran as fast as she could, pushing and shoving the onlookers out of the way as she went.

'Guys, you dicks! What did you do that for?' Some of the crowd were looking at the goons who decided that skimming a full bloody ice bucket across a room full of people was a great idea.

'Oh my God!'

'Is he dead?'

'Someone, call an ambulance!'

'Mr Wilson, start clearing the crowds out from the doorway!' The college staff were springing into action, the seriousness of the situation kicking in.

Calvin was lying on the floor, blood coming from a wound on his head. He was unconscious. Emily sank to her knees beside him, touching his face gently to try to wake him up. She felt arms trying to pull her away, but she shrugged them off. Glancing around her, she looked for the source of the trouble, and spotted a dented ice bucket on the floor beside him. 'Idiots!' she shouted in the jocks' direction. They were already being spoken to by campus security. She hoped they threw the book at them. Mrs Cheshire came into view, the medic on site, and she got to work checking Calvin out. He mumbled as he came to, his eyes looking dazed in their half-hooded state. Some of the onlookers were bored already, heading over to the bar area or outside, out of the way of the ambulance that was speeding its way over.

Emily didn't give a crap about any of them. She wanted the jock idiots dead of course, but they would get theirs. She reached for Calvin's hand and held it.

'Calvin, are you okay?' His eyelids fluttered. 'Calvin!'

'That … hurt …' he groaned, and Emily broke into laughter, which soon dissolved into snotty tears.

'I bet it did. What hurts?'

Calvin winced, but didn't answer; he'd lost consciousness again. Mrs Cheshire was looking worried. 'Hopefully the ambulance will be here soon.' That was when she noticed Calvin's arm. His wrist was bent at a very awkward angle. Mrs Cheshire saw her looking and leaned in close.

* * *

What seemed like years later, the ambulance arrived and Emily begged to be allowed to go with him, but a member of staff went to meet his parents at the hospital. Cover their arses too, probably.

Not that it was their fault, but Emily couldn't control her inner rage that Calvin was hurt. Emily found herself standing on the side of the road, blood from her hands now marking her dress in macabre handprints. She looked like a bad Carrie *remake. How did the evening go so wrong? Tonight was going to be the night. She was going to tell him that she loved him. Not as a friend, not even as a best friend. As the person she wanted to be with, above the billions of other people on the planet.*

Mrs Cheshire ushered her back inside for a cup of hot, sweet tea. The hall had been cleaned up, the offenders carted off by the police and the surrounding streets were full of cars and disgruntled party-goers heading home early or going on to other parties before their parents caught on to what had happened and started ringing each other's houses to check on where their kids were.

'Come on, love.' Mrs Cheshire was all gentle smiles and back pats. 'He'll be okay. He did a bit of damage but he'll mend.' Her eyes fell onto Emily's dress, and her smile dimmed somewhat. 'Such a shame about your lovely dress. Bit of hydrogen peroxide should get it out. Works a treat on my uniforms.'

Emily nodded dumbly, eventually dissolving into tears.

'Mrs Cheshire,' she said in between sobs. 'Can you ring my dad at work please? I just want to go home.'

79

Chapter 10

'I bloody well knew it,' Emily muttered when her mobile rang, cursing under her breath as she walked away from the tantalising bubble bath. After waking up feeling a little more than rough, and a little more than happy, she'd thrown her head into the wedding. The notepad had been out in force, and she had enough notes to write what she hoped would be a very structured piece – romantic, sentimental still, but muted for Joanna's palate. She knew they had some good photographs that would make it really pop. Before she'd known it, she was pinching some feeling back into her heels in the seat of her car, her nude high heels sitting on the seat next to her. They'd wrapped up early, and she'd fired off a text to Tim, asking him to come over.

He'd replied straight back.

Good news on the early finish. Can't wait to see you. I'll bring some dinner. Love you.

Her heart swelled. He knew she'd be tired, and offering to bring food was so him. He really was lovely. She couldn't wait to see him, sort things out between them. She'd missed him. The phone kept ringing and she growled at it as she hurled her sponge into the foam.

She looked once more at the hot, steamy water longingly. It

wasn't the caller's fault her whole body was aching, and she was a toe tip away from hot, sweet relief. She still resented them anyway as she threw on her dressing gown and reached for her mobile. 'Beth? Can I call you back, love, I'm just about to get in the bath.'

'What? I thought you'd still be at the wedding. What happened? Bridezilla attack? Dodgy quiche at the wedding breakfast?'

Emily grinned when she thought of her workday. 'Nope, I got what I needed and got the heck out of dodge. I'm determined to dazzle Joanna.'

'Em, nothing can dazzle that woman. She wants the big time, and Hebblestone is too sleepy.'

'Maybe.' Emily felt a flicker of defence for her hometown, and herself if she was honest. 'We Hebblestonians have our moments.' She frowned. 'If you thought I was still at the wedding, why'd you call? Everything okay?'

'That's what we were wondering.' She swore she heard her friend grin down the line. 'I was ringing to see if you felt better. You send me a couple of random texts last night, and a voicemail of you snoring like a freight train not long after.'

Emily's eyes bulged in her head. 'Really? What did I say?' She'd just shoved her phone in her bag that morning, wiping the notifications to spare her poor bloodshot eyes. What *did* she say?

'I have no idea. One looked like it was written in Klingon and the other was a GIF from that *My Girl* film, when the two kids kiss. Even Dave couldn't make out more than two words of it. Something about wanting to go next door, and castles.'

'Oh God. Weird. Sorry. I got a bit tipsy. I ended up meeting Calvin for a drink and I must have drunk-dialled you.'

'Lunatic. You do the weirdest stuff when you're on the wine.'

'How did you know I was on the wine?'

'I've shared enough rooms with you to know your telltale buffalo snore when I hear it. Did you have a good night? Any gossip? Did his wife leave him for the Ocado delivery driver?'

'No, nothing like that.' She went to check the living room as she tried to get her friend off the phone. It was all set up, clean and tidy. She'd run around like a lunatic in her underwear, getting the flat ready for the night. She smiled at her efforts. It had come together, and it hadn't cost more than a few candles either. The last thing she wanted to do was wow Tim and then have him keel over when he saw the receipt. 'It was good actually.' *I haven't laughed that much in ages.* 'I can't talk now anyway. Tim's on his way over. He's bringing dinner and I haven't got changed yet. I'm just about to hop in the bath. The wedding reception was a bit sweaty this afternoon.'

'How long does it take to get your bits washed and changed into sweatpants? Oh come on, Dave's at the darts tonight. There's bugger all on the telly.'

Emily laughed, shaking her head, and headed back across the hallway from her bedroom to the bathroom, where the heat from her hot fragrant bath called to her. Steamy fingers beckoned from the open door, and her tired and slightly still-pickled-from-the-night-before body walked towards the tub unbidden.

'Beth, honestly! Go read a book or something. I have to get ready.'

She didn't mention their planned meeting tomorrow morning at the clubhouse in the park. There was no way she'd get her off the phone then. What if Tim walked in? She hadn't even told him about Calvin yet, given the week they'd had. She didn't want him hearing it second-hand. She could hear a key in the front door of the flat. 'Beth, I must go. Tim's home.'

'Oooo, date night eh? Are you going to mention the wedding?'

'I was planning to.'

'Good. Tell him that you want your big day! That will pull you out of your funk, and I think Joanna would even see the merit in our very own wedding reporter getting hitched and the coverage it could bring. Just think!'

She felt a clench of something deep within her at the thought of her and Tim, smiling for the cameras, featured in the wedding section. It made her stomach roil. 'Okay, okay! Whatever! Now, naff off! Bye!' She jabbed the off button on her phone, just as she heard Tim calling her name.

'I'm in here, Tim, just getting dressed, sorry! Beth rang about work.' She shouted it through the bathroom door before she closed it and looked longingly at the still-steaming tub. She still felt rough, and her body was screaming at her to get in.

She could hear Tim walking around the flat, his voice calling out to her. 'I was thinking we could have an easy night. You sounded tired on the phone. What's with all the candles? Did the power go out?'

'No.' Emily rolled her eyes. She had planned to be wearing something silky when he'd arrived. A proper date night. 'I just thought it might be nice.'

'Oh, okay. Pretty. There's a show on tonight, about eight o'clock? Do you fancy watching it?'

'Err, yeah … maybe. I won't be a minute.' She pulled the stopper out of her bath, lamenting the hot, refreshing bubbly water as it gurgled down the plughole. 'Good day at work?'

'Not bad, the usual array of Saturday morning customers. I think our new savings packages are working, so that's been a good shot in the arm for morale.'

'Hmm-mmmm.' Emily made all the right noises as she freshened up in the bathroom, grabbing her clean yoga pants and loose-slung top and checking out her reflection in the mirror. It was a bit pointless dressing up now. She'd just have to try her new outfits on for him later. 'That's good. What did you get to eat?' Her stomach was now over the nausea; she was *starving*. She headed out of the bathroom, slipping into her bedroom to put a bit of perfume on. She still felt like the shots of tequila she and Calvin had drunk as nightcaps were seeping out through her alcohol-sodden pores. She was just about to leave when her phone beeped again.

'I thought we'd try that new Italian. I got us some lasagne and a bit of salad.'

Emily picked her mobile phone up, ready to text Beth back and tell her to bugger off. It was a message from Calvin. She clicked on the screen, and his words came up.

Hey Emily, thanks for last night. I am ashamed to say that I'm more than a little hungover today. You are a bad influence as always. So nice to see you. Calvin x

Her heart was hammering through her slouchy top as she read his words. It was strange to think of him out there, in the world, so close. Before this week he was just an old part of her life, something she pulled out of her memory banks from time to time when something sparked a thought of him. A whiff of aftershave from someone she passed on the street, an old film trailer that reminded her of a cinema trip together, laughing at the stories and flicking popcorn at each other. Now he was back. Single. Widowed. A father, no less. She'd expected him to be so different, but, last night, she'd realised that despite the years apart from each other, he was still the same Calvin Albright she remembered. The trouble was, she'd always had a crush on the teenage Calvin, as unrequited as it was. She'd wished for it to happen so many times over the years, but she was never brave enough to risk letting him in on the secret. It was too risky.

On reflection, years later when her heart had healed enough to look back, as a true romantic, she realised it was fate. Fate telling her that it wasn't meant to be. Last night, sitting there in that pub with him, surrounded by memories and people living their lives around them, she had realised that the crush hadn't entirely been extinguished, or dulled over time. It was very much still there, and she didn't quite know what fate was playing at. Since she'd seen him again, she'd thought of nothing else but the girl who knew him before, and what she would say to the woman in the mirror now. She could hear Tim in the kitchen dishing up their food, and knew she had to be quick. She felt bad enough not greeting him at the door.

I'm as fresh as a daisy. You must be getting old. I had a lot of fun too. Emily

She agonised over dropping a kiss on the end of the text, but after adding and deleting it a half million times, she left it off and hit send. He replied within seconds.

Cheeky. I'm only four months older than you, remember. Still on for grabbing a coffee tomorrow morning?

'Emily, you coming?'

'Yeah, just a second!' She called to Tim, fingers moving fast.

Yep, sounds good. See you at the clubhouse.

'Babe, you stuck in here? Food's getting cold.' Tim's head popped around the door. 'Come on, the show's nearly on.'

Emily stood there, frozen, phone in hand.

'I'm coming, sorry.'

'Oh okay.' Tim's bored look told her that he'd already tuned out. He found Beth a little much at times. Tim liked quiet, and Beth didn't know how to be. Besides, his head was half turned towards the television in the lounge. 'Come on then, quick.'

Emily followed him obediently into the lounge, dropping her phone onto her bed on the way out. In the lounge, the food was laid out on plates on the coffee table, the flat-screen playing an advert for life insurance. There was a bottle of wine and two half-filled glasses ready, and Emily took one as she sat down on the sofa. He'd blown the candles out, the corner lamp illuminating the room. When he saw her looking at the wisps of smoke, he shrugged.

'Sorry. They were reflecting off the screen a bit.' He took a seat next to her, picking up his plate and cutlery before she could lean in to him. She caught a whiff of the hot lasagne, and ignored her stomach a moment longer. Looking at Tim, she leaned in slowly and gave him a little kiss on the lips. He'd brought her dinner. He was lovely. She leaned in closer, nibbling his earlobe between her teeth. He kept his eye on the screen, but shifted in his seat. It was working. She continued her lazy exploration, licking gently along

85

the length of his jaw. He was clean-shaven as always, but she felt slight stubble as she kissed the corner of his mouth. Teasing him. He shifted again, and she moved closer. Another slow, just-there kiss. A twin right next to the ghost of the last one.

She continued till she was almost at the other corner of his mouth, and she felt his hand wrap around hers. He was squirming in his seat now. It really was working. She wondered where the feeling of elation had gone. She used to love to turn him on. It turned *her* on more than anything else. It made her feel like she had a little power over him. Her eyelids fluttered with the effort of keeping them closed.

She always wanted to make a man's eyes grow dark with lust. Get half lidded and horny eyes looking back at her. Knowing that she had done it. That she was the one woman who could wreck his life and make his dreams come true in one kiss. She saw it so often in the weddings she observed. The many, many pairs of once-single people, vowing forever with meaningful looks. She always watched the first dance for that look. When the intimacy of their bodies and the promise of the night to come shone in their eyes.

She couldn't think of the last time she'd seen a look anything like that in Tim's eyes, and she mourned the loss of it. She wanted it back. She kissed him again, this time pushing the tip of her tongue out and opening his mouth. He kissed her back and she opened her eyes, at last. His eyes weren't on hers. They were on the television screen. His lips came for hers, but she moved away. He patted her hand and reached for the remote, eyes never leaving the screen. She waited for him to do … well, anything, but he was absorbed by the screen.

'Seriously?' she asked. He didn't hear her. Her stomach growled defiantly. She felt like joining in a good old roar. But instead she said, 'The food smells amazing. This really from the new place on the high street?' She'd seen the takeout bags in the kitchen, but she was still surprised. Not his usual takeaway. He was making the effort too. He'd even plated her food up for her instead of using the takeout boxes.

'Yeah, a couple of the girls from work went last weekend for opening night. We got invited at the bank. They raved about it and with the vouchers they had, I got twenty per cent off.' He grinned at her, face flushed. He always got excited when it came to saving money. The best sex they'd ever had was when his ISAs matured. He was hot the whole weekend when that happened. That had been a good weekend, she remembered. *I wonder if he had the sexy hooded eyes then, when we reached for each other in the dark.* She tried to remember, but the food was calling to her.

She picked her own plate up and, starting to cut off a piece, she turned back and stared at him.

'Did the whole bank get invited?'

Tim's attention was still on the television screen, his mouth full of garlic bread. She noticed he'd got a tiny piece of red paper on his sleeve. It looked like a little Post-it. She picked it off him, willing him to answer the way she hoped he would.

'Huh? Yeah, I think they did. We get quite a few of these things through the post. The girls usually divvy them up and share them. We save a ton with the vouchers they send in. Wine's not bad, either.' His face was practically lit up now.

Emily nodded, taking a bite of the dish.

'So, why didn't we just go to the restaurant when it opened? We could have had a meal out.'

The adverts were ending, and Tim was turning up the TV. 'It's on! You ready?'

'Tim, answer my question. I don't want to watch TV. I wanted to talk.'

She was holding her fork aloft now, and she wasn't sure whether to put it on her plate or stick it through his eye.

'What question? Talk about what?' She could see him racking his brain for a forgotten anniversary, his brow furrowed. The show's music started, and his eyes were half on the screen. 'Martin's on now. Can it wait?'

'Martin?' Emily looked at the screen, and it dawned on her. The show he wanted to watch was a financial programme, run by a financial guru who was immensely popular among the public for helping them to save money. The modern-day equivalent of Robin Hood if he rocked a sharp suit and rode a briefcase. Tim loved him as though he were a god. 'Oh, Tim, seriously? We're having a nice meal, and you want to watch this? Why don't you just record it? It's Saturday!'

'I'm here now, ready to watch it. What would be the point in that?'

Emily looked at him and wondered what she had first seen in him, all that time ago. They were so different, but they'd always been that way. Opposites attract. *He* hadn't changed; he was as reliable and as sweet as ever. What was it? Why did little things get on her wick so much? She looked at her snuffed-out candles, and took a deep breath.

'The point is, we need to talk, Tim. Is this really it? Us watching TV on a Saturday night for the rest of eternity? I kissed you and you were more aroused by the Lurpak advert.'

'We don't have to be ripping each other's clothes off all the time,' he shot back. 'I didn't know you were feeling like that.'

'Yeah, well … I am … sometimes. I just think we need to make more of an effort, that's all. It irked me that you had an invite to a nice night out and you never said a thing. We could have eaten this meal out, together. Like a date.'

Tim sighed, pausing the show just as his idol appeared on the screen.

'What's wrong? Where has all this come from?'

His glasses were sitting low on his nose as he sat waiting for her answer. He looked like he was about to tell her off.

'Oh I don't know, Tim. Maybe I wish you didn't see life as a costing exercise. I take it the vouchers are for takeaway only?' His sheepish look told her they were, but she wasn't done yet. 'And the wine was free? So tell me, what's the point of saving all this money, if we don't actually do anything with it?'

'We're getting married! That's a huge thing, and we want to buy a house – all that doesn't come cheap, does it?'

'What about when I wanted to move in together? We could have saved double rent there.'

'I feel like this is definitely about more than lasagne.' He put his plate down and took her hand in his. 'I know we've been frugal lately, but it's only because I wanted to do it right. We have a plan, remember? I don't pay much rent anyway, having a lodger on the weekends, but we can do it right this way, eh? We just need to keep saving. Get married, and then we can buy our first home. Together.' He leaned in and kissed her gently on the forehead. 'Isn't that what you want in the big picture? Our projections are good, and if you get your little promotion, it might be even quicker.' He was looking right at her, and she didn't have the heart to tell him that she wasn't so steadfast in her conviction. The empty joint account proved it. They were both saving separately. Wouldn't they be doing it together if their future was so sure? Wouldn't they both go all in?

Tim was already back on his programme, wondering aloud where Martin got his ties from.

'Maybe you'll be lucky,' she said softly. 'He might have a tie discount code on his website.'

She'd said it as a joke, to break the tension and get them talking again.

'Yeah maybe,' he said, half over his shoulder, and his eyes turned square once more. She watched him discreetly unbutton his trousers, and she reached for her wine.

Was this really what romance looked like? It didn't look that way to her when she saw the people at the altar week after week. She didn't see mortgage rates, and five-year plans. Renting out the spare room on a weekend to lodgers for quick income, like

Tim did. He ended up staying at hers most weekends, meaning he earned money, and annoyed her with his own sedate plans for the weekends. Romance didn't have a plan. It was just there, infinite and cruel all at once. He was reliable when they'd met, and honourable. He'd never leave her. He'd never let her down. He looked after her and wanted a life with her. It was easy.

She'd been fresh from university, reeling from Calvin getting married, when she returned to her mother's Yorkshire puddings and her old room. It wasn't that she didn't love Tim dearly, they were just … different. Some sparks weren't as bright as others. Not everyone who fell in love immediately felt the thunderbolt. It wasn't guaranteed in life.

The uncomfortable truth was that the spark had never really been as bright for anyone but Calvin Albright. She had been ruined for all other men in her young foolish heart once Calvin had come into her childhood. Him being back had done nothing to disprove that so far, and now he was wifeless and home, while she was getting married. Jesus, it was like a chat show tragic headline. Maybe the castle walls had cursed the pair of them back when they were kids. One of her written made-up stories come true when folded and pushed into the castle walls, like he did when they were kids. He used to laugh when he put them into the cracks for people to find later, holding her out of reach while he tucked her tall tales inside nooks and crannies. He'd tuck in the odd note too, scribbled out of her sight. She'd catch him once in a while, when he thought her eyes were elsewhere. They were never elsewhere when she was with him. She always hoped to herself that they were his sketches he was leaving. People should see them too.

'Leave them, Ems,' he used to tell her whenever she begged him not to do it. 'Don't be afraid to be who you are. Let people find your stories. You should show people how good you are.' Maybe one of those stories wove some magic around them as they chased each other, breathless and giggling. Two best friends destined never to be happy at the same time. Little bits of paper, tucked alone in thick, ancient walls. She wondered what Tim would tuck there, if she had gone with him. She sighed away the feeling of revulsion that she'd compared them both. Calvin wasn't hers to compare anything to. Not like that.

'I don't like the sound of that sigh.' He looked across at her. 'I'm sorry, babe, I think we were in different moods tonight.' He gestured towards the candles. 'I wasn't thinking. We're okay though, right?' She searched him for a sign of desperation, horny eyes, anything, but she didn't see anything but concern. 'I might have gone a bit mad on the discounts lately.' He bit his lip, and she cradled his cheek in her palm. 'Not very sexy, is it?' He looked so deflated.

'I want us both to be happy,' she told him. She hated seeing him hurt. 'I just can't see the picture sometimes, like you can.' She flashed him a weak smile, and he dropped a kiss on her lips.

'I love you; you love me. We follow the plan; the picture will soon take care of itself. I know you don't always get it, but one day, we'll have the life we planned for. I promise.' She touched her nose to his, touching their lips together just enough to tease. She looked into his eyes, but they were closed. She pulled away. He patted her on the leg, reaching for his plate and jabbing the remote to un-pause Martin.

'Great. Do you want another bit of garlic bread? I don't want to gas you out later.'

'Sure,' she said, thinking about how she'd felt last night, sitting next to Calvin. She'd felt listened to, alive. Herself. Looking across at Tim, who was now worshipping Martin and eating with gusto, she knew she'd not felt that in a long time. Had she ever felt it with Tim, like that? That feeling of being truly cherished, valued? She thought of her phone, sitting there on the bed. Calvin could have replied.

'Tim?'

She heard a grunt, so she knew he was at least listening.

'I'm off to Mum and Dad's for dinner tomorrow afternoon. Are you coming?'

Tim shook his head, not bothering to tear his head away from the telly now the main feature was on.

'I can't, already said I would go to mine. Dad wants help cleaning out the garage. I thought I'd said, sorry. It's on the calendar.'

Emily waved him off. 'No, it's fine, don't worry. Mum wasn't expecting you or anything.' Tim nodded, before ignoring her entirely and devoting his full attention to Martin once more. 'You watch your show.'

* * *

Later that night, she found herself staring at her bedroom ceiling, wondering how long she'd been feeling like this, and why she had only just realised that her mood lately wasn't only about her stagnating career. She had pinned everything on how crappy work was, how unfulfilled she felt creatively, but with Calvin coming home and her telling him about her stories, she knew now that she'd been happily lying to herself.

She looked at Tim, sleeping softly beside her, and took him in. He was a handsome man, always was. He was an old-school man, a gent. Born with a suit and a copy of the *Financial Times* in his hand. He was methodical, kind, and driven. His parents had lived just this way, marrying after a long courtship. They'd followed the plan of family life down to the last detail, and Tim was as well rounded and as nice a man as one could ever meet as a result. He couldn't very well be anything else, with parents like his. They were lovely too, and adored their only child, and all his achievements. He was a good guy, a prime specimen of a man any woman would love to call her own. Almost every woman, it seemed. Not the insomniac currently laid next to him. She felt like they were so far apart, but she felt his breath on her arm and the contrast jarred.

Tim snored softly beside her, turning over in bed. She could hear him mumble to himself, and she waited till he settled once more before turning to face her nightstand. Her phone was sitting there on charge, and she reached for it and headed to the bathroom.

After flicking on the light and sitting on the toilet lid, she brought up her messages. Calvin had replied, and she felt like she was feeling the nostalgia all over again.

Yep. Hebblestone Park, 9 a.m. Another old haunt of ours, eh? Coffee is my treat.

Hebblestone Park. She'd not been there in a long time. Last time she'd been dragged there by her mother, who was trying to train her new pooch at the time, and she'd looked at the landscape and wondered how a place could contain so much of a person, without a hint of them being there. The air in the park that day crackled with ghosts, and she'd not been back since. She used the treadmill at the gym instead of running in the park like the other die-hard exercise enthusiasts. Who wanted to run with the ghosts of the park nipping at their heels?

She hadn't replied to his text. She'd had nothing to write back, and with Tim there, she felt guilty. The whole night had passed by without him even asking her about her evening out, and with everything that happened she'd completely forgotten that she hadn't told him about Calvin being back. She felt awkward, like her old feelings were tattooed on her forehead for everyone to read about. An old school friend moving back home? This was exactly the kind of thing that she should be able to tell her partner about. Hell, they could even have met up with him together.

The thought of Tim and Calvin standing side by side in the park looking at each other made her feel queasy though. Those two parts of her life, the past and the present together, felt weird. As though the Emily she was now was an affront to the Emily she once was.

She crept out of the bathroom, looking into the bedroom on

the way past and seeing Tim still fast asleep. She went into the lounge and, heading to the corner, she pulled a wicker lidded box out from its shelf on the end table and took it to the sofa with her. Tucking her feet underneath her, she placed the box next to her on the sofa cushions and opened the lid.

Inside was her youth. Old photos, ticket stubs from the P!nk concert she and Calvin had been to. She'd even gotten him to wear something pink to the event, she remembered. Clipped to the back of the stub was a roll of photo-booth photos. There had been one in the train station when they'd left the concert in Manchester and caught the train back home. She looked at the little photos, each one telling a slightly different story. In one they were hugging, their happy faces squashed together cheek to cheek. The next ones were goofy faces, tongues sticking out wild-eyed as they cracked each other up pulling their worst expressions. The last one: his bashful face up close, her lips on his cheek.

She grinned as she took the faces in. They were so happy that night. She remembered how perfect it had all been, like a dream date, and not a night out with her best friend to celebrate the end of their exams. Looking at Calvin, looking fresh-faced in his P!nk merchandise T-shirt, she studied the lines of his face. He really hadn't changed at all. He still had the same easy smile, the same little dimples in his cheeks when he really laughed at something.

She'd made him laugh in the pub, and he'd flashed them then. Her mother always told him it was his cuteness coming out. Looking at the old photo, knowing the man he was now, she had to agree. She looked through the rest of the box, finding little notes that they used to pass each other in class. Wrappers from the gum he used to keep in his pocket, just because he knew it was her favourite. Old birthday cards, tags from gifts he used to send from holidays with his family. She was almost at the bottom of her little memory trove when her fingers touched an envelope, and her hands stilled.

This is what's been keeping me awake. Sometimes being a

sentimental hoarder pays off. It was a finished handwritten draft, one littered with her frantic crossings-out. She'd kept it to remind herself of the words. They'd been a source of torture ever since.

Taking out the envelope from the rest of the belongings, she slowly turned it over in her hands. It was pretty worn now, from all the times she had taken it out and tortured herself over the years. She never knew what had happened to the original, but the fact it went unanswered was an answer in itself. *This is why I feel so weird. It feels unfinished, that's all. I feel unfinished. I didn't get the ending to the story like I thought I might have.*

The journalist in her always wanted to root out the facts. Opening the envelope, she took out the sheets of paper, the words looking faded. A copy of a letter that she'd pored over for hours. Typed her heart and soul into, finessing every word on the page. She didn't read it again now. She could hear Tim stirring, and she felt guilty enough already. She had a nice man in her bed, but here she was, skulking in the dark thinking about Calvin, who wasn't ever hers in the first place. She tucked the letter back into the box, and putting everything back into place. She grabbed a bottle of water from the kitchen fridge and padded back to bed. Tim was just opening his eyes when she slipped in through the door.

'Emily?'

'Sorry, did I wake you?' She slipped into the sheets next to him, and he pulled her body to his.

'It's okay. You thirsty?'

'Yeah, must have been the wine.' She offered him the bottle but he shook his head, tucking her into him as the little spoon. 'Go back to sleep, eh? Early start tomorrow.'

'Yeah,' he mumbled, nodding his head as sleep stepped up to claim him once again. 'Love you.'

He dropped a kiss on the back of her head, and she took a deep breath.

'Tim, I love you too, but I think we need to talk some more.' She could feel her heart hammering in her chest in the dark as she waited for him to say something. She found herself wanting to fill the silence, to explain herself. 'Lately, I just think that things feel a little different, you know? I know I've been busy with work and everything, trying to get this promotion, but honestly, it's more than that. I'm sorry, Tim, but I don't think it's working. I think I need a little time to think.' He didn't pull his arms away from around hers, but he didn't move either. 'To figure things out, you know? Maybe it's the wedding stuff, I don't know. Talk to me, please, Tim. I need to know how you feel.'

She put her hand on his, but there was nothing. A moment later, she heard a soft snore erupt from behind her.

'Tim? You awake?'

She turned to check, but he was fast asleep, oblivious. Emily sighed and waited for her nerves to subside.

'Damn it,' she swore softly. She looked at her sleeping companion, and then up to the ceiling as she pulled away from him again. 'Emily Hendrickson, you need to get your shit together.'

Chapter 11

Isaac's feet, which were only two sizes smaller than his father's and just as broad, were hanging over the end of the wooden bed frame, one sports sock still clinging to his left foot. It hung there like an abseiling man trying to get his crampons connected. Calvin frowned and knocked on his bedroom door again.

'Isaac, come on! It's nearly 8 a.m.!'

The sock fell to its death on the cluttered grey carpet, as the mountain started to stir. Calvin tutted, coming into the room and flinging open the curtains.

'Hiisssssss!' Isaac scowled as the sunlight hit him square in the face. 'Daaaddddddd! It's Sunday!'

'Yes.' Calvin grinned, opening the window to let some fresh air into the stale teenage-scented room. 'Sunday! The big game! Hebblestone Hounds versus Wakefield Jets. We need a win too – those Jets are pretty good you know. Their coach thinks he's Bielsa of course, but we can show them.' He sat down on the lump of duvet and laughed when he heard his son groan.

'Dad, it's a football match at the local park; it's not Wembley, is it? My old team didn't even kick off till the afternoon. It's against my human rights, this.'

Calvin jumped on the lump, and Isaac lashed out, kicking him in the back for his troubles.

'Human rights! I tell you, I used to love playing football! I couldn't wait to get out on a weekend, wind in my hair.'

Isaac's head and shoulders emerged from underneath the duvet mound. He looked like a toilet brush, his hair stuck up at odd angles.

'You sound so old.' He frowned as he looked at his father. 'What the hell are you wearing?'

'This?' Calvin brushed his hands down his smart outfit of warm cream jumper, a white shirt collar peeking out from beneath. He had his best dark blue Levi's jeans on, and his hair was freshly cut. 'Oh, it's nothing. I thought it needed an air-out. From the new stuff we got.'

Isaac lifted one brow in disbelief. 'It's footy. You look like you're going on a date.'

'Ha!' Calvin exclaimed. 'A date! Can you imagine! Ha ha. Hum. Ha. No, not a date.'

'Dad …'

'Yeah?'

'Why are you being so weird?'

Calvin shook his head and stood up abruptly, gesturing to the wardrobe doors with both hands.

'I'm not being weird. Can't your old dad just be excited about your match?'

Isaac hauled himself up out of bed, wrapping the duvet around him and slinking off to the bathroom.

'Yeah, but not this excited.' He sniffed the air, his head and feet the only visible body parts above the quilt. 'What have you got on?'

Calvin sniffed at his jumper, frowning. 'It's that new stuff you got me for Christmas, remember? Don't you like it?'

Isaac looked at his dad with an expression that left Calvin in no doubt that his son didn't approve.

'Yeah I like it, but did you bathe in it?'

Calvin pulled a face. 'Ah, well it's been a while.'

Isaac, still standing in the bathroom doorway, looked at his dad as if he'd been replaced by a pod person. 'A while since what?'

Calvin coughed and started to head downstairs. 'Er ... a while since ... I last wore it. Anyway, come on! We don't have time for this. Be in the car in twenty minutes, okay? We can't be late today.'

He could hear Isaac mumbling from the bathroom, and the tap go on. Well, he was up and doing, the house was clean, he was ready. Heading down the stairs, he took his long wool coat off the coat rack and checked his pockets for his keys, wallet, the usual. He'd already retrieved his wallet once, from the fridge. It was sitting there where the milk should have been. His head was all over the place this morning, and he'd been up before the birds with a nervous fizz in his gut. For once, he wouldn't be sitting alone watching, Emily would be there too. He found himself really excited for the day.

Walking through to the neat lounge, he laid his coat over the arm of the couch and headed to the bookcase in the far corner of the room. On the top shelf was an old wooden box. Pulling it out, he took the photograph from the top of the pile of belongings inside and put the box back. He'd spent the night before looking through the contents, but he really wanted Emily to see this particular photo. One from them in their last days, together. It had been one of his favourite photos for a long time. When he'd first arrived at university, it was all that kept him from packing up and going back home. Then they'd both been busy, and then busier with uni life, working and getting to know the new people around them. Then he'd met Diane, and life changed again.

He looked at the photo in his hands, smiling at the memory of the two of them. He could remember everything about that night, even the ending that didn't quite go as he'd hoped. Especially that. But still, it was a memory he would never forget. It had been one of the most important points of his life. We all have them, moments that are made when a decision takes a person on a whole new path. A dumping. A failed attempt at professing a long-harboured love. Death. Some were decisions, he reminded himself. Other things were out of their control, and some things couldn't be taken back. He thought of Diane again and realised that the pang of pain wasn't as sharp as before. He could remember the good times, over the bad. Moving here had made it easier to feel like his life with her was really over. It was a final step for them both, but then he'd stopped walking. Just for a second.

He looked again at the photograph, at his youthful and obviously petrified face. How glowing Emily looked beside him. It was one of the worst endings to a night he'd ever had, but when this photo was taken, he had been so happy. He couldn't wait to show Emily, see how she reacted. Maybe, some past events were traumatic, but they also lead to new paths. He could never regret how things had turned out. After all, he had Isaac, but he couldn't help thinking that maybe he might have a chance again. A fiancé made it a non-starter anyway, he reminded himself. *Slow down there, King of Missed Chances.* He had his best friend back in his life, but once again she was off limits to him, and he already knew he couldn't risk losing the friendship again. Breaking up an engagement wasn't exactly his style either. If he chose to make a move, another ice bucket would block his path – he knew it.

'Dad! I'm ready!' *Saved by the kid.*

'Yeah?' He headed into the hallway and was presented with Isaac, fully dressed and hair combed, coming down the stairs with one sock on. 'That was fast.'

'I get the idea you're in a rush,' Isaac groaned back. 'I've lost a sock though.'

Calvin pulled the missing sock off the radiator next to him and chucked it at his son.

'There you go, freshly washed. Come on, get a move on! Bacon butties are on me if we leave now.'

Isaac was already dragging the sock on with gusto at the mention of breakfast, so Calvin grabbed his coat and with a little cajoling and one forgotten sports water bottle debacle later, they were in the car and heading the short drive to the main park. Calvin kept to the speed limit the whole way, but silently cursed the Sunday drivers as he watched the clock on his dashboard slowly turn towards nine o'clock. He drove past the first car park area, near the ducks, and drove on up the hill towards the second set of fields, where the clubhouse sat at the side of the two football pitches the Hounds played on. For late April the weather was mild, sunny. The trees were full of blossom, the last of the daffodils providing huge splotches of yellow and orange colour to the emerald green hue of the grass and the wood from the trees.

'Here we are, come on – warm-up has started!'

Calvin pulled neatly into one of the spaces and whipped on the handbrake.

'Okay, Dad, I can see.' Calvin reached for his son's arm as he was reaching for the door handle.

'Listen, mate, before you go, I have someone coming to see me today. Emily, my old school friend?'

'The one you got drunk with the other night?'

'Er, I wasn't drunk—'

'You were! You tried to pay the taxi with your supermarket reward card.'

'You should have been in bed.'

Isaac rolled his eyes. 'I was asleep. Laura told me. She came back to get a book she left behind yesterday. You woke me up when you fell over in the bushes trying to get to the front door.'

'Oh, right. Well, anyway – Emily is one of my oldest friends, and I would like you to meet her today. I asked her to come for coffee.'

They sat in the car, looking out at the people out walking dogs, eating hot sandwiches and clutching refillable cups of coffee from the clubhouse tuck shop as they watched their teams limber up for their games. Parents huddled into clusters around the pitch, camping chairs and blankets spread out as they settled in to watch the game. Calvin could remember his own parents coming here once upon a time, when they were both healthy and happy. His dad would give the manager a shoulder to cry on half the time, after his wife had wounded him with her overenthusiastic commentary at the side of the pitch. It made him smile now, to think that he was keeping the traditions going with his own son. It meant more here than it did back in London somehow.

'Like a date?'

Calvin's stomach flipped at the question. It wasn't a date, but his stomach seemed to have other ideas. He felt nervous as if it was a date, but the reality was very different. He never expected Emily to be back in town, and single. It's not like he moved back to shoot his shot with her, but the news that she was here and getting married had floored him. He'd nearly fallen off his bar stool, and it surprised him how violently opposed to it he was. He hadn't even met this Tim guy, but he already didn't like him. It wasn't rational, but that was his gut talking. A bank manager too? There was nothing wrong with that, but he'd always pictured Emily happy in the world, loving her job. Writing her feelings, travelling. When he thought of the man she might be travelling with, he'd always pictured someone more creative, funny. Someone to make her laugh every day, and Tim didn't sound anything like Cal had imagined. Not that he had room to comment at all, but still.

Would she invite him and Isaac to her wedding? Cal shuddered at the thought. She'd never gone to his, but that was different. They'd lost touch by then. He didn't want to just fade out of her life again. He didn't want to be shut away from her again, and that meant he had to get his head around everything. Keep moving forward.

'Er no, not a date. Emily's engaged, actually.' There, it was out there.

Isaac, who had turned his head and actually looked interested at the date prospect, looked at his dad aghast.

'So no date? Just a friend?' Calvin didn't meet his son in the eye when he replied yes, both lost in their own thoughts. 'Do you want to meet someone, Dad?'

Calvin could see the clock was getting closer towards the time he was supposed to meet Emily, but he couldn't ignore the question. He sighed and turned to look at his growing boy.

'I think I do, yes.' He ruffled his son's hair, but Isaac brushed him off with a growl.

'I think you do too. Emily's just a friend though, yeah?'

'Yeah.' Calvin nodded. 'I don't think I ever told you about her. She was my best friend, all through school. She lives here. She's engaged to a bank manager fella.' He pushed down his irritation at the thought of Tim and shoved his swirling thoughts aside. 'She's a really good friend, so you might see more of her. That be okay?'

Isaac nodded, his look pensive. Calvin gave him time to process. After all, a new relationship affected him too. They were a team, and that came first.

'What does Emily do?' Calvin looked back towards the tuck shop and saw her heading into the park. She was dressed in a long pink wool coat, her long legs wrapped in dark blue jeans and cute black boots. Her head was moving from side to side, scanning the crowd for him.

'She's a journalist; she works at the *Hebblestone Herald*. She's here. You get off and join your team. I'll see you at half-time?'

'Don't forget my bacon butty,' he said, making Calvin laugh. They got out of the car, Isaac running off to join his team. Calvin watched him, and Isaac stopped, turning back to him.

'Hey, Dad?'

'Yeah?'

'If it's not a date, how come you look like you're going on one?' Isaac smirked at him. 'Have fun, Dad!' And he was off, laughing all the way to meet his teammates, who were all starting to run laps around the pitch to warm up. Calvin stared after him, feeling very transparent in that moment. Kids never did miss a trick, did they? He looked down at his outfit, but he had no comeback. Isaac had nailed it, and they both knew it. Looking at his boy now, so grown up, still looking out for his dad, his heart swelled with pride. He really was a good son. They were healing, slowly but surely.

* * *

Emily watched Calvin with his son as she walked closer to them. It was a shock, seeing Isaac in the flesh. He looked just like his dad; the same floppy hair, the same characteristic Albright cheeky grin. Whoever his mother was, she must have been so proud to call them her family. She felt a pang of something in her chest but couldn't put a finger on just what it was. Par for the course these days. Since her failed attempt at telling Tim how she felt, she hadn't dared to mention it again. They'd had a nice night, aside from the panic attack in the middle of the night.

She saw Isaac say something to his dad, laugh and run to join his teammates. Calvin was laughing too, shaking his head at his son as he watched him leave. She had only taken another couple of steps when he turned, and their eyes locked. Even from a distance, Emily felt the pull of him and her feet sped up a little in their excitement at seeing him again. They met halfway on the grass in front of the tuck shop. They both let out a nervous giggle, which was just so them she could have died on the spot.

'So, a football match eh? You do realise that you owe me a coffee and a bacon roll.'

'Oh come here.' Calvin laughed, taking her into his arms and giving her a big squeeze. 'I don't know why we always get awkward when we meet!'

Emily laughed, but she didn't answer. She was too busy inhaling the fresh scent of him, his aftershave enveloping her as his arms wrapped around her body. He felt solid, a little taller than Tim. She fitted into him like a glove. She always had. After a long moment, she forced herself to pull away.

'Oh, I don't know. Isaac playing for your old team eh? You must feel old.'

Calvin tucked her arm through his, and walked them both over to the tuck shop, where a small group of people stood queuing. 'Yeah, thanks for that. I didn't need reminding. How was your Saturday?'

Emily thought about her Saturday; mainly thinking about Calvin and the way he'd made her examine her life and wondering what Tim was going to say if she ever managed to get the words out.

'Aww, you know, nothing much. Work stuff.'

'Your dance card filled up this summer I take it?'

'Yep, diary is full. Always a wedding reporter, never a bride.' She laughed as she said it, but it fell flat even to her ears. Calvin must have noticed too; when she looked across at him she realised he was looking at her engagement ring.

'Not for long though, eh?' He nodded to the ring, moving to the front of the queue when the last customer departed with their purchases. 'Red sauce, no butter, right?'

Emily nodded, getting her purse out of her handbag. Calvin put his hand over hers, stilling her movements.

'Nope, my treat – I insist.'

He ordered two bacon sandwiches, a bottle of water and two coffees to go. When he had paid and chatted to the woman behind the counter, he took the drinks and food in his hands and led Emily over to one of the wooden benches that served as a picnic area for the park. Most people were by the pitch now, the game about to start. Calvin kept looking over at his son, checking on him, and it made Emily's heart swell. He was a good dad, always vigilant. She hadn't expected anything else.

'You turned out just like I thought you would, you know,' she said after a warming sip of coffee. 'Doing your dream job, being a dad. He looks just like you.'

'Poor bugger. He's a good kid. He makes things easy, to be

honest. Sometimes I wonder quite who the boss is though.' He took a bite of his bacon sandwich, moaning in delight at the taste. 'Oh man, they still know their bacon, don't they.' He took another wolfish bite, and Emily laughed as she tucked into hers. It was just as she liked it, the meat crozzled and well done. She hadn't had any breakfast, not trusting her stomach not to eject Cheerios all over Cal the second she clapped eyes on him. Her morning had not gone well. She'd slept through her alarm, and Tim's head wasn't on the pillow when she'd jerked awake. She didn't get a chance to tell him about her plans, and now she was seeing Calvin for the third time and he still didn't know.

She knew she needed to tell him Cal was back. The elephant in the room wasn't an elephant anymore when it was addressed. Simple. It would kill the crush-like feelings she was having, and then they could all just get back to normal. The niggling feeling in the pit of her stomach at keeping something from Tim was driving her mad. There was nothing going on; she had nothing to hide. Her stomach gurgled, and she took another bite.

Looking across at Calvin devouring his, she wondered whether he'd had to skip breakfast as well. The crowd behind them cheered as the whistle went for the start of the match. The pair of them turned automatically to observe, and they were soon sitting huddled together, facing the pitch. They chatted about the game, both of them cheering when Isaac scored the first goal in the first half.

'That's a tenner gone,' Calvin groaned as they sat back down on the benches. Isaac was high-fiving one of his mates as they got back into position. 'He costs me a fortune with his left foot.'

'He plays like you did,' she told him, watching Isaac's face grow serious as he zoned in on the ball. 'He loves it, doesn't he.'

'Proper football nut, but then Diane and I—' He looked down at his feet. 'Sorry. Didn't want to put a downer on the day so quickly. I have a habit of doing this.'

'What do you have to be sorry for? I'd like to hear about her.

She must have been proud of him too.' Calvin looked at her for a long moment, his emotions clearly wrestling across his features.

'She was. It feels a bit weird to talk about her with you now though.'

Emily's heart thumped in her chest as she played the sentence over and over in her head. It did feel weird, but she wanted him to be able to tell her anything. Just like before. Diane was a part of his life. She would never want to erase any of that from her friend, or their son. Besides, keeping secrets from each other never did any good. It led to unanswered words.

'It's not weird. We always used to tell each other stuff like this.' She fixed her gaze on him. 'That will never change.'

He nodded, a small smile on his lips.

'Thanks. She loved the game, for him really. And me, I guess. I like that you cheered him on. It reminded me of when you used to do that for me.'

Emily laughed. 'Oh God, I remember! Your old coach, he was a nightmare wasn't he? I used to love watching you play.' She touched his arm and left it there a moment. 'I'm glad you're back. It's so nice to have you both here. Mum will be really pleased. Dad too, of course.'

'How are your parents?'

'Same as ever, totally bonkers and never a dull moment. I'm going round theirs after, Sunday lunch.'

'Oh Lord, your mother's Yorkshire puddings. I can still taste them.' They both jumped to their feet as the crowd whipped up, but the ball shot wide of the goal by a few inches. They clapped and sat back down, their thighs touching each other this time. Neither of them moved away. 'Do they get on well with Tim?'

There it was. The first bomb. She could almost hear the "boom" sound as Tim popped into her head. Tim, who was right now round at his parents, helping his dad clean out the garage. While she was here, on a non-date that was sending her every nerve ending into overdrive.

'They get on great. Mum really likes him.'

'Just your mum?'

'Well, he's a bit quiet around company, like my dad. They just shuffle and skirt around each other unless the sports channel's on, and you know my mother. She loves making a fuss of people. Tim just goes with the flow. He's pretty laid-back.' She wondered what Dad would say when he saw Calvin. She just hoped that her face didn't display her feelings over it when they did meet. Her dad never missed a trick. She needed the past to stay that way.

Which reminds me, I have a bone to pick with them about their secret London trip.

'That's good. Bet they're really looking forward to the big day.' Calvin's eyes were on hers now, but she didn't look away from the match as she mumbled something vague back to him. 'Emily, is everything okay with you and Tim? I – I mean I don't mean to pry, but—'

The whistle signalling half-time sounded, and the people around the sidelines starting to filter towards the clubhouse again, bringing with them a fair bit of noise and an opportunity for Emily to escape Cal's question. She'd just been preaching to him about them telling each other everything, but here she was hiding her life away from his scrutiny.

'Dad! Bacon!'

Isaac was shouting to his dad across the pitch, and Calvin jumped up.

'Shit, I won't be a minute. Do you want anything?'

'No, thanks.' She waggled her half-full coffee cup at him. He nodded at her, looking like he wanted to say more, but he turned and jogged to the tuckshop instead to join the queue. She watched him leave, wondering what the hell she was going to say when he came back. A tap on her shoulder had her turning to see a mini version of Calvin staring at her. This one was rather sweaty, his hair stuck up in all directions, and he was half covered in mud.

'Hi,' he said jovially. 'I'm Isaac.'

'Hi!' Emily said, a little too shrilly. 'Emily.'

She held out her hand, and he looked at it, his brow raised. He raised his own hand, which was covered in mud and sporting a bloody scratch on his palm.

'Oh,' she said, retracting her hand. 'Do you need some help there?'

Isaac wiped his hand down the inside of his shirt, shaking his head.

'Nah, it's nothing. Listen, I need a word with you, and we have to be quick.' Isaac's eyes darted to his dad, who was stood in the queue talking to another dad. 'You work at the newspaper, right? The local one? Dad said you worked there, writing stories about people.'

Emily, wondering where the heck all of this was leading, nodded along mutely. Isaac's face lit up, and after checking on his dad, he started talking.

'So, I uploaded a video to my YouTube channel, trying to get Dad a girlfriend, but I only have gamers on there really, and no one could help. Dad won't let me have social media, so I was thinking you might be able to help me.' Another furtive look towards the clubhouse. Emily followed his gaze and saw Calvin looking at them both. He waved, and she waggled her fingers back at him.

'So this video, asking for a girlfriend for your dad, you made it?'

He nodded, a bead of sweat dropping off the end of his nose.

'Dad doesn't know, but I really want to help him out. Can you help me do something? Oh God, Dad's coming!'

Calvin was indeed now making his way over to where they were.

'Isaac, I don't know that your dad would like this. I don't really think I should be the one to—'

'He will when he meets someone! Dad's really sad, even here. I know he wants to meet someone, and if you tell him, he'll stop me.'

Isaac was giving her a puppy dog expression now, and she could see Cal getting closer with each step. She was cornered. *This serves you right, you lunatic! I told you nothing good can come of this!* Her inner consciousness was positively snarling at her. *See, see what words can do! A pen is a weapon capable of cutting deep.*

'Emily, Dad says you're his best friend. I know you don't know me, but I know you care about Dad too. Will you help me, please? Will you help me make him happy again?'

I do care about him. That's half the problem. His son was so lovely. What kid cared about his dad like Isaac did? He knew Calvin inside and out, and he made it sound like Cal was lonely. She didn't want that for him. She wanted him to be happy, regardless of her swirling emotional opinions on the subject. She could help Calvin, and maybe even reignite her own romantic spark again.

Calvin was almost within earshot now, so she dug around in her bag, pulling out a compliments slip from work, with her last quick shopping list written on the back.. She wasn't about to rat Isaac out to his dad either, so she had to be quick.

'This is the advertising desk email. Send me the video and I'll see what I can do, okay? Mark it for my attention. But I really think you should tell your dad.'

'Tell me what?' Calvin was standing there holding out a brown paper bag to Isaac. Isaac took the sandwich and tucked into it like a trash-can racoon.

'That I should get fifteen quid for each goal,' he said smoothly between bites.

Emily swallowed hard and pulled herself together. 'At least – with the rising cost of living. I would review it again next season.' She winked at Isaac, and he gave her a thumbs up.

'I like her, Dad, she should hang around more often.'

Calvin beamed at this, and Emily looked at his innocent, unknowing face and wondered just how many lies she could keep up with.

'I'd like that too,' Cal said, taking them back over towards the benches. 'I think you two are going to get along like a house on fire.'

Isaac and his dad started dissecting the first half, and Emily sat there, watching them both interact. There was clearly so much love and affection there, but it was more than that. They respected each other. The way they laughed together, she couldn't imagine them going through what they must have with Diane's passing. Seemingly, it had strengthened whatever bond was already there between father and son. Looking at Calvin, she realised that she could help. She could help Isaac with his quest and help Calvin to meet someone too. She wanted that for him, didn't she? She could help him, and she should, but the thought made her feel so ill she couldn't bring herself to act quite yet. Why was doing the right thing so bloody gut-wrenching?

'Better go. Coach is calling us over.'

Isaac finished the contents of his water bottle, refilling it with the larger plastic bottle his dad had given him. He gave them both a beaming smile and headed off to meet up with his teammates.

'Nice to meet you, Emily!' he shouted as he left. 'See you soon!'

The second half of the match started, and Calvin turned his attentions back to her.

'Well, I think he likes you. Do you want anything else to eat, or another coffee maybe?'

Emily shook her head, still playing the conversation with Isaac over and over.

'No, I'm good thanks. He's a really nice kid. You must be so proud of him.'

He grinned at her, and she felt a flutter of butterflies in the pit of her stomach as she watched his whole body animate when talking about his child.

'He's amazing. It's been tough, but I think things are starting to get better now. It helps being here, and meeting you again, well, I think that just made it for me. I think to be honest, I've been a bit lost.'

'Really? You not enjoying being back home?' This was it. This was the moment that Emily had been waiting for since Isaac told her his idea. She needed to know how Calvin felt about it. 'You seem really happy together.'

111

Calvin's gaze was fixed on the distance, his lips pressed together in thought as he watched his son play.

'We are happy, but it's not always been easy. I think we both shut down a little bit. It's taken a while to get back on an even footing. Since then, I think I've just been getting on with things, but it's not quite the same. Once Isaac's in bed, I sit on my own most nights. I've watched every box set going.' Emily laughed softly, but she could see he was in pain, and even to her, admitting how he felt wasn't coming easy. 'Oh wow, that was a bit deep wasn't it?' He snapped himself out of his melancholy mood and, standing, offered his arm to her.

'Fancy a quick walk around the park? We won't be missed for a while.'

'Sure.' She took his arm and they turned left, walking away from the pitches towards the duck pond. The grass was still slightly damp from the rain the night before, the dew leaving patches of water drops on her suede boots. 'Have you been dating at all?' Calvin tensed beside her, but she pretended not to notice. 'There's nothing wrong with dating, Cal; you're entitled to have a life.'

They sidestepped an older couple, walking arm in arm in the other direction. The couple nodded their heads, saying hello as they passed. Cal turned to look at them as they went by.

'I know that, and I want that. It just feels a bit weird. For us both I think. When I got married, when we had Isaac, I just assumed that was my life forever. Raising our son, working at my old firm. Diane was fit and well, till she wasn't. I guess no one wants to bury their partner at any age, but when it happened, it just felt as though my story was over too. Like it ended with hers, but she never saw it that way. She was quite annoying about it, to be honest.'

'Diane wanted you to move on?' The more she heard about Diane, the more Emily wished she had gone to the wedding. Been part of their lives in some way. She had a feeling that she would have really liked her. Calvin was an excellent judge of character;

he always was. She knew Diane would have been a special person. How could she be anything else, to gain his heart? 'You talked about it?'

Cal ushered her over to an old dead tree that provided seating with its carved, gnarly roots. They sat together, their thighs pressed side by side as they watched the other visitors of the park walk around, play games and feed the ducks around them. An occasional quack penetrated the chatter of people, the wind rustling the trees above their heads.

'She was sick for a while, not a long time, but enough to know what was going to happen. She was a financial planner, so her brain was all switched on with settling her affairs the minute the consultant had finished speaking. She didn't want me to be … well, like this I suppose. She was sending me dating app adverts the week before she passed. I just never wanted to consider it back then I guess. It felt like something that was far off in the distance.'

'And now?' Emily's words sounded choked to her own ears, and she realised she had been holding her breath since he'd started speaking. She locked eyes with him again, and his cheeks were flushed.

'Well, I've never really been one for putting myself forward.' He looked at his hands when he spoke, playing with a receipt from his pocket. 'It's cost me before.' His jaw flexed as his teeth clenched. 'Now, I don't even know where to start. Dating is different to when I did it, and even then it was different. Diane and I just kind of fell into our relationship. It was easy. Now everything's about manscaping and avoiding double denim, and that's before you even ask a woman out.'

'Come on, you must have had some offers.'

'I have had a couple of awkward conversations with one or two mothers at the school gates, and one of the temps asked me out for a drink on her last shift, but I haven't done anything about it yet.'

'Not your type?'

'A little forceful, I think. One of the school mums tried to marry her daughter off to Isaac in the process. It's not really my scene, being out there. It's all a bit tragic, isn't it?'

Emily looked at her childhood best friend and wondered how a person could be so unaware of just how great they were. He still had no clue how amazing he was, even now.

'Not at all, Cal. You lost your wife; you're only young. Humans are not made to feel lonely. That's not what love should be. You should get yourself out there, see what feels right.'

Cal pulled a face, shrugging his shoulders and getting to his feet. He reached for her hand, and she placed it in his, letting him pull her to her feet. His eyes fell on her ring, and he touched it once with the tip of his finger. She caught the sadness in his eyes and looked away.

'Sorry, this is the last thing you want to be talking about. You get it though, right? You have that with Tim? That certainty that you're with the person you should be?'

He'd phrased it as a question. This was her chance. She should tell him. Everything. About her confusion about him coming back home, and her doubts about Tim, her career. The answer to the question she'd never asked to his face. This was it. *Say it. Be honest.*

'Yeah, I get what you mean.' *Coward.* Her inner voice was a snarky one today. 'You'll find that, Cal – I know you will. No one deserves to be happy more than you and Isaac.'

He smiled at her then, tucking her arm through his again as they headed back to the match.

'Thanks, Ems. You're right. I'm sure it will happen soon enough. Fate's a bit of a nightmare, isn't she?'

They were back at the bench now, and Emily watched Isaac fight to get another goal for his team. She thought of his plea for help, and all thoughts of spilling her own troubles vanished. She was engaged, and that was that. She felt suddenly stupid, standing there. Crushing on the same guy she had crushed on for most of her childhood, when he was in such a different place. Calvin had responsibilities now, a son to raise. He was just starting out again; she couldn't mess with that for anything. She wouldn't, and she knew that she needed him in her life. From the second she'd seen him in that coffee shop, she'd been happy. Sure, he'd spun her little world on its axis by settling back home, but she knew without a doubt one thing. One thing that her teenage heart still knew the beat of. She would rather have Calvin back in her life as a friend, than risk ruining anything they had.

'Yes, you could say that,' was all she replied to him. 'Listen, I'd better go. My mum will be expecting me.'

She was early for her mother, but she needed to get away. She felt like she'd ripped open the stitches on an old emotional scar, and she wanted to lick her wounds away from his eyes.

Cal looked a bit disappointed, his smile fading. 'Oh, that's a shame. We were going to have a drink in the clubhouse. I was going to ask if you wanted to come.'

'Sorry,' she cut him off. 'I can't. Another time?'

Calvin's smile brightened. 'Deal. How about one night next week? We could go to the movies or something?'

Emily nodded, getting her car keys out of her bag so she wouldn't have to look at him.

'Sure, sounds nice. Call me. Say goodbye to Isaac, okay?'

She made her goodbyes and resisted the urge to run across the fields to the sanctuary of her car. She kept her walk casual, turning to give him a wave before she turned into the car park. When she looked back, he was watching her. She waved, and he slowly lifted his hand in response. When she got to the car, she rolled her windows down and slumped back in her seat.

'You are an idiot, Emily Hendrickson. An idiot. You hear me? You can't get involved in this. You have your own stuff to deal with.'

She eyeballed her reflection in the rear-view mirror and jumped as a figure appeared at her driver side window.

'Arrghh!'

'Sorry! Sorry!' Calvin was standing by the car door now, hands held up in surrender. 'I didn't mean to startle you. Who were you talking to?'

'Huh? Oh … no one! You just startled me.'

Cal held out a photograph through the open window. 'I forgot, I was having a look through some old stuff recently and I found this. I wanted you to have it.'

Emily, still trying to recover from him appearing at her window, took the photo from him and turned it over in her shaky hands.

'It's from the prom. I have some more from the castle too.' He shrugged, looking away, and it made him look seventeen again. 'Still unpacking some bits.' The castle. Their first and last proper kiss had been in the castle grounds. It was the result of a spin the bottle game, but still. Hebblestone Castle. It was one of the town's few attractions. One of their favourite haunts. She remembered days spent there, in the sunshine. Him sketching castle redesigns on his sketch pad, her beside him creating love stories about the people who might once have lived there. The tucking of notes into castle walls and the chasing. Long lazy looks across the blanket on the grass.

The photo was of the two of them standing in her mum's front room, just before they left in the limo. In the photo, they were smushed together, his arm around her shoulders. Their faces were full of smiles, but she could see the nerves hidden in her expression. Looking at Calvin, she noticed that he looked a little nervous on the photo too. It was probably just her mother, and her attempt to take over the night. She pushed away the memory.

'I couldn't believe it when I found it.' Calvin's deep voice stirred her from her memories. 'We look so young. Isaac's been digging around in the boxes the last couple of days. I think he's been looking for bad haircut photos to show his mates.' He laughed when he said it, but it made Emily think of the video again. Was Isaac planning to release more? She needed to get her head straight, and fast. Isaac's plan felt like a boulder rolling down a hill. She needed to get out of the way or get crushed in its path.

Emily was taking in every detail of the photograph, wondering what the younger versions of themselves would think of what happened to them both. Looking at the faces she knew so well, she never imagined that they would not be in each other's lives. Having him back in her life, with Isaac to boot, just felt right. She didn't want anything to affect that. She knew already, after less than a week of having him back, that him not being part of her life again just wasn't acceptable to her.

'What's the matter? Shocked into silence at our glaringly awful fashion sense?'

'Hey, speak for yourself.' She laughed, holding the photo out to him. He waved her hand away.

'No, it's for you. I made a copy. I thought you might like it.' She had her own copy of course, in the box with the rest of their childhood story. She'd not looked at it in years. She couldn't bring herself to. Not after the way the night ended, and how it changed their paths forever. Looking at it now, she realised it was a good memory. The girl in the photo was so happy to have Cal. She knew how she felt. It warmed her heart to think that they both loved the photo.

She looked again at the snap, and a question came unbidden from her lips.

'Are you lonely, Cal? Even here?'

Cal's head snapped back as he took in her question. He blushed, his hand rubbing at the back of his neck, a gesture she recognised from old.

'I guess I am, Ems.' His lips curved into a half smile. 'Pathetic, right?'

'Not even a little bit. You deserve to be happy.'

'Thanks. I think so too.' He cleared his throat. 'So, movies next week? I promise not to get all maudlin on you.'

Emily nodded, grateful of the change of subject.

'Give over. I'm looking forward to it.'

'Me too,' he replied, his eyes locking with hers once more. 'I'm so glad to have you back in my life, Ems.'

'Me too, Cal.' She stopped herself from saying more, as usual. 'I'd better go. Mum will be waiting.'

He nodded and waved her off. The instant she turned her car around the corner, she pulled over and dialled Beth's number. If she was going to keep detached from this, and help Isaac and Cal she was going to need all the help she could get. That, and a double helping of her mother's Yorkshire puds.

Chapter 12

Emily's parents' bungalow was on a little cul-de-sac of bungalows filled with homeowners who saw gardening as an Olympic event. Her dad Dennis was one of the more extreme competitors, and as she pulled her car up to their home, she could see him pruning the hedge. He turned to her as she got out, pointing with the tip of his shears in the direction of the kitchen window.

'Hi, love. Give your mum a minute, she was murdering Dolly Parton's back catalogue a bit ago. I hate that bloody Alexa thing – I feel like I've got two wives. She's always singing with the bloody thing, and she set reminders for my blood pressure pills! I swear, I wouldn't need them if they both left me alone!'

'Hi, Dad.' Emily laughed, manoeuvring the stabby implement from his grasp and hugging him to her. 'Sorry again about the Christmas present. I'll buy her smellies next time.'

She felt him grunt and grumble in her arms. Looking over his shoulder at the flower-filled garden, she changed the subject.

'Garden looks great though, Dad; flowers are really looking good.'

They both headed indoors, her dad pointing out his favourite blooms in the garden along the way. As she entered the kitchen, Emily's stomach grumbled as the waft of Sunday lunch enveloped

119

her nostrils. It hadn't been long since her bacon breakfast, but she was never too full for her mum's cooking.

'There you are! Dinner's not long, you know!'

Her mother hugged her, pulled off her coat and bag, and steered her to the table in one fell swoop.

'I'm early, Mum. You said one o'clock.'

'Did I? Oh well, you're here now. Tim at his parents' again?'

Emily nodded. 'Yep, garage clear-out duty.'

'Ah, that's good of him. Just us then, eh?'

'Yeah, just us.' Emily side-eyed her mother as she started to plate up the dinner. She could hear her dad whistling from the bathroom. 'I saw Calvin today. Do you need any help with lunch?'

'No, love, everything's in order. Just your dad to do the gravy real— You saw who?'

She whirled away from the hob and a roast potato fell from her fork and hit the floor. The dog was in it before it landed, and it spent the next few minutes picking it and dropping it, too hot for his eager little tongue. Her mother ignored the comical commotion, her jaw on the floor.

'Calvin. Are you sure?'

'I think I remember what Calvin looks like, Mum. You look a bit hot and bothered. Glass of wine maybe?' She got up from her seat and headed to the fridge. Her mum always had a bottle of wine on the go. She called it her cooking wine, although none of it ever made it into the recipes she concocted. Emily pulled out the ornamental sloth-themed stopper and poured two glasses, aware and slightly enjoying the fact that her mother was still looking at her agog. 'Will Dad have a beer?'

'Does a bear do its private business in the woods?' Her dad entered the room, leaned into the fridge and yanked out a can of beer, kissing his daughter on the forehead. 'What have you done to your mother?'

'She's seen Calvin,' Carole answered for her, and Emily watched her parents closely for signs of either of them ratting the other out. They loved each other, but she felt pretty sure that her mother would crack first, and probably take her dad down with her. One shot fired, two nosy little birds with buckshot in their hindquarters.

Dennis's eyebrows were the most expressive thing on his face, but Emily saw that no surprise registered there.

'And? How long till dinner? Have I got time to water my pots round the back?'

'No, you haven't.' Carole swatted him with the tea towel she was holding after putting down a platter of fresh steaming green beans and baby carrots on the table. 'Where did you see Calvin?'

Her dad sat down at the table and gave Emily a sly wink. She looked back at him stony-faced.

'The coffee shop in town, you know, the one near my office. Did you know he's moved back?'

Dennis coughed and reached for the Sunday paper. Her mother shot him a dirty look, and Emily almost blew her cover by laughing out loud. Bringing the last of the dishes to the table, her mother sat down and started messing with the napkins on the table.

'We had heard something, but you know what gossip's like.' Her mother stole a glance at her, and Emily smirked.

'Oh yes, I know all about gossip. Where was it you went on that London trip again?'

'Which trip? We had the *Cats* one, and the *Matilda* thingy at Leicester Square?'

'Yeah, and then we went to that spa hotel for the weekend, remember, Carole?' Her dad was looking pretty sheepish now, her mother throwing lots of not-so-secret shut-the-hell-up-Dennis looks his way. None of them were picked up by her dad of course. He was still no closer to understanding his wife's secret little handshakes and eyebrow Morse code. She heard her mother tut, and only just resisted the urge to laugh at the pair of them by smushing her lips together as if she was holding in some awkward wind attack. Emily had never wished for anyone to shit themselves before, so this was a first. Especially on a Sunday. It was so much fun watching them squirm like little worms on a hook, but she did actually want to hear the story at some point.

'The summer I lost out on that promotion at work again, remember?' she pressed, still feigning a certain degree of innocence. Her second of many losses. 'You went to London then I recall. A couple of years ago?'

Her dad coughed again behind his paper. His eyebrows shot up above the edge, like two little dogs trying to bolt a fence. *Got ya.*

'Give it up, Mum, I know you were there. Cal told me. What I've been wondering to myself since is why didn't you tell me?'

Dennis folded his broadsheets and patted her on the hand.

'You weren't going, love, it wasn't a thing. He didn't exactly send you an funeral invite, did he? You'd just had that upset with work; you were off on your travels. All happy and excited and that. You weren't speaking to Calvin by then.' That was about the depth of his knowledge on the scale of female emotion. Happy, excited, or that. 'You remember, Carole, she got those things put in her hair? Came back all full of spirits or whatever.'

He made it sound like she'd been off finding herself in the foothills of the spiritual hills of yonder. What she'd actually done was gone on an all-inclusive holiday to Mallorca and drowned her sorrows in sunshine, sweaty armpits and tequila sunrises with her girlfriends. She had wanted to get away, not focus on the fact that she'd lost another chance of progression, and the girls had collectively wanted to mark their own successes. Namely engagements, promotions, and new careers. A bit of a contrast, but she'd had a good holiday. She'd done that before, she remembered. When Cal was getting married. She'd jetted off then, danced her tiddly bum off on a few dance floors and cried in various club toilets with her university mates. She'd started at the paper the week she'd touched back on British soil. She'd been firmly planted ever since. Holidays abroad were definitely NOT on the sodding five-year plan. Emily rubbed at a split nail on her left hand, giving in and ripping the shard off with her bare teeth.

Her mother was watching her like a hawk from across the table.

'Why are you mad anyway?' Carole's eyebrows were playing their own game now, namely trying to scowl Emily into submission and winkle out her secrets. 'You know we loved Calvin's parents, God rest 'em. They couldn't be there to support him, so we went by proxy. Beef, Dennis?'

She hadn't thought of that. She'd just thought of her own guilt at not being there when she'd heard, and the pain at the thought of actually *being* there. Seeing him go through that, and her being a stranger to him, unable to comfort him like she once could have. Like when his dog Rusty got hit by the delivery bloke from the grocer's. He'd only lost a leg in the end, and half an ear, but she still remembered how Calvin had screamed when it happened. How he'd crumpled to the ground beside the setter's prone little body. She couldn't imagine anything worse, yet she knew it must be. She thought of losing Tim, but then she felt like the worst person in the world. Who imagined their other half dead, to see how they would feel about it happening?

She was tired, and hungry. That was it. Random thoughts need food. Her parents started filling their plates, and she followed suit.

'Are you mad we went?' Her dad said this in between shuffling forks full of Sunday dinner into his face. Her mother reached for the wine.

'I'm not mad, I just didn't know you went. I'd wished you'd told me. I didn't have a clue. I wouldn't have gone on holiday.'

'How is he – Cal?'

She took a moment to answer, seeing her dad's eyebrows twitch from the corner of her eye. They both looked away when she put her head up from her plate. She felt like she was being interviewed, and they'd still not said why they kept it from her.

'He's good. We had a great catch-up. He's doing a lot of redesign work in Hebblestone at the moment actually.'

Dennis sliced into his meat, the knife scraping on the plate.

'He was always a smart one, those drawings he did. What's his son like? We didn't speak much at the funeral. The poor little bugger just seemed to stay close to his dad.'

Her dad said it matter-of-factly, as he usually did, but the thought of Isaac in a dark suit, clinging to his dad, made her throat catch. He was so like Calvin when she'd met him today. She could already see the man he was going to become. She felt an urge to cuddle him or something. 'He's lovely actually, just like Calvin really.' She thought of his plea for help. 'Maybe a bit bolder.' *Room to talk, missy!* Her subconscious jeered her once more.

'We should have him round. We were saying that the other day, weren't we, Dennis?'

'Were we?'

'Yes, dear. We were. Why don't you come too, Emily? Be like old times.' Her mother filled up her glass once more.

Emily went to say yes, but then thought of Tim.

'Er sure, yeah. He hasn't met Tim yet, though.'

'Well Tim can come, can't he? And Calvin's son! The more the merrier, eh?' She jumped up suddenly, running off into the hall. Seconds later, she came back with a pamphlet for the local Indian restaurant, The Golden Poppadom. It was outside Hebblestone, a huge purpose-built place with parking, situated on the outskirts of the motorway. People drove for miles to come and eat there. 'I tell you what, why don't we go here one night? They've just revamped the interior. I've been meaning to go. They open back up soon. Shall I book a table?'

'Oh I don't know, Mum – I'm pretty busy with work. Listen, I'll talk to Tim and let you know, okay?'

'Oh, all right, love. Let me know.' She put the pamphlet down on the table and resumed her dinner. 'Dennis, your sleeve's in the gravy again.'

The rest of the dinner went on as normal, and her parents didn't mention Cal or Tim again. Her dad's eyebrows twitched a few times in her direction though, and when she got home later that afternoon, the restaurant pamphlet was sitting in her bag. On it was one of her dad's notes. He'd written on it: *It would be nice to do this. Let me know, Dad*

Oh great, she thought to herself. They were both in on it.

Chapter 13

Monday morning came sooner than Emily felt prepared for. She took extra time getting into work that morning, slapping on her war paint after a sleepless night, wondering how she was getting to get through helping Isaac, while still keep her distance. After lunch with her mother, she'd gone home and hidden out in the flat for the rest of the afternoon. Tim was supposed to come round after lunch with his parents, but he'd sent her a text saying that his dad was dragging him off to the pub and he'd sleep at home.

To his credit, Tim did phone her later on, to say goodnight. She could barely hear him over the noise of the football match in the pub though, so they didn't talk for long. She thought that the night to herself would give her some clarity, but she woke up tired and irritable. After parking her car in the office car park, she pulled out her handbag from the passenger seat and, smoothing her grey suit down, she took a deep breath and then headed into the foyer. She'd barely gotten to the lift when a text from Beth came through.

Heads up, Boss Lady wants a word.

She read the text as the lift doors closed, Malcolm from accounting giving her a nod as she clicked the button for her floor.

'Good morning!' he said jovially.

She eyeballed him. 'Is it? I never noticed.'

He chuckled. 'Monday blues, eh?'

'You could say that, Malc. How's Joy getting on?'

Joy, his daughter, had gotten married at the Hebblestone Hotel the previous year. It was one of the best weddings she'd been to that year. She'd been so much in love.

Malc's face lit up at the mention of his eldest daughter.

'She's great. She and Kyle are having a baby. Did I tell you?'

Emily beamed at him. 'Wow, that's amazing! Congratulations. A grandad, eh?'

Malcolm pulled a face, the dark black frames jumping on his nose with the movement. 'Oh God, I know. It only feels like two minutes since I was marrying her mother. How's your plans coming along?'

Emily's smile vanished as quick as turning off a light. 'Oh well, you know. Tim's busy with work; I'm trying to get a features job. Never any time is there?' She shrugged nonchalantly.

Malcolm wasn't fooled. 'For the things in life we really want, we make the time. You'll get it done.' The lift for her floor opened, and she almost cried with relief. 'It's worth every bit of effort.'

'Thanks,' she said, flashing him a smile and backing out of the lift doors. 'Give Joy and Kyle my best wishes, won't you.'

'Will do,' Malcolm called as the doors closed behind him. 'Have a good one!'

As soon as the lift doors closed, she frantically tapped a reply to Beth's message.

Am here. Where is she?

The lift door dinged. A voice in front of her answered the question quicker than Beth could text.

'Good morning, Emily. I've been waiting for you. Can I see you in my office please?'

'Joanna! Good morning. Er, of course.'

Joanna had already grabbed her under the arm and steered her into the direction of her office, right at the back of the main office.

The minute she got in there, Emily could see that something was wrong. Very, very wrong. Annabel, head of PR was sitting there. She racked her brain for what could be wrong, thinking back to the last few events. She hadn't made a faux pas somewhere, had she? Had she pissed a bride off with one of her write-ups?

'Please, sit down, Emily. You look worried!' Joanna was acting weird. For one thing, she was offering her a chair to sit down on. Usually, her mantra was chairs were for wimps. She made everyone stand in her room, and she sat on a bright blue birthing-ball-looking thing and did squats at her desk every two hours to "keep her glutes activated". The woman was the definition of efficient.

Emily gave the chair a quick once-over, but she couldn't see any booby traps, or nails sticking out of the cushion pad. She nodded politely to Annabel, who nodded back with an equally creepy wide smile. She felt like she was Alice in bloody Wonderland, the Cheshire cat in stereo looming over her.

'Is everything okay?' she asked finally, unable to take the polite grinning for any longer.

'Well,' Joanna said, 'you've been asking for an opportunity for a long time now, and I finally have something for you. It's your chance, Emily, and it's a big one. A project, just for you.'

'It really is,' Annabel cooed next to her, her head nodding rapidly with her enthusiastic agreement. 'It will be wonderful for raising the profile of Hebblestone too, especially with the wedding season pull-out in the mid-August edition.' She was getting excited thinking about whatever it was now. Emily could see her cheeks flush, and her hands were punctuating her words with more gusto as each syllable rushed out of her mouth. 'We might even need some more pages, Joanna, for the extra advertising!' The last three words tumbled together in an excited squeak, and Emily was still none the wiser.

'I'm sorry,' she addressed the women as professionally as she could, feeling like she was looking for a white rabbit to show her the door out of this weird Monday. 'What project are you talking about?'

* * *

Walking out of Joanna's office sometime later, feeling like she was about to throw up, she looked around the office. With one glance around, she knew just where to start too. Beth knew. Emily knew as soon as she saw her. She didn't even put her bag down. She was still holding it under one arm from the meeting. Her arms had been frozen in place the minute Joanna started talking, with little squeaks and chirps occasionally from a very excited Annabel.

One look from Beth as she left that office was enough to make Emily storm over and yank her by the arm, clean off her chair. Beth whinged and whined all the way to the lift, and each time, Emily's grip on her tightened. Heading down the long corridor, sending colleagues and the FedEx bloke fleeing to the nearest exit, she growled and pulled her friend over to the staffroom. The staffroom at the end of the hall that was kept for work-related meltdowns and awkward conversations with HR. And, come to think of it, a hook-up room at Christmas parties run on the budget of the petty cash postage tin. The woman currently struggling to get free of her grasp could attest to that one. Dave still had the photocopies from their office tryst on their fridge at home. Much to Emily's horror every time she went round for a cuppa.

'HR's in there.' Beth laughed, well, she tried to laugh. She was trying to stay on her feet with her mate dragging her along like an IKEA rug. 'Brenda came to work after switching her tea with her husband's again. She was found in her cleaning office, eating Wotsits and talking to the mop.'

'What, again?' Emily asked. 'That's like three times now! What the hell's in that tea?'

Beth tried to shove her mate off, make a run for it back to the office, but Emily gave her a second to think she was winning, and then charged at her. No one in the office murmured as outside, Emily rugby-tackled Beth to the floor, and got an elbow in the side for her trouble.

'Oof!' The two women landed on the floor, Emily picking Beth up like an oversized designer handbag and steering her back to the lift.

'That hurt, you knobhead.'

'I don't care. You deserved it.'

'Did not!'

'Yes you did. Wait till we get to the lift. Stop making a scene.'

'Me making a scene?' Beth tried to turn to look at her, but her mate shook her head and pushed her head forward.

'Eyes forward, traitor.'

They passed the staffroom door, and they could just see Brenda wrestling with Kamil from HR. Brenda was throwing bright orange crisps at Kamil, who was shielding himself with a cushion and trying to back his way to the door. He was trying to calm her down. As they walked by the door, they heard Brenda yell, 'No, Kamil, I won't let you win! Sod off, corporate overlord! You will not take my crisps. You will not take my freedooooommmmm!'

Both women just got past before Kamil burst through the door, cushion still in hand. He was covered in orange dust marks. He looked like he'd been paintballing. He held his body against the door, his back sagging to the floor. He spotted the two women just as his bottom hit the polished tile. His face looked desperate, pleading.

'For God's sake, don't open this door for a bit. Bert's sent Thomas – he's on his way to pick her up.' Bert was Brenda's husband, the handyman of the community and part of her cleaning business. Brenda's Best she called it, and her little van was always seen around the place. Thomas was their son, and occasional parent when they got into scrapes. The two of them were such a pair, the office was never dull when she came in to work.

130

'Tea again?' Beth confirmed.

'Yep, she keeps forgetting which tin they keep her Earl Grey in.' Kamil wiped at his brow. 'Falling out again?'

Emily, who was still holding Beth captive, nodded. Beth just rolled her eyes. 'Apparently. What's in that tea, anyway?'

Kamil laughed again, brushing himself down but only managing to make himself look more like an Oompa-Loompa.

'I don't know, but Bert hasn't got glaucoma anymore.' Beth cackled with laughter, and Emily found her anger building once more. Bloody Beth and her bloody ways.

'Thanks, Kamil, we have a meeting to attend.' She cut the pair of them off and headed to the end of the hall with renewed determination.

The lift doors opened for Emily like the Red Sea parted for Moses, and she practically chucked her now quite angry mate into the tin can. The two women glared at each other, Emily's foot tapping ten to the dozen. The instant the lift doors closed, all pretence of professionalism went out of the window.

'You leaked the video to Joanne! What the hell did you do that for, you silly cow!'

'Silly cow! I still have your heel print in my arse!'

'Oh shut up, I only touched your arm. Why did you tell her? You must have known who the video was about!'

'Of course I did.' Beth rubbed her arm theatrically. 'I saw the photo. I knew it was Cal! I thought you'd be happy. When it came through to the work email, I thought it was meant to be! You need a shot, you know him, you can help. This is your chance, Emily. I sent it from your email.'

'What! Why didn't you just answer the phone yesterday? I wanted to talk about it first, before it got out!'

That was why Joanna had wanted to speak to her, not Beth. She hadn't mentioned Beth at all. She thought it was her email. 'So, she doesn't know I know Cal.' She'd thought as much, but having it confirmed was still a relief. 'Wait … you sent it from my email?'

Beth shrugged. 'Yeah, it's your story.' Her frown dissipated, her fingers tucking her crumpled blouse back into her skirt. 'He's your friend. I thought I was doing a good thing.' Her eyes narrowed, and Emily looked away from her penetrating gaze. 'Actually, why are you mad? You want to help him, don't you? I watched that video so many times, Emily. That man sounds lonely to me. He's a catch, and you could help him AND get a promotion!'

The lift doors opened, and Gavin from accounts went to get in.

'Occupied!' Emily growled at him, and he took a step back. His glasses twitched on his nose as he stared at the pair of them open-mouthed. Beth clicked the button to shut the doors, and he disappeared from view.

'Of course I want to help him, but it's complicated! And I have a job, and this shouldn't be that …' She was pacing up and down now, small steps filled with frustration. 'It's not a project, I mean he. He's not a project, Beth, he's a person, and he's a dad and … and … it's just complicated.' She sagged against the lift doors. Her shoulders hunched over with the stress knots tied across her shoulder blades. 'And now Pandora is bloody singing her head off outside of her ruddy box, and I've got no idea what to do.'

'Well, ragging on me wasn't the best idea you've ever had. I don't get why you're so mad. What did Joanna say?'

'She's talking to legal, but since the YouTube video was out in the public domain, it looks like we are clear to run the story. She loves "my" idea of featuring it for the paper.' She winced. 'I'm going to tell her I changed my mind.'

'You can't!'

'Why not?'

Ding! The lift doors opened, and Emily fell straight backwards, ending up flat on the floor and looking at the feet of the people in the corridor. Namely Joanna's feet. Emily felt her skull hit the tip of her heels, and she looked up sheepishly.

'Brainstorming, ladies?' Emily bounced back up onto her feet, stammering and stuttering. She shot a look at Beth, who was giggling behind her hands. 'Good fun, Beth?'

Beth stopped laughing and straightened up. 'Not bad. Emily's just working out the kinks.' She flashed them both her super fake professional smile, the one that she always used to get out of everything from parking tickets to unpaid overtime. Emily fantasised for a moment about what it would be like to put a kink in Beth. She could get a fair few kinks in if she tied the little loudmouth into a knot.

'That's right.' She smirked back, her eyes as dead and cold as she could make them. Beth's lip twitched. *She was bloody well enjoying this.* 'We need to be sensitive.'

Joanna waved her off with a manicured hand. 'Oh of course, and that's why we have you! With the wedding season, we can really capitalise – I mean prioritise this boy and his dad – we could run a lonely-hearts column even! Best get to work, ladies!'

Before either of them could murmur a word back, Joanna was off, positively bouncing down the corridor on her heels. She loved it when she had a local scoop. She fancied herself something of a Rupert Murdoch at times. The office often joked that she prayed for an alien spaceship to land in Hebblestone, or a celebrity sex tape scandal. Anything to lift the kudos of the town beyond its quiet profile in the local media.

The corridor fell quiet, and Emily got back into the lift, pressing the button for the lobby.

'What are we doing? Staging a walkout?' Beth went to click the button for the office, but Emily body-blocked her.

'No, we're going to get a coffee, on me. I need a bacon sandwich and a hot minute to figure out what I'm going to do.' The lift doors opened. 'What *we're* going to do.'

'Oh no, you can count me out. I've done my bit.' They walked out into the morning sun, turning towards the coffee shop. 'You need this, Emily.'

'It's too complicated, I—'

'It's complicated because you're not happy, and you're scared to ask for more, Emily. It's not rocket science. That's why you kicked off. I had a feeling, but this just confirmed it. You like Cal, don't you?!'

'Of course I like him; he's a good friend.'

'Well why don't you help him then? Go for it, get the scoop! Calvin will be easy to match. Come on. He's a catch. It's Hebblestone.'

'I … don't know …' Emily stammered. Beth was right, but she didn't get it. If she did this, she'd be saying goodbye to Calvin again. She couldn't see him with another woman; she knew she couldn't. 'I don't think it's a good idea.' *Lamest. Excuse. Ever.* Beth's loud tut obviously agreed. 'Where's your bloody sparkle gone? I saw a glimpse of the old you, mate, and I know I take the piss, but I love you. I knew you wouldn't do anything to hurt anyone, and you know him so well. It's got to help, surely? I did this FOR you, Emily. Someone has to make a bloody decision. I am sick and tired of watching you waste your life being unhappy!'

'How do you know what I want, Beth?' She was shouting now, both women getting more and more frustrated with each other. 'You did this without even thinking about it!'

'How do YOU know what you want? Emily, you never just *go* for it. It makes me so mad! Tim is nice, but you just … gave up.'

'I did not. I've been working my arse off for this promotion! Joanna kept saying no.'

'Because she knows she can browbeat you! You're such a good writer, but you never write anything but work stuff. You never tell Tim you're fed up with him penny-pinching, or being out so much, or tell him that you want to book the wedding. I don't even think you want to marry him. It's just something to do. Something to make you feel like you're happy. You never open your bloody mouth, Emily! I did this to make you do something. You have to go for it, or you will end up being known for nothing but your bloody cardigans!'

134

Emily was shaking her head furiously, but Beth stepped closer and grabbed her by the shoulders.

'Listen, I didn't do this to hurt you, but the boy in that video wants help. It sounds like Calvin is lonely, Emily. If nothing else, you can help him – but think about why you reacted why you did. If he's just your friend, then why wouldn't you want him to meet someone? You want to help that boy, right? Make a decision Emily, and go for it!'

Emily wanted to deny it, to scream back that she was talking bollocks, and that she could jolly well bugger off with her ridiculous notions. She couldn't though, because as usual, Beth had called her on all of it, and she didn't want to admit it. The fact that it had only just registered in her own brain made it hard to articulate her words at the present time. *I never take the leap.* She thought about that night at the dance. She'd missed her last shot then, and it had gone downhill from there really. She knew that, but right now, it was pressing down on her chest. Hard. She knew she needed to woman up, but now, it was even messier.

'No answer for that?' Beth's grip was still firm, but her expression had softened a little. She didn't look like she wanted to throttle her anymore, which was an improvement. 'If you really want to help the pair of them, the first thing you need to do is be honest with yourself about what you really want. You need to talk to Tim.'

'Tim hasn't got anything to do with this.' She looked her friend in the eye, but Beth's dulled before her.

'Mate, if you really think that's true, then I can't help you. I've said my piece now.' She shook her head a little, throwing her a sad smile. 'I'll get the coffees and the butties. You just have a minute.'

The doors closed behind her, and Emily was left staring after her, moving aside for a lady dragging a tartan shopping cart behind her.

'Sorry,' she mumbled, lost in her thoughts. She felt like she was on fire. Looking down the row of shops, she brushed her hair back into shape and set off walking. She walked right the way up to the high street, not stopping till she felt the cold chill of air conditioning prickle over her neck as she entered a familiar building. It was as neat and as uniform as always. Advertisements of interest rates and mortgage deals hung suspended from wires in the windows, the tills and cashiers all uniform in their choice of colour scheme and hue of depressive stuffiness. A bing sounded, and the small queue of people, walking around a taped-off barrier system that was about five miles long, all shuffled up one space. She looked around and saw Pippa.

Of course she'd see Pippa first. She'd probably seen her on the CCTV and bolted out of her office.

'Hello, Emily, er … to what do we owe the pleasure?' Her top lip was positively twitching, her head whipping back towards the counters.

'Hello, Pippa, I'm good thanks. I just came to see Tim. He in the back?'

She was already making a beeline for the back office, Pippa at her heels.

'Err, yes but employees only, policies … you know.'

Emily nodded, not stopping till she reached the keypad.

'Not a problem.' She shut Pippa's stutterings down by pressing the intercom button. A second later, the door buzzed and she pushed it open. Pippa was half a second behind her, but Emily slid through just quick enough for it to slam shut.

'Hah!'

Emily couldn't help it. Pippa always got on her wick no matter what she did. She knew that everyone had a work wife; she had one herself in Beth. The fact was Pippa obviously harboured something more than friendship for Tim. It wasn't this as such that ticked Emily off, it was more the way she looked at him. She always looked at him as if he was God's gift to women; she hung on his every word. Pippa was young and impressionable. To her Tim was the consummate alpha male. He wore suits, he was well spoken, everyone he encountered liked him. He had a good job, one that he was clearly passionate about, and Pippa was cut from the same cloth. She didn't see the bank as Emily did. To them it wasn't a boring building, one where very necessary but very boring things took place. They saw it as a beating heart of a business, part of the local Hebblestone community.

The truth was, when Emily looked at Pippa, she saw what sort of person she should be with Tim. Could be still if she would only take the time and make the effort. It was his career, his passion. She should support it. They should support each other career wise, right? *Little writing job.* That's what Tim called her job. More than once. Calvin and Tim were very different. Calvin always loved her writing. *Don't compare, don't compare.*

To Emily, Pippa was the ideal woman for Tim, and what woman would want that in her life? Tim was hers. She didn't like the fact that there was someone else in his life better suited to him. Half a second later, the door buzzed again and a very annoyed-looking Pippa came stomping through.

'Emily, please let me announce you?'

Emily turned to the woman and, sighing, nodded slowly.

'If you like,' she relented. 'It's hardly necessary. I'm not about to rob the bank, am I?'

'I know,' Pippa was trying to soothe her now, her eyes darting back and forth between Emily and Tim's office door. 'He's just had a bit of a morning that's all. You know what things get like around here. It's not all deposits and withdrawals you know!'

From the tone of her voice, she made it sound like they were doing secret rocket-building missions in the back, a secret cohort of money men tucked into a cupboard somewhere out back, brokering world-changing secret deals. From the queue that Emily had clocked on the way in, the clientele that morning seemed to consist of Val from the sandwich shop ordering change bags and half of the blue-set brigade out to get their pensions and spread their wealth among the cluster of local businesses on Hebblestone high street. It was hardly *Wolf of Wall Street.*

'I see,' Emily said, her eyes focused on the closed office door. 'Hectic day then, eh?'

'Oh yes,' Pippa preened. 'But you know Tim, he's a steady hand at the helm of our ship.'

Emily didn't answer her. She was currently too busy trying to conjure the image of Tim, dressed in sailor's gear, steering a ship out on the open ocean. Pippa at his side, rigged out in the latest seasons season's nautical must-haves.

'I bet he is. Can I go in now? I do have to get back to work myself, as it goes.' She gave Pippa her best pointed look and, sidestepping her, she put her hand on the handle and walked into the room. Tim was on the phone, and his face registered no surprise at seeing her there. He'd buzzed her in. She turned to Pippa, flashing her an in-your-face grin. Pippa huffed, a little high-pitched "huh" that sounded like a clown with the hiccups. Tim threw her one of his usual smiles, raising his finger to tell her he wouldn't be but a minute. He was talking about something to do with regulations and borrowing rates, and Emily took the opportunity to try to gather her own thoughts.

Any minute now, and Tim's phone call would be over. She needed to get this out, tell him everything. Well, not quite everything. She had never told him about the dance at college; she'd only ever given him the highlights. Sure, Tim knew that Calvin existed, but only in an abstract way. He knew that they were best friends all through childhood but had lost touch. That much was true. He'd seen the photos at her parents' house, frame upon frame of days out, theme park rides they'd screamed on together. Calvin was, and always had been, weaved into her early years. Like a gold thread of running stitch through the quilt of her existence. Calvin had always been there. Until he hadn't.

Now that he was back things had changed, and the lines separating the different parts of her life were blending, the colours running into each other and creating whole new rainbows of colour. It was only a matter of time before Tim knew about Calvin's return. Emily was amazed he didn't already know, given their close-knit community. In that town, one that felt so much like a village, nothing got past the local folk.

A few months ago, Audrey Appleton had mistakenly sent out a photograph of her bare bottom to the complete email list of the parish church council. From the official parish email account, and unsigned. What she had wanted to do was to innocently send the photograph to her dermatologist daughter, who lived in Australia, so that she could assess a worrying lump. The resulting furore on the town Facebook community site resembled something akin to a witch hunt. Cries of "whose arse is that?" rang louder than the church bells for a full fortnight. Audrey, embarrassed and mortified about showing her derriere to the local community, soon felt not only relief at the fact that a few thousand people declared the lump to be safe and nothing but a pimple, but also gratitude.

Angela, the owner of the local yoga clothing store was equally thrilled to have Angela be the official model of her newest line of tight-fitting buttock-lifting yoga pants. Apparently, not only was half of the town's Facebook population well versed in skin care, they also loved a pert-looking behind in a pair of yoga pants. TikTok leggings had nothing on the Hebblestone lot; it was already old hat to them by then.

Pippa was still hanging around behind her. Emily could practically feel her nervous breath on the back of her neck.

'Thanks, love, we shan't be a minute and then he's all yours.'

Pippa looked behind her at Tim, but Tim did nothing but wave her off with a set of waggly fingers. She looked rather dejected as she left but Emily couldn't bring herself to care at this moment in time. After all she was only here to see her fiancé. She hadn't broken any rules and it wasn't as if she did this in work time any other day.

Pippa practically peed in a circle around the bank every time

Emily got a little bit too close to their section of the high street. She'd mentioned it to Tim before, the fact that his assistant and work colleagues treated him as though he was some kind of Greek god. All Tim had done was laugh and brush it off, throwing her another one of his "oh, Emily" looks. The kind of look that left her feeling like a blethering idiot. Tim often had a way of doing that, however unintentional.

She knew what she wanted to say to him. She'd planned it out in her mind. When she was in front of him, the words just disappeared, leaving her tongue-tied. Or worse, mute. She couldn't really blame him of course; he didn't understand her job or dreams any more than she did his, but that had never seemed an issue before. They were different people with the same goal, or they were when they started out as a couple. She just assumed that eventually things would work out. Opposites attract and all that. You only had to watch a rom-com to see two characters so different from each other meet and fall in love.

Sure, that difference often made for hilarious incidents and heartfelt moments, but this was real life. Was being married to Tim for the rest of her life really what she wanted? It couldn't just have been due to Calvin's return. It wasn't like she'd pined for him all these years. She hadn't stalked his Facebook; she hadn't tracked down his wife and son. She never sank to the ground and pleaded with the heavens to give him back to her. She'd had a crush on her childhood friend, and it hadn't worked out. She'd never got to tell him face to face. She'd pictured him reading the letter over the years. His expression as he read her words. She still couldn't believe he had never answered, but decided that he'd been trying to spare her. He didn't feel the same. It happened to people every day.

It was hardly earth-shattering. Half the teen movies and films were on just this subject. The fact was that Calvin had seemed so abstract, so removed from her life as it was now that seeing him there had shone an unwelcome light on her existence. It had also reminded her just how lacking in lady balls she actually was. When *she thought* of the younger, shinier version of Emily, the one that Calvin had known so well, she realised just how much she had changed. Everybody changes. We all become different versions of ourselves. We break off pieces of ourselves; we hand them out like candy to others. Sometimes our experiences change us for the worse and not the better. Trying to reconcile the teenage version of herself with the more adult version Emily saw in the mirror every morning had made her realise how much she had changed as a person.

She wondered how Calvin's experiences had changed him. After all his wife was dead, he had no doubts about her. Death was the parting factor in their relationship, and it wasn't something that Emily could ever understand. There were certain clubs in life people became a part of, clubs with high membership fees no one wanted to pay. The dead parents club, widow club, the divorce gang. When you asked a child what they wanted to be when they grew up not one of them would ever say any of this.

Calvin had changed – she knew that. What surprised her most was just how familiar he still felt to her. He probably wouldn't be very flattered to hear this, but Calvin Albright was a comfy sweater to Emily Hendrickson. He gave her comfort and warmth and reminded her of home. His big gangly frame felt like home to her once, her forever house of muscle and love, cheering her on. And she knew it lingered. Their conversations had been awkward in the beginning, sure. She didn't pretend otherwise, and neither had he. She'd been like an awkward teenager around him, all fluttery heart and shaking hands. It was probably why he didn't seem to notice the change in her as much as she felt it within herself. To him she was just Emily, his goofy friend. She wasn't back in the friend zone; she'd never left. The thought made her heart lurch. Tim spoke and jarred her from her thoughts.

'Emily? This is a nice surprise. No wedding work today?'

Emily found her teeth grinding against each other before she could stop herself. She resisted the urge to bristle and gave him a warm smile instead.

'No, actually I'm rushed off my feet. We have a big new project in. Joanne wants me to take the lead. It's actually why I'm here.'

'Oh no, Emily, please don't say that Joanne's roped you into something ridiculous to do with the weddings bit. I did tell you; she's been looking for a huge scoop for a while.'

Emily felt her hackles rise. 'Actually, Tim, not everything is about flipping weddings, or you. I came out of work today to tell you something. Relating to my work. You know that silly little writing job thing I have that pays my rent? The MA I have? The 20k student debt?' Tim opened his mouth to speak, his hands reaching up to loosen his grey silk tie. A telltale sign that he was feeling stressed. Possibly hen-pecked. And panicked about hearing about the student debt again. It made his spreadsheets quiver. He was probably wishing for Pippa to storm into the room, spinning a pen on a chain around like a medieval mace to save him. She filled the gap before he could recover and try to placate her. She didn't mean to come across as so hostile, but her anger was fuelling her courage via the adrenalin rush pulsing through her veins.

'Anyway, The thing is, the feature. Well, actually it's about Calvin.'

Tim looked at her blank-faced.

'Albright,' she continued. 'Calvin Albright. You know my friend from school?'

'I thought he was in London?'

'Well yeah, he was for a long time.' She looked away from Tim, taking in the room and buying herself some time to clear her thoughts. There was a photo on his shelf, of him holding a big cheque. He was standing next to an Elvis impersonator. In the background, Emily knew she was inside the bank, seeking out a third glass of free cheap plonk while Tim did his photo opportunity and Pippa followed him round like an eager beaver. She should have been in the photo. Why did she do that? She should have paid more attention. That was her problem.

'So where does he live now?' Tim looked around the room, as if Calvin was suddenly standing in the room. 'Here in Hebblestone?'

'Yeah, here. He moved back a few weeks ago and his son has kind of roped in the paper to help him a little bit.'

'Ah I see. That's nice – little family project.'

She could see that Tim was focused back on his computer screen now, and she crossed the room to stand in front of him. He reluctantly pulled his gaze away from the screen.

'Sorry, can't ignore head office, but it's nothing. Why do they need your help?'

'Joanna gave it to me.' She couldn't lie, and that was true at least. He frowned, but she kept going. 'So anyway, I just came to tell you that. I might have to work a few late nights, early mornings. Maybe a couple of busier weekends. I'll still be doing the wedding stuff obviously; this is just kind of extra.'

'Oh?' Tim's ears had pricked up now. 'So if it's extra it means extra pay right?'

Emily looked at him blankly. 'I don't know, but that's hardly the point is it?' She didn't know actually. Joanna had just talked about the "opportunity" and not a guarantee of promotion. She couldn't profit it from it anyway; she wouldn't. She realised with a shudder just how it might look to Cal though. Her cashing in on his misery, exploiting his son. *Oh God, this is getting far too complicated.*

Tim sucked air in through his teeth, picking up his pen from the counter and tapping it against the wooden surface.

'Well it makes sense, surely? What's the point of doing the extra work if you don't get the money?'

Emily felt herself getting angrier but she managed to keep it under control. She wasn't going to give Little Miss Perfect Assistant outside any ammunition, and she didn't put it past her not to be listening in behind the door. The thought of this only served to make Emily angrier, and she felt her fists clench at her sides.

'I'm helping my friend – Calvin. He was my best friend for years, all through school. Mum has photos of him all over the house. He was practically like her son.'

'Well.' Tim swallowed, and Emily bit her tongue. The son comment was mean, but it was true. 'Yes of course, it's lovely that you're helping your friend, but do we have the time? Not to mention the energy? I thought you wanted to plough on with the wedding saving?'

'I did want to plough on with the wedding,' she retorted. Her voice was rising with her anger. 'You never showed any bloody interest, other than to moan about the cost of everything. Besides which this is for work, not for pleasure. It's my job. Joanna has given me no choice.' *You didn't try though, did you? You just stood there, trying to stop your knees from knocking together like a telltale beating heart.*

'And what is this project exactly? Some kind of destination vow renewal?'

'Calvin isn't actually married,' she said softly. 'He lost his wife some time ago. He just moved back to the area with his son. It's his son who contacted the paper to ask for help. Joanna gave it to me – well in a roundabout way – and I want to do it. I want to help him. Plus, it's a feature. A real feature with a real by-line, my name in the by-line for something other than a wedding, christening or bar mitzvah. This is my ticket to promotion too.' Not that it was relevant to her in this case, but she felt like she needed to prove herself to him somehow. This was not going well. She felt her steam start to recede.

Tim stood up from his desk and took her into his arms. He'd gone a bit quiet since she'd started speaking. He didn't even glance towards his desk.

'I'm sorry, I didn't mean to come across as being snippy. I just worry about you in that job. The prospects never seem to come to anything. You work so hard. If you can help your old friend and gain some brownie points with Joanna I say go for it. We can manage without the extra money.'

Emily's heart sank into her Pixie boots. She'd told him but she still felt like she should have said more. She wrapped her arms around him loosely, choosing instead to say nothing.

'Why didn't you tell me he was back, before all this? Have you seen him?'

Now was her chance. She could tell him what had been burning a hole in her chest when she looked at him.

'I didn't get a chance at first, and then with the other stuff … I was going to tell you tonight.' Tim froze, and behind her she could hear the door being opened. Perky little Pippa's voice broke the silence.

'Sorry, Timothy, but Mr and Mrs Elliot have just arrived for their appointment. Shall I tell them you'll be right out?'

'You should have knocked, Pippa,' he near growled. 'I need a minute.'

Given that Tim was still hugging Emily to him, and she had just interrupted a private moment, Pippa then went one further in being annoyingly intrusive by stepping into the middle of the room and practically throwing Emily towards the door. 'Shall I see you out, Emily?'

Emily looked at Pippa as if butter wouldn't melt.

'No need, dear, I know the way. Tim darling, we can talk about this more later.' She turned her back to Pippa. 'I do need to talk though. After work, at home.'

She didn't look him in the eye. She could practically feel Pippa watching their every move.

'Okay, darling, I'll ring you later.' Tim dropped a distracted kiss on her lips and headed back to his desk to collect his paperwork for the appointment. He punched a brown plastic cup off the corner of his desk, showering water over his whiteboard. He didn't acknowledge the action. Both women headed out into the corridor, Emily taking larger than normal strides to make her exit as she waited for Tim to look at her again. He didn't; he stood with his back to her, shoulders slumped.

'It's funny isn't it,' Pippa said as she was almost at the outer door.

'What is?' She was almost back at the keypad door. She had no time for snark.

'Oh nothing. I was just thinking how funny it is that you talked about home, yet you still don't live together, do you?' She laughed, a little tinkling annoyance. 'However do you figure out which "home" you mean?' The accompanying smug look on Pippa's stupid, perfect face left Emily in no doubt. Not only was Pippa hankering after her fiancé, she also thought their relationship was as stuck as Emily did. She felt the need to defend herself despite her own inner turmoil.

'Oh yes, I guess it is a little strange from the outside. We know what we mean though.'

'I guess you do; still, I bet you can't wait to live with him.'

'That's the plan!'

Emily waved goodbye to her and strode through the bank. She felt slightly shaken, but she'd done what she set out to do. She just needed to speak to him about where they were going.

Calvin was out there now. She'd told Tim about him, and about the project and some of what it entailed. She was breaking down the barriers between her worlds but she wasn't sure how she felt about it yet. It had to be done – she knew it was inevitable. She couldn't have kept all of the parts of her life separate forever. It was already confusing enough trying to work out why she felt like she had sleepwalked through the last few years of her life.

She hadn't been happy for a while, long before Calvin had arrived back home. She'd had moanings and grumblings. Cold feet about the wedding, their whole living situation. His long-winded plans for the future. The difference was she'd ignored these niggles for the most part before. The ones she'd noticed. Now, with everything that had gone on recently, she just couldn't silence the old Emily any longer. Correction, she could silence the old Emily. The old Emily was seemingly happy to float through life with Tim, in her job chasing weddings every summer. The old cardigan-wearing Emily she had morphed into since coming back from university.

She didn't believe the stigma of staying in a small town; she had been born there but she'd left. They all had. Calvin had met Diane, had their son and a whole life. He'd still come home, feeling the old connections of his roots. Emily loved her home, and she wanted to travel and see things. She wanted to write articles that mattered, stories of love that inspired and lifted others. To her, life was where you wanted to be. A person could live their entire lives in one tiny place and fit many lives' worth of experiences into it. Others could travel the world and still have nothing to tell.

The issue wasn't her life, but her own stagnation within it. The fact that she floated like a "Yes Day" idiot sometimes had led her to today, as it does everyone. The fact was at this moment in time she was losing her fiancé, feeling jealous of his assistant, feeling things she hadn't felt in years and still she didn't have the tools to get herself out of it.

As she walked through the foyer of the bank, her phone rang. Pulling it out of her pocket she saw the office number light up. *Tick-tock, Emily,* she thought to herself before pushing the green button. *You need to get your head together.* At this rate, she wasn't going to have the by-line for the headline article. She was going to *be* the headline and she wasn't in any hurry to subject herself, or anyone else, to any further gossip-worthy thoughts.

She needed to shut the hell up and snap out of it. She had her own life to sort out, and she couldn't even think about dragging Calvin into all that. This was her chance to help Calvin, to help Isaac, and to help herself. She just had to keep it together long enough to convince herself. After all Calvin was her childhood best friend. Whatever happened, his happiness deserved to be protected, and not just for his son.

Chapter 14

A beautiful morning, and Hebblestone parish church was bustling with people. Set back from the main road, the church was a majestic-looking building, restored and kept pristine by the devoted parish churchgoers. Today in particular, the May weather taking on a balmy summer vibe, it looked lit up in the sunshine. The rays of light shone through the windows, lighting up the coloured glass panels of the ornate windows. Emily stood at the bottom of the path, off to the side of the slow trail of wedding guests, just to take it all in. Geoff's camera went off behind her. *Thank God for Geoff*, she thought to herself. Her photographer mate kept her sane on the days when she wasn't feeling very "yes to the dress".

'Gorgeous today, isn't it?' he said jovially, laying his camera back against his chest by its strap. 'I do love weddings here. Nothing like a church wedding in Hebblestone, eh?'

Emily nodded, not taking her eye from the building before her. She'd imagined her own wedding here a half million times, but she knew that Tim wasn't overly keen on the idea. Well, what he'd actually said was that it was "rather twee" and he didn't want to break tradition. His family tradition was to go big, it seemed. His parents were married on a cruise liner. Somehow she couldn't see her mum and dad being cooped up together with another few dozen guests. It was not something she wanted to think about. Besides which, Emily had always hated the thought of cruises. What was so fun about being sat like a sardine in a tin can for weeks on end, looking at nothing but each other and shuffleboard timetables? Nope. Not for her. Tim got seasick anyway, luckily.

They'd figured that one out when they'd tried the pedalos at the local country park. The lifeguard had to fish Tim out after he panicked and fell out of the boat. A duck had flapped its wings in his direction a little too close and that was that. He'd gone arse over tie into the water, and Emily had to be towed back to shore with everyone watching. It was hilarious. Tim was really upset about it. He didn't like ducks much now. She sent him duck memes when she was bored at work sometimes. She wished they'd just been able to agree on their wedding. It had been a big part of why things had stalled. Their ideas of the big day didn't match up much beyond the bride and groom, and the guest selection.

'The bridal car is a few minutes away,' the vicar could be heard telling some of the wedding party. 'Please, take your seats inside ready for the service to begin.' The last of the mingling guests made their way into the building, and Geoff hung back to snap a photo of the bride and her father. She idled long enough for the rest to leave, Geoff and the vicar standing at the church gates to wait for the wedding car. Emily took a deep breath, and slowly made her way up the long stone path to the church doors. She imagined herself, just for a moment, not in her outfit of smart pastel blue shoes and blue printed summer dress, but in a wedding gown.

As she slowly made her way through the doors, she put herself into the bride's shoes. Just for that moment. The inner church doors were open, the groom standing facing away from the entrance, facing the altar. Standing to the side of those doors, she wondered what her wedding would be like for the millionth time. Before, when she was younger, she'd spent hours thinking about the life she would lead. What it would lead to. A new job, a new home, the aisle. She'd been a confident young girl, and over time, she'd lost that. Just a little. A chip, here and there.

She looked once more at the excited congregation, and the man tapping his foot rapidly as he laughed nervously along with his best man. Who was probably ribbing the crap out of him at this moment about cold feet, and whispering ball and chain jokes. It was a world that she'd lived in for so long, observing, recording. Detailing the little touches and the moments that made life interesting, memorable. The father of the bride, crying into a hanky as his daughter danced with her new husband. The flower girl sneaking a kiss from the startled little page boy under the cake table, their mothers searching for them with nervous looks in their eyes. The single men and women, hoping that some of the romance of the day would rub off on them.

She loved the romance and promise of it all, but she realised, she just couldn't see her and Tim getting married there. She couldn't see them at the altar at all at this point. It just seemed like a someday thing, and not a certainty, and the longer it took, the less shiny and hopeful it felt. She hated that. She wasn't a girl for a long engagement, and she knew that Tim would never want to get married so traditionally. It was about the only part of getting married where he wasn't traditional. He loved the big events, so obviously he wanted the wedding to be the same. She was the same with her ideas. They just needed to talk, to get it out in the open. See whether their differences could be smoothed over.

She wondered whether Calvin ever thought of getting married again. He'd look so handsome, up there at the altar. His dimples showing with his happy smile. Her smile faded. She might have the misfortune to be standing here one day, watching Calvin marry again. The lucky woman who read her article and snared his heart. Her words, sealing her own fate again. She felt a lump in the back of her throat so thick she couldn't breathe, and she wiped at her eye.

At least I'd know for certain he'd read the words this time.

The white-ribboned wedding car had arrived, and Emily stepped out from her vantage point to slink into one of the pews in the back, a couple of seats away from Geoff. She always kept a notepad in her bag, and had her voice app for quick dictation, but she did that later, in snippets. The actual wedding march, the anticipation, she didn't miss any of that. She filled her creative well with the atmosphere, and then it bled out onto the page. Today was no different, and the atmosphere was just as exciting as ever. Something had changed though. The congregation were settling down now, the ceremony about to begin. The vicar was in place, looking expectantly at the doors, the groom's gaze focused on the altar. She slid closer to bridge the gap between her and Geoff.

'Geoff,' she whispered. 'Do you ever get bored of doing this?'

Geoff thought for a moment. 'I sometimes wish I did his gig.' He nodded to the private photographer the couple had hired, who was taking some interesting-looking shots of the church, the flowers, and the guests. 'Bit more freedom. I photographed a dead weasel yesterday. Apparently it had terrorised some of the gardens on Cliffe Court, and an unnamed vigilante had stoved its little head in and shoved it into the community garden bin.' Emily looked at him in horror. He nodded, his gaze flicking to the door now and then waiting for the wedding party to take their steps down the aisle. 'It was awful. I mean, how is that news?'

Emily shook off the image Geoff had catapulted into her head.

'That's horrendous,' she replied, keeping her voice low. 'I didn't mean the job though, I meant the whole thing. The declarations of love, the milestone moments, you know? We're a bit like passengers on someone else's happy trip.'

Geoff chuckled, earning a sharp look from a woman in a big hat in the row in front. Emily smiled and looked apologetic. The woman turned round to face front again and took half the sunlight with her.

'Someone's not feeling the love today. You're normally bouncing off the walls at these things. Especially in this church. Bit of a busman's holiday for you, I suppose. Me and Stefan never really saw the point really.'

'It's only a busman's holiday if you are in the bloody thing in the first place. We haven't planned anything yet, and I'm not sure I can muster the energy to even bother anymore.'

Geoff looked across at her, patting her hand with his own. 'Mate, we've worked together long enough now. You've not been right for a while.' He noticed the vicar nodding his head, and they knew it was time. 'If you're not happy in life, you have to change it. Trust me. The rest of your life is too long a time to be unhappy.'

'You and Stefan are so happy though. And Tim and I are happy too.' She bit at her lip. 'I think. We could be. If he changed. And me. But why change things drastically when I could just make it worse?' The organ started up, and the congregation collectively turned their heads to look at the incoming bridesmaids, and the main event. Geoff stood to take a couple of aisle shots, and leaned in close.

'Ems, darling. If you were happy with how things were, we wouldn't even be having this conversation. Have you talked to Tim about any of this? I thought you were doing okay. You got that new project!'

The bride entered, cutting off her opportunity to answer as the congregation collectively gasped as they took her in. She never answered Geoff; she didn't know how to answer him anyway. She knew what she needed to do, but she didn't relish the details of the hows and whens. The talk with Tim loomed large in her thoughts. As the whole room watched the bride, Geoff snapping away beside her, her eyes were firmly on the groom.

This was what kept her going in life. Amidst the job frustration, all the Tim stuff, Calvin. The first look. The moment when the groom turned to look at the woman who he had chosen to spend his entire life with. It never mattered how long the couple had been together, what number marriage this was to them, how many kids they shared. The first look was universal, and it couldn't be faked. It was when you saw a man in love, adoring the woman he loved as she walked towards him. She looked at the groom, his face teary and lit up from within, and she saw Calvin standing there. Just for a moment. Just for an inkling of a second, her imagination had her in that dress, walking towards Calvin. Watching his face change as he took her in. It wasn't Tim's face she saw at all, and that told her everything she needed to know. She needed to give her life a huge kick up the arse, and she was going to bloody well get on with it. Hallucinations weren't good. At this rate, she was a dancing baby away from Ally McBeal.

* * *

Later that day, freshly showered from work, she changed into sweats and got to work. Sipping a glass of wine on her couch, she got out her laptop. Beth had wanted to talk to her all afternoon, and she'd managed to dodge her questions by staying out of the office at the wedding and ignoring her after-work calls. She had a pitch to present, and the sooner she got started, the quicker she would stop dilly-dallying with her life and make some decisions for herself. Tim was due round any minute, and she was finally going to tell him that she wanted to take a break. To figure things out, to concentrate on work and what *she* really wanted. To see where he stood with the wedding.

Her phone rang again when Tim was twenty minutes late. She was watching Isaac's video for the millionth time. It was still unseen really on there, only a few hits. Most of them she knew were from her. She went to turn her phone off and saw Tim's name on the screen.

'Hello, you lost or something? What's taking so long? I said I would cook, save you queueing at the chippy.'

'I can't come tonight, Ems. Sorry. Problem at work.'

Emily's heart sank. 'What sort of a problem?'

'Er, well I can't really divulge that, but it's nothing serious. I just need to double-check a few things. I'll not disturb you. I'll call at the pie shop on the way home, get something to go.'

The pie shop on Hebblestone high street was a late-night attraction to the pub-goers and late-night workers. Where else but in Yorkshire could you get pie, chips and hot sweet gravy at 2 a.m.? It knocked the spots off a kebab.

'Really? I can wait up. I did want to talk. I can eat now; you get your pie and come over, eh?'

'I'll be too tired to be any company, honestly.'

'Tim, about Calvin.'

'Yeah?' His pitch went higher. 'What about … that?'

'I just feel weird about not telling you before, I'm sorry. I really think we need to talk. We have a lot of stuff to sort out.'

'I can't tonight, I really can't. I'll call you, okay?'

'Okay.' She nodded redundantly into the phone.

'Listen, I have to go.' She could hear a murmuring female voice in the background.

'Is Pippa there?'

'Yeah, she's staying behind to give me a hand. We're pretty slammed.'

'Okay, I'll let you go then.'

'Ring you tomorrow.' And with that, he was gone. She stared at her phone, and then rang Beth. She picked up after half a ring.

'Finally! Where've you been?'

'Oh just at a wedding, full of love. I was waiting for Tim to come round, but he's just cancelled. Some kind of work emergency with Pippa in tow.'

'Eugh,' Beth chimed in.

'I was going to tell him I want a break. From us. From the engagement. Till we both know where we're going.'

The theatrical gasp through the phone told her that she'd finally managed to shock Beth. 'I know.' Emily swigged her wine again, waiting for Beth to get it together. 'I need to get it out now.

It's giving me heartburn.' She tapped her palm against her chest, rubbing the acid feeling away.

'Sure it's not the wine?'

'Don't trash-talk my friend like that. Wine is always my friend.' She flicked the TV on, a rescue show playing where dogs were matched to hopeful owners. She saw a young lad trying to make friends with a rather dappy-looking rescue dog, and she thought of Isaac. *He'd love a dog, I bet.* 'I've been trying to write the pitch Joanna asked for. I have till 2 p.m. Wednesday to file final copy, and Calvin doesn't know yet. What the hell am I going to tell him?'

'And back to Calvin.'

'Back to work, you mean. If I'm going to be single, I'll need the money. I'm not sure Tim's going to get on board with what I have to say.'

'Money? For what? You live like a church mouse. How much have you got in the bank now? Enough for a wedding and a bloody house deposit no doubt! Why don't you just tell him you want to move forward? Single?' She heard her friend shuffle on the line, obviously adjusting her position.

'At this point,' Emily pouted, looking back at the screen where the boy and pup were making friends. 'It might be easier to fake my own death. He might actually listen then. Properly.'

'You serious?' Beth's tone changed slightly.

'It was a joke.'

'A dark one.'

'I feel a bit dark tonight. Another night of not getting this off my chest.'

'Ah see, Tim might thwart the bank robbers a bit early, be on his way over in the Plonker Mobile.'

'His car's not that bad. I'd better go – I need to get some work done.'

She watched the TV for a bit, watching the terrier finally accept the family with a few face licks and a waggy tail. She looked at the little thing, so happy. And now she was jealous of a poor little dog who had had a horrible life and had now got a new life. It wasn't as if he'd walked out of a relationship.

'I'm going mad.' She poured herself another glass, choosing to forget it was a school night. 'Plonker Mobile. Ha.' She giggled belatedly at Beth's quip. She had a point. One of the cashiers had probably lost a tenner at cash-up time. Tim was the captain of *SS Financial*, after all. She pulled out her phone, and dialled his number. He didn't pick up. She called again, but just got the same. He'd have his phone shoved in a drawer in his desk – she knew it. Either that or Pippa had turned the ringer off and she was going all single white female.

She tapped out a text to him a half dozen times, very different texts ranging from "answer your phone" to "we need to talk. I'm not happy, Tim." All of them got deleted swiftly. Instead, she wrote: *Tried to call you. Speak tomorrow.* She didn't put anything else, she was far too riled up at this point to even think straight. Joanna wanted her pitch for the article first thing, and she needed to get it right.

Putting down her phone and the wine, she went to the kitchen and clicked on the kettle. It was going to be a long night. And she was going to have to avoid Cal if she was going to have any kind of professional distance.

Chapter 15

Three days later, the paper came out, and the online piece containing a still of Isaac's YouTube video was already gaining clicks on the website. That sunny May Thursday morning, the news desk fielded two calls: both asking for details of the mystery man. The paper had obscured their faces in the end to protect their anonymity, but people weren't stupid. It was easy to find information out, especially in Hebblestone. She knew it would only be a matter of time before it caught on.

The next day, the calls doubled, and then trebled, and the hits kept coming. Emily kept checking the tally on her phone the whole way into the office building from the car, and she could see the hits and shares ticking over. It was gathering speed, and Hebblestone wasn't a town to shy away from a bit of excitement. The streaking bobble hat man was a hit for weeks after he ran around the castle moat a couple of years ago. "Mr Winter" as he was affectionately known to the locals, was a local celebrity for such a long time that there was even talk of the mysterious star being asked to switch on the Christmas lights. The Mayor of Hebblestone, who normally did the honours, was rather put out to say the least.

'Have you seen the hits?' Beth asked the second she got to her desk. 'Emily, have you seen this?'

'Seen what?' she tried, but Beth was on to her.

'You know what! Your mate is getting to be hot property! We've had people messaging our news desk all morning, wanting more details about the kid and his dad. Have you seen him?'

Emily logged in to her computer, opening the piece on wedding traditions and new trends she had been working on for the next issue of the pull-out supplement. She read through the first few lines, but then her emails booted up and the notifications started coming through. She muted them and began writing, ignoring Beth as best she could. 'No. I haven't, not yet. He doesn't know.'

The truth was, she'd shied away from everyone in her life since Monday. She'd barely spoken to anyone, least of all Calvin. Luckily, he seemed to understand, and she knew that he was busy. The new shopping centre was taking up a lot of his time, and Isaac's social life was seemingly hotting up too. They'd been texting each other a lot, mostly him trying to get her to come to the cinema to watch some Godzilla-type flick that sounded both awesome and terrifying. She'd cried off with work, which had been true, but really she knew she would have to tell him if they were face to face. Isaac had emailed her a couple of times, but he was still keen for his dad not to find out quite yet. Something about being grounded for the century when the football season was in play. All teenage angsty stuff. She felt terribly guilty.

God, was this what being a parent was like? No wonder Calvin was uptight about his son sometimes. She tried to focus back on her work, but the words seem to swim on the page. She almost wished she'd just let the names be released, but she'd fought hard to "make it more interesting". Well, that's how she'd sold it to her boss.

Beth's phone rang, and Emily almost fainted with relief at the distraction.

'Advertising, Beth speaking. No, sorry, we can't give out personal details. The email on the video is the main contact point for getting in touch. Ha ha, no we don't know that either.' Emily turned, and Beth was trying not to laugh as she dealt with the caller on the line. 'Shoe size? How is that relevant?' The caller must have responded because Beth's eyes widened. 'Oh, yeah. Well, I see your point, but again, we don't have any personal details at this time. The Herald will be covering the full story though, so be sure to keep buying the paper!'

She got rid of the caller, grinning triumphantly at Emily the second the call disconnected.

'Can you believe the brass neck on that one?'

'Are they all like that?' Emily asked, already dreading the answer.

'No, of course not! You always get a few odd requests with things like this – it's par for the course. We've already started getting letters from people interested though. I never realised Hebblestone was such a lonely-hearts club. This could be amazing, you know. If you really run with this story, it's going to get Jo's notice for sure. Think of your promotion!'

'I don't know, B, it feels wrong. What is Calvin going to think about all this? I know Isaac's heart is pure, but will his dad be happy about having his life hijacked? He's doing well but this might really upset him. He and Isaac haven't exactly had it easy, have they?'

The phone rang on her desk and she groaned as she saw the familiar number come up on the screen.

'Hi, Tim,' she answered, gesturing to Beth to be quiet. 'Everything okay?'

'Oh fine,' he said jovially, a hint of humour in his normally professional tone. 'The story about the boy looking for a new mum is getting a lot of attention. I've never had as many people come into the bank in one morning. Half of them just came in to chew the fat. I even got asked if I knew the family.'

'You didn't say anything, did you? And he's not looking for a new mum. That's not what this is about.'

'I can't exactly say I know Cal, can I? I've never met the guy.'

The silence down the line made Emily uneasy. 'Are you mad about that?'

Bethany was working back at her desk now, but one glance at the set of her shoulders gave her earwigging away. Emily looked furtively around the office, but everyone else was oblivious to her discomfort.

'No, not mad.' Tim sighed heavily. 'I guess I'm confused as to why you hadn't mentioned meeting up before. Or told me about what kind of article it was. I didn't realise it was this big a deal.' He cleared his throat, and she could hear him shuffling. He was pacing; he did that when he was having an awkward phone call. She could picture him hopping uncomfortably from one foot to the other.

'Are you shuffling?' she cut in. The noise stopped immediately.

'No, of course not. Are you going to answer my question, or avoid it? Come to think of it, you've been a bit like that all week.'

'I haven't been like anything; I'm busy – that's all. What was the question?'

'Why I haven't met Calvin yet. I'd like to meet him; he could come to the wedding!'

'We haven't set a date yet, Tim, so I can hardly send an invite, can I?'

She tried and failed to keep the snark out of her voice. She felt like a cornered cat, lashing out to protect herself. Why did he suddenly mention the wedding unprompted?

'Well, about that. I do think that perhaps we've waited long enough. I know you've been getting a bit fed up with all the planning you wanted to do, and me refusing to book anything. I have a feeling that the chat you wanted was about that? Why you've been a bit distant? I'm sorry, Em, I really am.'

So, he'd noticed. Oh, the irony. He made her sound like a bridezilla, but still.

'It's not that, Tim, I—'

'No, it's okay. I get it. You're a true romantic. My parents reminded me of that the other day, at lunch. My mum always reads your little pieces; she really likes them. She made a good point.'

160

Ignoring the "little pieces" barb, which was always how he referred to her work – or "little job" – she focused on the secondary shot he fired.

'And what point was that?'

'Well, I guess I just realised, it can't be easy doing the job that you do. Watching people week in week out, year in year out, pledging their lives to each other while we … well plan for the future I guess. Maybe I didn't get how long it would take, with everything. I mean, we are engaged, Emily. The plan is to get married. That is still the plan yeah?'

'I don't think we should really talk about it on the phone. How about later? I could come to yours?' He was finally opening up, but this wasn't the time. And Beth was eavesdropping, making Emily sweat in her chair.

'Badminton tonight, sorry, darling. I do think we need to talk about this though; I really do. I do think it's overdue and for that matter I'd like to meet Calvin too. He's important to you, obviously, so I should meet the man.'

Beth, who had been sipping at her cup of coffee at her desk, spluttered loudly. She began to have a frantic coughing fit, coffee streaming out of her nose and tears rolling down her face. Emily said to Tim, 'I'd better go sort her out. I'll call you after work?'

'Just … wait one second. Next time we both have a night free I'll take you out. No vouchers, no early bird specials. Just you and me, a nice meal, an expensive bottle of wine. We can talk about the wedding. Bring our diaries and put something concrete in action.'

Beth was still coughing her head off. 'I don't know, Tim, I think it's past just looking at dates. We need to talk, but I can't now. I'm sorry. I need to go.' She put the phone down before he could get a word out in response. She felt so sad about it all. How had they come to this? Badminton too. He sounded like he really wanted to sort things out, but couldn't he have cancelled it for her?

'Well, that went well.' She reached across the length of her desk, grabbing for the man-sized box of tissues and turning to come to her friend's aid. Beth, who looked like she'd leaked coffee from every orifice on her face, had unfortunately regained the control of her voice.

'You think that went well?' She reached for a handful of the large tissues and started to dab ineffectually at her ruined clothing.

'Ohh shit, Dave is going to be so mad. He bloody loves this outfit. That did not go well. I've had less uncomfortable smear tests, and that's bloody saying something. So, he knows about Calvin then? Why don't you just get the two of them to meet?'

'How did you hear what he said? Bat ears. And also – are you insane? I don't want the two of them to meet. Ever!'

'All right, that sounds realistic. Come on, this is bloody Hebblestone. You fart and everybody knows what you had for dinner. You have literally zero chance of that ever happening. Why don't you just get out from under it. Take charge of it! Book a table somewhere – invite the pair of them and see what happens. It is going to happen anyway, Emily. You know it, I know it, the whole bloody town knows it. So he swaps a few stories with Tim about when you were kids. It's nothing too embarrassing, is it? This story is getting bigger every minute. We have had people coming to talk about it on our website from all over. This is going to go UK-wide you know! People are loving this story. Isaac is a superstar! Plus, Calvin is a hot hot widower! What woman doesn't want a piece of that action? Come on, mate. If I didn't have Dave at home, I'd probably consider it myself if I didn't know you. Do you really think he's gonna end up single at the end of this? Not a chance, mate. You need to get in there quick. If that's what you want. I would be in like Flynn if I were solo. Still good about the wedding eh? He's listening to you!'

'Didn't you hear him just now? He wants to name a date. I've been waiting for this for years, and now all of a sudden, he's Mr Let's Plan. I just don't know what I want anymore, Beth, and this is all spinning out of control. I need everything to stop.'

'Emily Hendrickson, how many times have I told you … Life

does not wait for any man, woman or dog. You can make all the plans you want; you can procrastinate all you want. Do you think old Father Time gives a shit? You do know what to do.'

Joanne, never one to avoid walking into a loaded room, appeared from nowhere at the side of their desks. She was positively bouncing on the spot, her red-soled shoes jiggling on the carpeting.

'Have you seen the numbers this morning? Head office have been on the phone four times already. Four times! I haven't heard from them so much since we had the flasher in town!'

Beth, for once, seemed to sense Emily's mood and stepped in. She shepherded an exuberant Joanne away, murmuring about how busy Emily was and how committed she was to the project. Joanne was like a nodding dog at her side. Emily took the opportunity to relish the silence for a moment, gather her thoughts. A second later, she almost fell out of her chair when her phone vibrated in her bag. She grabbed for her handbag, instead knocking it to the floor with her shaky fingers.

'Shit.' She mumbled a few fruity expletives, sinking to the floor on her knees and reaching for her phone. Turning the screen to face her, she saw Calvin's face come up. He was calling her right now, and she didn't know what he knew. She'd been like this every time since the article had landed. She took a deep breath and pressed the green button.

'Hi, Calvin.' She tried to keep her voice as neutral as possible, though she could hear the fear in her own voice. 'Everything okay?'

Chapter 16

Walking into Hebblestone High School earlier that morning, Isaac waved goodbye to his dad as he drove away. Isaac looked for Kai. He didn't have to look far; his best friend was sitting on one of the benches outside the sports hall. As Isaac walked over to his friend, he noticed a few looks and double takes were being thrown his way by the other school students. He shrugged his bag off his shoulders and took a seat next to his friend on the bench.

'Have you seen all the things online about your dad?' Kai looked around furtively for any teachers who might be overlooking them, and then reached into his blazer pocket for his mobile phone. Shuffling closer to Isaac on the bench, he brought up the link from the newspaper website. Underneath the article, after the video screen where Isaac could see his own face as he sat in his bedroom, were a whole load of comments and questions from the viewing public. Some of them were silly comments, others were genuine questions from all over the UK, and a couple beyond. Kai was positively bouncing on the spot as he scrolled down, his eyes constantly flickering from the screen to Isaac's face.

'What did your dad say about it?'

'I don't think he knows yet. There's no way he knows. He hasn't mentioned anything. I think he's been pretty busy with work – the marketing campaign for the new shopping centre is taking all his time at the moment. Plus he has a new friend at the newspaper. Remember me telling you about Emily? He keeps texting her and laughing his head off. He's been doing stuff in the house too. I caught him singing while he was hanging the washing out the other day.'

'Hasn't she told him about it yet?'

Isaac rolled his eyes at his friend.

'She hasn't told him yet either. I asked her not to. She's pretty nice. I hope Dad's not mad at her when he finds out.' He thought for a minute about Emily. They'd only had a brief chat, a few emails, but he liked her. His dad was happier lately. He was a bit sad she missed the cinema trip, but the film was awesome. 'Nah, there's no way he knows. He would be mad for a start, and instead he's been a little bit happier lately.' Isaac thought about his dad's moods. It was true, in recent days he had seemed decidedly chirpy. He'd stopped ordering new clothes online, and last night he'd found him sitting at the computer looking at interior design websites for inspiration. Just that morning, as they were leaving for school, a courier had arrived, dropping off several boxes and bags full of odd-shaped items. 'I think to be honest having his friend here is helping him. He's not going to be mad, is he, Ky?'

Kai looked at his friend, the very epitome of tact evident on his features.

'I don't know, mate. When I told my mum about it this morning she thought it was really romantic. Like dead romantic, and she even said your dad was a bit fit. But then my dad came into the kitchen and he wasn't that impressed. He said it was pretty embarrassing that a teenager needed to advertise for his own dad to find a girlfriend.' Kai looked at Isaac's stricken face and laughed. 'My dad's a cynic though, and my mum says it's just because he's unromantic.'

'And what did you dad say to that?'

'He made a comment about not needing to buy the cow when

you were getting the milk for free, and so my mum slapped him around the head with a tea towel. Come to think of it, are you sure you want to get your dad a girlfriend? It's pretty cool at your house, and my mum and dad do nothing but fight and moan about who's doing the dishwasher, who's more tired, and who forgot to put the bins out.'

'Yeah, I'm sure. My dad deserves to be with someone nice. He was happy with Mum, but Mum's gone now. She's never coming back. I know everything seems cool to you at my place, but the house is just not the same with only us two. My dad is defo not the same, and besides, I'm not going to be around forever. If I'm going to be some kind of intrepid explorer, I need to know that my dad is going to be okay. I don't want to be worrying about him being bored on his own. Kai, I know your mum and dad fight. The fact is my mum and dad used to fight too. It wasn't always hunky-dory, but I even miss that. My dad always leaves his shoes in the hallway, and now there's no one around to tell him off. I think that makes us sadder than it should. I know that he's going to be mad, but Emily will talk him round I think. She said she would help, so she must think it's the right thing for Dad too. Dad said that when they were growing up around here, they were the bestest of friends. He trusts her; he talks about her all the time. If anybody can turn him round and make him take part in it, she can.'

A teacher started walking their way and Kai quickly put his phone away.

Isaac threw him a mischievous look. 'Besides which, if he wants to kill anyone, I'm hoping he'll go for her first.'

The teacher passed by, and both boys stood as the bell sounded for registration. As they walked towards the science block to go to tutor group, Isobel fell into step beside them. Isaac could feel his cheeks flush in her presence, and he wished Kai would walk faster and leave them to walk together alone. Kai, seemingly ignorant as ever to his friend's poor youngling heart, did no such thing.

'Have you seen Isaac's dad? Is he famous now? Is your dad still with your mum? If not – maybe you could set the two of them up? How cool will that be eh? His dad, your mum?'

Isaac felt the urge to punch his friend in the throat. Isobel made a loud yuck sound and rolled her eyes at Isaac. She looked just as disgusted at the thought as he did.

'Nah, my mum and dad are still together thanks. I did see the article though, Zac. How's it going?'

It took Isaac a full thirty seconds to regain the power of speech. Whenever Isobel looked at him, he always seemed to lose his train of thought. He turned into a gibbering idiot in her presence every time, no matter where they were. Class, the gym, the cinema. The last time they'd been in a group to see the latest film at the cinema in town, relating to their history topic, Isaac had been so jittery he had managed to spill his entire bucket of popcorn before they even got out of the foyer.

'I don't think he knows yet, but I'm sure he will before too long.'

At that moment, Mrs Tonka, one of the modern foreign language teachers walked across to them as they entered the block.

'Good morning, Isobel, Kai.' Her gaze came to rest on Isaac. 'And good morning to you. I see you're quite famous this morning, Mr Albright.' She gave him a simpering smile. 'How is your father today? Do pass on my kind regards, won't you? Parents' evening soon, eh? Do tell your father I would be happy to have a meeting about anything he would like to discuss.' She gave the children another winning smile and headed off. Kai, Isaac, and Isobel all looked at each other in horror.

'Well, whether your dad knows or not isn't the issue. The issue here is not getting your dad shacked up with one of your teachers. Can you imagine seeing Mrs Tonka in a dressing gown over breakfast every morning?'

'Not on my watch.' Isaac looked at the retreating teacher's back and shuddered at the thought. Kai had a point. He was trying to get his dad a girlfriend, but he had to like the girlfriend as well, right? He'd never really thought about it before, but this woman would end up living with them forever. Hopefully of course. He thought of his mother with a pang. He knew that it was a bit of a task; he wasn't stupid. But the new girlfriend would be a mother figure, he supposed. He didn't linger too much on the thought. He'd think about it later, when it was an actual thing.

'He's got a point, Isaac.' Isobel looked suddenly serious. 'My auntie Cheryl went on a dating site a couple of years back and she ended up with the biggest moron. My mum says that internet dating is dangerous. You can't let your dad be attacked by all the women in Hebblestone.'

Isaac thought back to the gaggle of women who always seemed to swarm around dad on the school run. Both of his friends had a point, and he needed Emily's help to control this situation. Once his dad was in the full picture, they had to make sure between them that the woman that Calvin chose in the end was someone that they could all live with. He couldn't imagine going from living with his mother and father, to living with some horrible woman who turned his dad into a simpering idiot. They were getting on better at home now, not as many awkward silences. No more crying quietly at the dinner table when a song on the radio jogged a painful memory. The Albright males of the household were healing.

When he started this video campaign, he did it for a reason, and that reason still stood. Isaac made a mental note to himself to contact Emily after school. He had her number at the paper. He could perhaps catch her when Calvin was busy making dinner. They needed to vet these women. He deserved nothing less.

'She's right, you know. They have those sucker fishes on the internet too,' Kai added.

'Catfishes,' Isobel and Isaac said together.

'Yeah.' Kai nodded. 'That's them. They pretend to be someone completely different. My mum watches a show about it all the time at home. She calls it her ironing time.'

Isobel's cute little brows raised as she looked across at Isaac.

'You said the lady at the paper was helping you, right? And you're still getting the emails from the address you created, right?'

'Yeah, till Dad finds out. Emily told me not to check without Dad being there. I didn't expect it to be this popular so quick though. I can see the YouTube comments. I thought he might have had a bit of time to get used to the idea.' He looked stricken for a second. 'I really think he might kill me.'

Kai laughed, but Isobel reached over and grabbed his arm. Her fingernails were painted with clear polish, sparkly bits shimmering as they caught the light. She had a rubber bracelet on, just peeking out from her uniform, her favourite local band's logo written across it.

'I think it's really brave. Your dad might get mad, but he won't stay that way for long. If his best friend is going to help you too, get her to read the emails with you. Give her the log-in. She can help you get rid of the Mrs Tonkas of the bunch.'

It was simple, and genius. Emily was a professional romantic, after all. Dad had said as much. She cared about Dad. It made perfect sense. 'Do you think she'd have time though?'

Isobel nodded. 'Friends are there for each other. I bet she'll make time. Let's ask her, after school! Meet me at the far bus stop, okay?'

'I can't,' he shouted after her. 'Dad's picking me up!'

She ran back to him, pulling a pen from her bag. Taking his arm, she rolled up his sleeve and after pulling the lid off her pen with her teeth, she wrote a number on his arm.

'Call her tonight then and let me know how it goes!'

She was off, bag on her shoulder and running to her classroom before either boy could blink, let alone reply. They both stared down the corridor, watching her leave.

'Do you think she meant both of us?' he checked, not wanting to make an idiot of himself.

Kai tapped him on the shoulder, giving him a knowing look.

'Mate, I think I'm busy tonight. COD war. You two have fun though, yeah? Ring me after; tell me how it went.' He made a girly-looking "call me" motion with his hands, pushing his lips out in a huge trout-like pout.

Isaac blushed, knowing that Kai was being a good wingman for him. He really was becoming a best friend. And Isobel was … oh, Isobel was just – lovely. Every time she brushed her arm against his, or sent him a note, his heart would sing. He was really starting to like it here and he just hoped that all his efforts were going to pay off and not leave him and his dad a laughing stock. They headed off, and Isaac found himself wishing the day away.

* * *

Calvin was knee-deep in designs for one of the shops in the new shopping centre when he noticed the girls in the office were a little giddier than usual, even for a Friday. His office door was open as always, and he could just make out a congregation of some of them around his assistant's desk. He tried to return to his design, which was for a new comic book shop a local business was opening. He'd decided to add him to the promotional material as one of the showcase shops. Give the guy a boost. He'd been in their year at high school, and the guy was sweating over opening up premises with a sick mother to support. The rates for a shop in that particular complex weren't cheap either, even with the regeneration funding the city had received. He wanted to help the guy out. He knew what it was like to lose a parent, and if he had either of his here, he would move heaven and earth for them.

The women giggled again, and he saw a head turn in his direction. What was going on? He finished saving the latest draft of his design on the computer, picking up his coffee cup. The minute his bottom left the chair, the women scattered like antelopes from a prowling lion. He walked down the corridor and headed to the kitchen. Ryan and Bill were already in there, tucking into their lunch. The two men stopped talking the instant he walked into the room.

'Morning, gents.'

'Good morning, Romeo!'

Bill sniggered like a teenager beside him. 'Give up, Ryan, it's a good thing.' He cleared his throat. 'Sorry, we're just being daft. Some of the comments on the article were a little … well … amusing. That's not to say that you won't find someone though, of course.'

'Yeah, of course.'

Calvin frowned, moving to the coffee machine to get his caffeine fix.

'I don't know what you're on about, gents. Do you know what's happening out there, by the way?'

They looked at each other sheepishly.

'Ah well, it's the article. From the video Isaac made?'

'What?' Cal's phone buzzed in his pocket, but he ignored it. 'What article?'

His phone started buzzing again, short little bursts. Horrified, he looked at the number of notifications on his screen.

'Bill, what the hell is going on? What video? What has Isaac got to do with it?'

Josie, one of the office girls, tentatively put her head around the kitchen door.

'Morning, everyone.' She looked straight at Calvin, and he nodded at her jovially. His phone was still tinkling away in his pocket. He covered it with his hand, not that it did much to muffle the sound.

'Morning,' Calvin replied, feeling the pressure to reply since his two friends seemed to have forgotten how to speak. 'Everything okay out there?'

Josie looked a little shy for a moment. 'Oh, it's just … us girls wanted to say that we wish you good luck, with the search and everything. We're all rooting for you.'

Ryan piped up a "hear, hear" in the background. The notifications were still pinging, and Calvin finally connected the two together. This was about him, and whatever it was, it was obviously out there.

'Er … thank you, Josie.' He put his coffee cup down on the counter and walked as calmly as he could out of the room. 'See you later, guys,' he called over his shoulder and closed the door behind him. The women in the office, and the men for that matter, all suddenly looked very urgent. Much shuffling of papers and tapping of keys erupted the second he'd stepped foot out of the ruddy kitchen. Out of the frying pan and into the fire. He smiled at a couple of people who dared to make eye contact, and once he got into his office, he sagged against the closed door.

'What the hell is going on?' he said to the empty room. 'Isaac …' Something about Isaac and a video. His hands grabbed for his mobile, activating the screen with his thumb and scrolling through the notifications. The many notifications. Oh God.

'Oh dear God.' It was about him, wanting to find a girlfriend. People had replied, people he knew. People he didn't. People who typed in languages he didn't even understand. *What the hell was going on?* There were lots of mentions about Isaac, and the video. Lots of people talking. He found a link, and clicking it, his YouTube app fired up. Isaac's face filled the screen, half covered by the little white play symbol. He stood and peered through his door. His office colleagues seemed to have lost interest, thankfully. For the minute at least. He went over to his desk, reaching into a drawer for his headphones. He sat back behind the door, not wanting to be interrupted and wishing there was a lock on his office. Plugging the earphones in, he hit the play button, and braced himself as Isaac's voice filled his ears.

He watched it twice. Shock at his son's actions quickly turned into admiration, and fear, and a punch of gut-wrenching pain to boot. The way he spoke about his mum, and about him being lonely, it just brought home how much the lad had seen in his life. How caring he was. How bold. Just like his mother that way. That was when the tears came. His own son had stepped up to pull his old dad out of his rut, and that made him feel so ashamed of himself. He'd dragged the kid to Yorkshire, away from his childhood home, his friends, everything he knew. All for the promise of a new life, and lo and behold – he still hadn't really done anything. Apart from meet Emily of course. Finding her again had been amazing. She was a breath of fresh air, breezing right into his life.

It clicked then. The paper. He came out of the video app and googled the paper website. He remembered seeing their banner on one of the links. It hadn't registered before, but now it was screaming at him. The website popped up, and the link was right there. Clicking through, he read the whole thing. Including the by-line. Closing the net, he scrolled through his numbers and hit the green button.

'Cal? Is there something wrong?'

Cal hadn't thought past hitting the call button. He realised a little too late that he didn't have a bloody word planned.

'I saw the article,' he blurted. 'What's going on?'

'Er, Cal – I'm at work at the minute.'

'Meet me then, after work? Isaac's staying out tonight with a football mate, sleepover and then training in the morning. Come to mine.'

'Cal, I—'

'Emily, you printed an article about me without telling me. I think we need to talk. Seven, okay? I'll text you the address.'

Then he did something neither of them had ever done to each other. Not on purpose, at least. He put the phone down. She dialled back, but he ended the call without answering, and after firing off a text with his address on to her, he turned his phone off. He hauled himself off the floor, went over to the wall and yanked the internet cable out of the wall. It was only then

173

he felt himself breathe, but he could still feel eyes on him from outside. He couldn't cut the internet to the building. Could he? No, of course not. He picked up the phone on his desk instead and dialled his assistant.

'Hello? Yes, hold all calls please. I'm going home for the day to work.'

He put the phone down again. He was getting good at it. He gathered his things together and fled the office as quick as he could. He made it to the foyer without speaking to anyone. Larry the security guard, a huge titan of a bloke, patted him on the shoulder as he scrambled for the exit.

'Mr Albright, right on! Good luck, my friend.'

'Er … thanks,' he mumbled, fumbling in his pocket for his keys. He dumped his work stuff in the boot, and he didn't take a breath till he had driven out of the car park and put work in his rear-view mirror. He turned on the radio by way of distraction.

'… he must be desperate though, surely?'

'That's a bit mean, and we are live.' Calvin turned off the high street, heading through the familiar streets and avoiding eye contact with anyone at the traffic lights. He'd kept the windows closed, even though he was melting in the warm weather. He felt like a hothouse cucumber.

'I disagree, I think it's lovely. This family deserve a bit of happiness. Don't you think? Hebblestone deserves a bit of cheer too I think.'

Calvin frowned. Hebblestone FM, the local radio station, didn't normally have such heated debates.

'I agree, Doris, and thank you both for calling in. That was Doris and Frank, everybody, from Leeds – they had differing opinions on the latest article from the *Hebblestone Herald*. Call in to tell us your opinion—'

He turned the radio off quickly. Jesus Christ, it was on the radio. Calvin suddenly felt sick. He needed to think. Why the hell was Emily involved in this? Why hadn't she told him? Isaac was in big trouble, but he knew his reasons why. The tear-jerking reasons. He could blub all over again at the thought of the video. He'd made a massive effort, to say the least. How could he be mad, really? But Emily … he thought about how busy she'd been this week, and something in his heart stuttered. Was she just using him for an angle? He dismissed the thought the second he had it. No way. Emily would never do that.

There was something else at play here. Isaac must have spoken to her, somehow. He thought back to the clubhouse that day, the pair of them bonding. The little sod. He was mad now! No more bacon butties for his progeny, that was for damn sure. He could have cereal and bloody well lump it! He suddenly felt like he was the sole parent of someone who could give Artemis Fowl a run for his money. He jabbed at his stereo, putting on his favourite Killers album from the CD changer. "Mr Brightside" started to play, and Calvin started to laugh hysterically.

'You have got to be kidding me!'

He jabbed the button off and drove the rest of the way home in seething silence. After pulling into his street, he parked the car in his drive and left everything but his phone and the keys in his hand back in the car. He knew he wasn't going to get much work done this afternoon.

'Hello!' A sudden voice from the bushes had his keys flying out of his hand.

'Gah! Hello?'

A couple came out from behind the hedge that divided the properties.

'Sorry, love,' the woman said. The retired couple from next door, they'd been quiet to live next door to. Calvin had heard them laughing together out in the garden on sunny days and seen them coming and going together in the car. They looked nice enough. Grandparent-like, which they were of course. They regularly had visitors with car seats and toddlers in tow. It was nice, a bit of life to listen to, even though it made their own house seem so much quieter. 'I didn't mean to scare you! We just wanted to say hello and ask if you were all right.'

Her husband nodded at Cal, and he found himself nodding hello back.

'Er ... I don't know what—'

'The article, love. The video your lad made. We saw it today. We just wanted to see if you were okay, because ... well ...' She trailed off, and Jim picked up her cue.

'Alice was—'

'We—'

Jim's lip twitched. 'We, well we were worried that you might be feeling a bit – exposed. You see, this is not our first marriage. We both lost our partners.'

Alice took her hand in his, and he held it tight. It looked so natural between them. A fresh little wave of loss came over Calvin. He missed that.

'We actually met through a bereavement group online.'

'Anyway,' Alice interjected. 'The point is, we both know how hard it is to take the next step, and we just wanted you to know that. And also, not to be too mad at your lad. If you don't me us saying. He's a good lad.'

He was a good lad. Calvin never tired of hearing it from other people though. He was touched that they'd reached out to him. He had no idea. They looked like they had been together forever.

'Thank you – I mean that. I'm afraid I'm a bit in shock about all this. I didn't know about it. I think my friend at the paper helped him.'

'Emily's your friend?' Alice's ears pricked up. 'Emily Hendrickson? Oh, we love her. She covered our wedding, didn't she, Jim?' She elbowed Jim full pelt in the side. To his credit, he didn't even react. 'Tell him, Jim! Emily's lovely isn't she?'

'She is lovely. She did a lovely little write-up. Nice woman too.' He studied Calvin for a minute. 'Shame she's not single, eh?'

'Yeah,' Calvin replied. 'Er ... no, well – she's got a – Tim.'

'Yeah, we met him. He came to collect her at the end of the night.' Jim's face said it all. 'He's a bank manager.' He said it like you would introduce a rectal thermometer salesman. With more than a hint of disgust. 'Never liked bank managers.'

'He never has.' Alice giggled. 'That guy who sings those insurance adverts gets right on his wick too. Well, we'll let you get on with your day. We just wanted to catch you to say that really. Our door is always open, okay?'

Jim stepped forward and put a fatherly hand on his shoulder. 'Good luck, son.'

He felt for a second like they were waving him off to war. Then again, judging from the comments he had scanned through, he'd been thrown into something that felt a bit like a battlefield. He hadn't even dipped his toe in the dating pool yet, and now he had to do it in public? Eugh. He was back to mad again. He made his goodbyes, and headed straight for the shower, stripping his work clothes off as he went. He almost felt like he needed to start his day all over again. He didn't put the radio on this time. He needed the silence and the hot feel of the water to think about how he was going to play this. He could phone his friends back home, but then that would spread the news. He didn't want London catching wind. They might even bloody share it to their pages, and then he'd be even more viral. Him, a graphic designer specialising in marketing campaigns. Marketed as a sad lonely widower by his only child, who was secretly a bloody evil genius at making him crawl out of his rut.

He needed to get it together. He was picking Isaac up in a few hours, and Emily was coming over tonight. She had better bloody come too, or he was going to her. Tim be damned. He could always take Jim with him as muscle.

The shower gave him the white noise to think. He knew what had bothered him so much. He knew that Isaac loved him to pieces, and he was touched by his actions. Mortified beyond belief but touched. It was Emily. The fact that she'd not said anything to him. The fact that it was another ice bucket to the head. He knew what had annoyed him. It was the fact that she wasn't bothered. Isaac had gone to her for help, and she'd helped him. She'd cocked up, but that was Emily. He knew her way of thinking. She'd done what she'd always done. She'd helped him. He'd told her himself that he was lonely. That's why she'd been asking. *Me and my stupid bloody heart.* He'd harboured the stupid thought for half a second that she might have just got a pang, having met the grown-up Calvin. The more confident Cal, the one he'd wanted to be that fateful prom night.

But no, she didn't of course. She just saw him as a friend, a BFF. Best Friend Forever. A sad single friend who needed her help. That's what pissed him off the most. He'd felt something off since they'd met back up, with her and Tim. She never talked about him, not really. She never showed any excitement when she did refer to him. The wedding was barely mentioned, and when he brought it up, she deflected the subject away. He'd thought, well, he'd hoped that perhaps she'd actually liked him back for once. Nope, he could already hear the ice bucket coming his way. She didn't feel a thing, obviously. He banged the tiles in frustration, and stewed under the steam a while longer.

By the time he got out, he'd shampooed his hair three times. His fingertips were like prunes, but as he dried and changed into a pair of jeans and a T-shirt, he'd calmed down enough to deal with the general public again.

It was early Friday evening, warm May weather shining through the windows. It felt pretty normal, a normal day. He was picking up his son and his footballer friend Owen from school, work was good, he had plans with his childhood best friend later. Crushing disappointment and media exposure aside, things were moving on finally. When he ran over it in his mind, he was doing okay. He was happy. This wasn't too bad. Maybe he'd overreacted. Maybe that's just how things were done these days. Influencers shared their whole lives, didn't they? They shared everything from what washing powder they used to what gender their unborn children were. It was the digital age after all. *Not everyone met in a bloody bank. What kind of meet-cute is that.* He hadn't mentioned it to Isaac yet, not in front of his friend. He'd have to wait till they were alone. It might give him some time to think about what he was going to say. He didn't want to raise Isaac's hopes for nothing. The kid was obviously hellbent on his plan.

He passed the park and drove up to Owen's little estate. Just past the turnoff, there was a little parade of shops. Hebblestone was a lover of little shops, and there were many dotted around the place. People seemed to prefer to shop local rather than tramping to the bigger towns that surrounded them, and the shop owners loved their customers right back. As he indicated to make the turn, Owen suddenly jumped up at the window like an excited spaniel.

'Oh my God, is that your dad?'

Calvin tried to control the car as he craned his neck to see what Owen was exclaiming about.

'What? Isaac?' Isaac was no help to Calvin. He was busy trying to stuff Owen's head into the crack in the upholstery. Owen, oblivious to what he had caused, was trying in a very muffled voice and in between bursts of laughter to ask his friend what was going on. Calvin spotted what the lads were looking at, and he felt his face erupt with heat. On the sandwich board outside the gift shop that sat on the corner, where they normally displayed the latest local gift ideas, was a huge picture of his face. Calvin's face from the company profile. Someone had printed it out and stuck it to the black-painted surface. Underneath it read: local man looking for love. Buy him the perfect gift here!

Oh dear God. He'd become an advertisement. He'd pulled to a stop now, groaning heavily as his head slowly came to rest on the steering wheel. Both boys sensed the change in mood and stopped squabbling.

'Oh God. Oh no. Oh Lord.' Each phrase was punctuated by Cal's head hitting the steering wheel. 'Oh God. I'm a sandwich board advert. I mean, first I was a video, and now my face is on a sandwich board. I'm screwed.' Another bang of his head under the steering wheel. Isaac leaned forward and patted his dad on the shoulder. Calvin looked across at him, the imprint from the steering wheel leaving a pink line of stitching imprinted on his head.

'Dad, are you okay? People are starting to look.' Calvin's head popped up like a meerkat's, and sure enough, there were a few people starting to look from the board, to their car. Probably because the owner of the car had just seen his own face on the side of the road and then decided to pull over and have a mini mental breakdown. He gave them a weak wave and then ducked down as low as he could. 'Dad?'

Calvin hadn't spoken yet, he had pulled away and headed the car to Owen's house again.

'Dad?'

'Is your dad okay?' He could hear the whispers from Owen. The poor kid probably wished he'd got the bus now.

'I'm okay, Owen,' he said finally, just as they pulled up to the house. 'Hey, will you do me a favour? Take Isaac's footie stuff in for me, eh?' Owen didn't need asking twice. He took the bags Calvin passed him and was out like a shot into the house. 'Have a good night!'

'You too, Mr Albright,' he called as he ran for safety. 'Good luck, Isaac.'

Owen was obviously far more observant than Cal. He'd worked out that Isaac had something to do with it quicker than the man raising him under the same roof had. The car door closed behind him, and the two Albright men were left sitting in the car on the driveway.

'Dad, I—'

'I'm not mad, son, it's okay.' Calvin took off his seatbelt, sighing heavily. 'I wish you'd had done it another way, but I get it. I watched the video. A lot.'

'You did? How did you find out? I knew she'd tell you.'

Calvin thought back over his white-knuckle ride of a day.

'A mate at work.' He turned to face his son, and Isaac suddenly looked very little in the back seat. Calvin saw a flash of him sitting there when he was younger. Little chicken legs poking out from his toddler cat seat. His hair. Long, dark like it was now, but fluffier. Curls of babyhood. He shook his head to dislodge the image from his mind. 'Are you okay?'

He knew he himself felt like an ant under a magnifying glass. Isaac shrugged. 'I just don't want you to be mad.'

'I'm not mad. Well, I was a little surprised. Why didn't you just talk to me about it?'

'I tried, Dad, but you never want to talk about it. You just got sad. I wanted to help. Our house is massive.'

'The house? What's that got to do with it?'

Isaac folded his hands on his lap, something that his mother used to do when they were talking. It took his breath away.

'It's just me and you, that's all. The house in London was more fun. I thought our new house might be good, but it doesn't feel the same. I heard you crying, Dad, at night. When we first moved. You still do sometimes. I do. I just thought that maybe if you met someone, you'd—'

'Feel better?' he asked gently, and his lad nodded slowly. 'I'm sorry you had to go through all this, I really am. It breaks my heart.'

Isaac jumped forward in his seat, closer to his dad.

'It's not your fault; you did everything you could, Dad. For both of us. I do like it here too. Emily's nice, and she seems to make you happy. These last few days have been different.'

'Emily helped you, didn't she?' He didn't argue that he was happier with her in his life, but that felt confused now.

'I don't think she wanted to. Her friend at the paper did it really. Emily said I should tell you, and not look at the emails. I thought she'd blabbed.'

'Emails?' Calvin's face paled. 'There's emails too?'

Isaac got his phone and tapped on the screen a few times.

'From the video, yeah.' He showed Calvin the screen, and the email icon had 562 at the side of it; 562 emails. 'It was only a few this morning!'

'There's 562 emails! Isaac, how the hell are we going to read all those?'

'We can get Emily to help! I was talking to Kai at school, and—'

'Kai knows?' Calvin put his head in his hands, but Isaac was excited now. He didn't see his father's panicked demeanour anymore.

'Yeah, Kai knows, and Isobel! She even gave me her number; she's dead excited. And Kai's mum says that some of her mates would give you one too, whatever that means. I think she means emails.' Isaac's innocent little face jabbered on as Calvin died slowly from mortification. 'So they must be in there. Issy says that we should give the emails to Emily and let her go through them to get rid of the rabbit killers and stuff.'

'Bunny boilers,' Calvin corrected, his voice a strangled squeak. 'That's really the truth? Emily said that you shouldn't do it?'

Isaac rolled his eyes. 'Dur, Dad. I'd already done it on YouTube. I've made another; I just need to upload it.'

Calvin's eyes popped. 'Excuse me, it might just be my old ears, but did you just say you made another video?'

* * *

Much, much later, Calvin was feeling a little bit better. Sure, it could have been the beer he'd drunk while cooking his favourite curry, or the fact that he'd muted his notifications on every device in the house until the end of time. It could be the fact that he'd spent the last few hours shopping, cooking and throwing the various bits of home décor that had been stacked up in boxes on the porch around his home. It looked good too, even if he did say so himself. And he had. Several times. After he and Isaac had hugged it out, he'd not stopped. He'd taken himself to task.

He checked the clock. Just before seven. He turned the curry down a little and was just about to reach for another beer when the doorbell went.

Chapter 17

'Hi.'

'Hello, Calvin.'

'Calvin, before you say anything, I—'

'Calvin, I'm a mess. I think I love you, and you coming back has twisted my melon, man.'

No. No. No. She'd practised all the way over in the car, her jean-clad knees knocking together as she drove to the address on the text. She felt chilled to the bone, even in her wool jumper and black jacket. She could feel the goose bumps all over her body catch on the material as she walked up the path and rang the doorbell. Nothing she'd practised had felt right, and now she was just a girl, standing in front of a door, begging it not to open.

Calvin opened the door, a glass of wine in his hand. She could smell spicy food. He looked gorgeous, dressed in a simple pair of jeans and T-shirt. Which was irritating at this moment, because her mind was already blank. Now, she had no chance of keeping her head in the game.

'Hi, come in.' Her legs somehow carried her over the threshold, and then the door was shut behind her and all thoughts of escape left. 'Come through. Don't bother about shoes or anything.'

She'd already started tugging off her boots, so she finished and followed him into the kitchen. The table was set with two places in the dining area.

'You hungry?' He was pouring wine into another glass now, ushering her to one of the place settings and plonking her down on the chair. The wine was placed in front of her, and he headed back over to the kitchen. 'It's just a curry, nothing special.'

'Have I walked into a parallel universe here? I thought you were mad.'

Calvin came with two plates of curry and rice, a stack of naan breads on a separate platter. He got to work putting them down, finally settling in his chair, glass back in hand.

'I was mad. I am mad, a little. Why didn't you tell me?'

'Isaac asked me at the clubhouse that day, and to be honest I just didn't know what to do. I didn't want to break his trust. I didn't expect this, but Beth and Joanna got involved before I could get a handle on it, and then it was just out there. I'm really sorry.' She took a glug of her wine, relief flooding through her when he reached for her hand across the table.

'So you didn't want to do it?'

'No!' she said violently. 'No. I feel awkward about the whole thing.' Her eyes widened at her admission, and she felt his eyes on her. 'You know, because of the work thing.'

'Sure,' he said, a sly smile spreading across his lips. 'The work thing.' He locked eyes with her. 'I think I'm beginning to understand. Isaac told me what happened, and I pieced the rest out of the paper.' He nodded to the bin. Emily laughed.

'I deserved that.'

'Isaac wants you to deal with the emails, from the video.'

'Oh.' Emily's face dropped. 'Is that why I'm here? Are you going through with this?'

Calvin's brows furrowed. 'What do you mean? I mean, it's out there now. I sort of have to, don't I?' He looked a bit confused, as if the thought had never occurred to him before. *Such a good dad*, she thought ruefully. 'Isaac would be heartbroken if I didn't try, right?'

Emily knew without a doubt that it was what Isaac wanted. Cal's own words kept coming back to her. He'd told her he was lonely. She could feel his sadness, like always. That's why she was doing this. It wasn't about her.

'I think you should try, but only if it's what you really want. I know you want to meet someone, and I … saac just wants you to be happy. Do *you* want me to deal with the emails?' Her eyes narrowed when his jaw clenched hard.

Calvin picked up his fork and he looked pointedly at her plate.

'After dinner, and a couple more drinks. At least. We can look together.'

Emily picked up her fork. The food did smell good.

'Can hardly say no, can I? I was expecting an executioner, not a meal.'

Calvin's laugh filled the air, and Emily relaxed. He had forgiven her, which was great. The night had suddenly got better.

* * *

'Dear Lord of all that is holy, what on earth is that?'

Calvin was glaring open-mouthed at an email photo attachment he'd received. They'd spent the best part of the last hour wading through the emails, printing out any that were possibles. The wine had made the trip with them to the couch. Emily sat cross-legged next to Cal, leaning across him to scrutinise the image.

'A cat I think. Must be a cat lover.'

'Thank God for that. I wondered what the hell I was looking at.' Cal felt himself sag with relief.

'Right? There's some really interesting people in here.'

186

'Interesting is a bit polite, isn't it? Can't you remember that one with the tea cosy obsession?'

'Oh yeah, she was a bit strange.' He saw her amused grin and smiled. *It was nice, having her here.*

'More wine?' He held the bottle out.

'Driving,' Emily moaned. 'And I have another wedding tomorrow, plus an evening reception. I need to keep my head straight.'

'Good point.'

Calvin put down the bottle, leaning in closer to her and clicking delete on the cat photo. 'Thank you, next.'

'Okay, not a cat lover.' Emily brought up the next email. 'Okay, this one looks promising.' She started smiling at Calvin like an unhinged maniac.

'What, a normal person? Who is it?' He gingerly leaned in, but she covered the screen with her hands. 'Hey!'

'Don't spoil the surprise! This is a good one, trust me. Remember Mrs Evancliffe, from secondary?'

'Yeah … vaguely. Liked those long pendant necklaces? When she turned quickly in the corridors you got twatted in the face? That Mrs Evancliffe?'

Emily was shaking with laughter now, clutching her sides. 'I forgot about those necklaces!' She held her stomach, sloshing the last bit of wine from her glass onto the carpet. 'Oops, sorry.'

Calvin shrugged it off, dabbed at it with his socked foot.

'Don't worry, I live with Isaac. He sheds like a Siberian husky. What about her?' A look of dread crossed his sexy face. *Sexy face indeed.* She put her wine glass down and waited for him to guess.

'Go on, I'll give you two guesses.'

'Oh, Emily, you and your two guesses. The rest of the world usually get three!'

'Three is far too easy. Come on!'

'Her granddaughter emailed in.'

'Nope,' Emily was trying her very best not to crack. 'Last go!'

'Her daughter?'

'Nope!'

'No.'

'Yes!'

'Oh my God,' Calvin reached for the wine. 'Mrs Evancliffe sent an email? What did she say?'

Emily was hysterical now. 'My stomach, my stomach. I can't breathe.'

Calvin wrestled the laptop closer, and leaned in. 'Oh my God, she basically gave me a school report! What the hell?'

'It's absolute gold! I swear, this would be the funniest article!' She leaned in, feeling Calvin pull away from her side.

'You're not going to print these, are you? I didn't think that you'd do that.'

Turning to Cal, she realised what she'd said. 'No Cal, oh God no. These emails are private. I wouldn't do that.' She saw his jaw clench. 'Did you think I'd do that?'

'Well, you printed the article.' He finished his glass, and she saw it then. He was mad. Really mad, despite what he'd said earlier. Glistening-eye, twitchy-limbed mad. 'I didn't think you'd do that, either.'

'I told you about that; we rehashed it at dinner. You know I didn't have an opportunity to say no. Joanna makes Anna Wintour look like Alan Partridge. If I'd said no, I would have probably lost my job. She's always pratting on about how many people she could cull with the click of a button.'

'It's not about that; I just wish you'd told me. Before. All this.'

'You'd have stopped me!'

'I wouldn't!'

'Calvin, you almost stole a sandwich board today because it had your face on it. You told me that yourself. I know you're going along with it, but there's no way you wouldn't have tried to stop it. It's only because of Isaac you are even considering this.'

188

'You make me sound like a wimp. Was that it? Poor old Cal, so sad. I don't need pity, you know. I've had enough of that gut-rot to last a lifetime, Emily. I was just fine!'

'No you weren't!' Emily objected to his rewriting of the facts. This conversation had turned so quickly. It wasn't like them. The wine, maybe? She wanted to calm down the situation, but she couldn't bite back her words. 'You told me you were lonely, and Isaac asked for my help, and he said you were sad. He begged me to keep it quiet, and I'd only just met him! I didn't want to betray his trust like that, Calvin. What was I supposed to do?'

'Tell me! Talk about it!'

Emily stood up, gathering her things. 'Oh, I knew you weren't okay. This is a bad idea.'

'Yes!' Calvin punched the air triumphantly. 'She gets it! This is a bad idea. You should have told me.'

'Your son made the video, Calvin; it was already out there.'

'Yeah, and you announced it to the bloody world and never thought to mention it! What is wrong with you?'

'What's wrong with me?' Emily stabbed herself in the chest with one of her boots as she headed to the hallway, collecting her bits and making her escape. 'What's wrong with you! Have you seen my other boot?'

Calvin found it under the coats rack and brandished it aloft. 'Why didn't you tell me? You avoided me all week, and I thought – well it doesn't matter what I thought. You were just hiding from me because of all this.'

She held her hand out for her shoe, but he moved away.

'Look,' she sighed, exasperated. 'I'm sorry. I know it was dodgy, but I just sort of got … swept up. I should have told you, but I just couldn't find the words. It's been a bit of a weird couple of weeks.'

'You're telling me,' he agreed. His shoulders sank. He was breathing hard through his top, and she could see him inhaling sharply. 'Don't go. Please. I hate it when we fall out. I just don't like secrets between us, Ems. I never did.' He looked down at the floor, sighing heavily. 'They take a toll, that's all. I don't want to argue. This is not us at all. I do need your help with the emails, and you did say you would help Isaac.'

'You played the son card, nice.'

'Thanks, I thought so too. I just freaked out.' He held his hands out, offering her the boot with a rueful smile on his face. He looked so bloody adorable, she couldn't help herself.

'I was freaked out too, you know.' She took the boot and covered her face with her hair as she put it on. 'It's been weird, seeing you again after all this time. And now this – I just don't want anything to come between us.'

She was back on two feet again, and Cal was right there, up close.

'Nothing's going to come between us. Ever. It just wasn't like you; I felt a bit betrayed.'

'Betrayed?' Emily felt sick. 'Cal, I would never betray you. I did it for you. Sure, I didn't really want to do it, and I acted like a chicken. I just want you to be happy. You deserve someone who makes you so happy.' She reached up to touch his face, and she saw his eye fall on the ring once more. He always seemed to look at it.

'What about Tim? Does he make you feel like that?'

'Sure.'

'Sure? That's it?'

'Yeah, of course. Listen, I'd better go. Early start.'

Calvin looked at her disapprovingly but she patted him on the chest and headed for the door.

'I'll go through the rest of the emails. Let me deal with this, the paper I mean. Beth lives for this stuff. Just let us do it, okay? I can ask Isaac to check the possibles once they're vetted, and I'll make sure he's safe.'

Calvin just nodded at her. She was almost out of the door

when she heard his parting shot. She thought of nothing else in the car on the way home. It kept her up half the night and snoozing through the wedding festivities the day after.

'We're both chickens, Emily. Remember that.'

She didn't know what to say to him. She already knew how much of a coward she was.

Chapter 18

The following week, Emily and Tim caught a taxi from her place to meet Calvin and his new date at the restaurant. Giuseppe's was your typical Italian chain restaurant, complete with awkward stereotypes of moustached men and check linen tablecloths. People didn't come here for that though; they came here for the good food and the easy, comfortable surroundings. Tim was grumbling beside her on the back seat, moaning about the expense of a taxi. In front of the very annoyed taxi driver.

'I'm sorry, but I just don't see why we couldn't have taken one of the cars. What's the point of the extra expense?' As he said this he jabbed his finger towards the cab driver. Emily heard the driver mutter something under his breath about biting fingers off. For a moment she half wanted to see him do it. Another sign that this evening was going to be a total and colossal nightmare from start to finish. Emily wasn't new to going along with things in life: jobs, relationships, awkward dinner dates that she never wanted to go on in the first place. It was very on brand for Emily Hendrickson.

Even so, tonight had to be the lowest point. She was going to have to spend the entire evening with her fiancé, her child-hood best friend who she was secretly in love with, and some desperate woman who had replied to a YouTube advert from a pubescent boy. Well, that was nasty. Even her inner thoughts were quite vicious this evening. A sure-fire sign that she was in full-on fight-or-flight mode. She turned to Tim and resisted the urge to slap him by sitting on her hands. She wasn't looking forward to this at all, and he wasn't in the best mood either. He had been odd lately. Very odd.

'Because I didn't want to drive, Tim! What's wrong with wanting to have a drink with a meal? It's only a tenner each way for a taxi. I didn't think you had that much of a tight arse.'

'Twenty pounds here and there adds up, Emily. It all costs money, and I have a full tank of petrol in my car. If we are going to book the wedding, we're going to need big deposits for the better offers.'

Emily sighed and opening her bag, pulled out a twenty and shoved it across to him.

'There you go, problem solved. And if you don't mind, tonight I don't think we should mention the wedding.'

Tim didn't move to pick up the note. She looked him in the eye and registered hurt in his. She was taking out her jealousy on the wrong person. 'Well, you know how it is. Calvin being a widower and all? His new date might not want to hear about that either. It might be a sticky subject. That's all I meant.'

Tim nodded slowly, but his expression was far from impressed. She turned and looked out of the window, trying to cover her thoughts.

'So who is this new date anyway? Do you know her? Does Calvin?'

'No, she was one of the people who responded to the video article. She seems nice, normal. Isaac seemed to like the sound of her.' Isaac had in fact been positively giddy about his dad meeting this one. She was called Sophie Clement, and she lived on the outskirts of Leeds. She was single, a radiologist, and a mum to a girl six months younger than Isaac. On paper, she seemed like a normal person. What troubled Emily wasn't that she might not be normal. It was more that she would be. And more importantly, that Calvin would think so too. This was the first date, but what if that was all it took? Not to mention the fact that the entirety of this uncomfortable exchange would be witnessed by not only herself, but also by her fiancé.

Emily had never had the best of poker faces, so when the subject of driving to the restaurant had come up, she had put her foot down. Firstly, there was no way in hell that she was going to get through this evening sober, and if Tim drove, she risked him watching her get drunker and drunker as the evening went on and having her feelings all over her face. No. No driving for either of them tonight. She needed both of them lubricated to get through it. Anaesthetised if you will. At this moment in time, if Amazon sold tranquilising dart guns with next-day delivery available, she would have found herself having a one-click predicament. She wasn't quite sure that Tim, given his erratic moods of late, would forgive her for darting him in the ass five minutes before they were due to leave. She already had enough explaining to do.

They still hadn't spoken, him blaming work for being tired, busy or just not interested in talking about anything but weddings. Having her job had its uses sometimes. She'd thrown herself into work, and had spoken to Cal daily about the work she was doing. And other things. They often rang off after an hour on the phone, when she'd only called to check on a detail.

'So you and Isaac have seen details of this woman, but has Calvin seen anything?'

'He's read the letter she sent in. I think he's trying to roll with it for Isaac's sake.' He'd been a bit quiet about the whole thing to be fair, since their argument anyway. He seemed far more interested in the prospect of meeting Tim, which terrified her even more. 'I can't see this going anywhere.' Radiologists were boring, surely. Sure, she sounded cool, accomplished even. It just didn't suit Calvin. *Liar, liar. Bum's on fire. Stop it.* She was regretting bringing Tim now, but it was impossible not to between both their insistences. She felt like he had an edge to him tonight. Something was brewing between them.

'He said yes though, Emily. He must want to meet someone. Maybe he liked the cut of her jib.'

'Maybe,' Emily muttered noncommittally. 'It's only a first date. Just a meal.'

Tim reached across the seat and put her hand in his. 'Well, sometimes a first date is all you need. People forget sometimes. It can be that simple.'

She knew he was thinking of them, of their first date. She smiled at him weakly, and he kissed her hand. The taxi pulled up outside the restaurant, and the pair of them got out. Tim paid the driver and Emily turned to face the doors, and her fate. Calvin was standing outside the entrance. Just looking at him standing there took her breath away. It was like she always forgot how handsome he was. As if she half expected the gawky teenage boy she knew to pop back up. The gawky boy she'd also thought handsome throughout her childhood. Just looking at him gave her a warm feeling.

'Hi,' he said softly, taking a step towards her. Her own feet never stopped. She turned to see where Tim was. He was still standing in the same spot, his mobile phone pressed to his ear. He looked across at them and gave her the one-minute finger. His gaze lingered on Calvin a little longer than was necessary or socially polite, and then he turned away to concentrate on his call.

'Hi, sorry about Tim. He had to take a call. Bank business, you know.'

'No problem. My date apparently isn't here yet. Remind me why I'm doing this again?'

'Because Isaac set you up, and you agreed.'

'Ah yes, my son. And his partner in crime, my best friend.' He chuckled softly when she did a little bow. 'I remember now, it's all coming screaming back to me.' He chuckled, and Emily laughed with him. Already they were back to their easy selves once more, and it made her bloody heart sing. She could hear Tim talking in the background and found herself getting annoyed at him. He'd been so insistent on them coming.

'Shall we go inside, get a drink and take the edge off perhaps?'

'Sounds good.' Calvin beamed. 'But what about Tim?'

'He can buy his own.'

Emily brushed past Calvin and led the way inside.

The restaurant was quite busy, the easy-going chatter and laughter of the customers surrounding them the second they walked in. The smell of the food enveloped their senses, and Emily's stomach rumbled. They walked over to the bar area, Calvin giving their names to a passing waiter to inform them that they had arrived. The waiter asked if their party was complete, and Calvin shook his head. The waiter invited them to get a drink and scurried off to deal with the rest of his patrons. Looking at the door, there was still no sign of Tim. It wasn't unusual. He helped on a few local boards et cetera, so he was often called out of office hours. It was probably a badminton league emergency or something equally as obscure. He was driven in what he cared about.

'Busy, isn't it. Food smells good.'

Emily nodded along with him, two bar stools becoming free just as they inched forward. Calvin placed his arm on the small of her back and walked them both forward. He pulled out the stool for her, waiting till she sat down and got comfortable before he took his own seat. Emily was suddenly very aware of her outfit. She had gone and bought a brand-new dress for tonight, red with a heart neckline and a side split down one side of the dress. It showed off her legs as she sat down. Thank God for quick fake tan. She was wearing a pair of red suede low-slung heels to finish the outfit off, a black strappy handbag dangling from her shoulder.

'Thanks. Drink?'

He waved her off. 'On me.' The barman nodded in his direction, and Calvin ordered two single whiskeys without hesitation. 'And what do you want?'

She laughed. 'Whisky is fine. You okay?'

'Nervous, to say the least. Plus the fact that she isn't here yet is even more worrying. What if she saw me outside, and ran for the hills?' His face was almost comical to watch, the fear evident across his features.

'She's seen what you look like, you berk! Besides, you look gorgeous.' The words were out of her mouth before she could stop them. His eyes widened.

'Thank you.' He leaned in a little, and she saw his gaze drop to the flash of leg showing through the slit in her dress. 'You look beautiful. You always do. I love the colour.' The way his eyes met hers gave her the impression that he liked more than the colour. She felt like her whole body was on fire.

'Everything okay? Between you and Tim I mean? There seemed to be a bit of tension outside.'

'I don't think I've got long enough to tell you to be honest. I don't know … I just, sometimes I think we're just a little bit too different.' *Wow, where had that nugget of truth come from?*

'I see what you mean, about the difference thing. He isn't quite what I pictured for you, I must admit.'

'Really? Who did you think I would end up with?'

'Not him.'

Emily didn't know what to say. She should defend him, and she knew it. Shouldn't all women defend their men?

She was still figuring out what to say when an attractive redheaded woman tapped Calvin on the shoulder. 'Calvin?'

Tim appeared beside her, an odd little smirk across his face. 'Guess who I found loitering around outside. Sophie! Sophie, this is my beautiful fiancée, Emily.'

He made an odd little game show movement with his hands, making Emily feeling momentarily like a prized speed boat on an old cheesy programme.

197

'Sophie, hello! I'm Emily Hendrickson, the reporter from the paper?' The woman beamed at her. *Damn, she seemed nice.* 'This is Calvin Albright of course—' she darted a dirty look at Tim '—and of course you've met Tim, my other half.'

'Delighted, madame,' Tim dipped into a theatrical bow gesturing wildly with his arms. Sophie giggled, and Emily tried not to vomit into her own mouth. One look at Calvin told her she wasn't the only one. He looked positively green at this point, and his eyes were darting wildly towards the restaurant exit. When she looked back at Tim, she was startled to see that he looked as though he was thoroughly enjoying himself. He had had a bit of an edge to him lately, she remembered.

Beth had mentioned something in the office a couple of days ago about male rivalry around females. Emily wondered whether Beth had had a point. Was Calvin making Tim act all interested lately? He had been talking about the wedding recently, and that was after Calvin had been on the scene. Was his sudden urge to rush her up the aisle just a way of securing her against thinking about Calvin? Tim was many things, but he wasn't stupid. Far from it. She looked him in the eye and the smirk was gone. Emily looked around for the waiter that Calvin had spoken to. Spotting him, she waved her arm towards him trying to grab his attention.

'Everything OK, darling?' Tim was positively simpering now. Sophie was talking to Calvin about the quality of parking outside the restaurant. Tim spoke loudly over them both, and Emily saw Calvin's jaw clench tight.

'Just trying to find the waiter, I'm famished.'

She stood up from her stool and went to stand by Tim. Sophie sat in her seat without even drawing breath, going on to chat about local things the kids could do in the area. Calvin looked quite comfortable, so she went back to looking for the waiter. After a moment's thought, she leaned in between the couple and grabbed her whisky. Calvin shot her an odd look, but she didn't dare look his way. She necked the whisky in one large gulp, half slamming the glass back onto the bar.

'Everything okay?' Calvin asked. The waiter chose that opportunity to sidle up to them, looking at Calvin in question. The little git, where did he come from? She'd been looking for him for the last fricking ten minutes.

'Excuse me, sir, is all your party here now?'

Calvin looked around him, and she saw his lips twitch. She felt a bit stupid herself now. She was acting like an idiot, and Tim was definitely playing a game of some sort.

'Er yes,' he said jovially. 'Yes, we certainly are.'

* * *

They were sitting towards the front of the restaurant, near the windows, and for a moment Emily wondered what it would look like from the outside. Looking in, as it were. She would prefer that view if she were honest. It was weird actually sitting at the table. The table was a round, checked affair, a candle stuck in a wine bottle on the table to arty effect. Bread and oil were brought with the menus, and Emily ripped off a chunk and got to work. She was starving. She'd felt too sick to eat earlier and now she was ravenous as a result. Tim was perusing the wine list, Sophie chatting to him about her favourite tipple. *Chatty Cathy.* Emily rolled her eyes, reaching from the bread again. Her hand hit something soft and warm. She looked up in surprise and met Calvin's eyes.

'Sorry, you first.'

'No, you go. You look hungry.'

'I am as it goes.' She ripped off two even-sized chunks of bread, passing him one and taking the other between her fingers. They both dipped the bread into the oil, their fingers brushing against one another in the close proximity. 'I didn't get much time to eat today.' Partially true, she had been very busy. Isaac had dropped another video and was promising more. The latest one was all about Calvin and his likes and dislikes. He'd used some of their old home videos, and people had gone nuts for the candid snapshots of Calvin, and their lives in London.

The saga of Calvin Albright and his intrepid filmmaker son showed no signs of losing the public interest anytime soon. In fact, it had brought out somewhat of a romantic aura around the town. They'd already had a couple of videos sent in from other people, wanting to get their loved ones a partner. They had a few funny ones too. Elvis from the butcher's on the corner had advertised his wife. He'd even offered a free beef roast joint every week for a year to the person willing to take her on. They hadn't used it yet of course. Joanna was ambitious but even she would draw the line at inciting a murder by beef joint incident. Imagine the headlines.

'Oh, work keeping you busy?'

'Yeah it's been bedlam. The video was great. I liked your Elvis impersonations particularly.' She gave him a daft grin, and he flashed his pearly whites in return.

'Uh-huh-huh,' he joked, curling his lip at her. *God, she wanted to bite his lip. She needed another drink.*

She realised that Tim, sitting next to her, was watching them now and so she resumed eating her bread and pushed all carnal thoughts about lips away.

'Quite a few weddings this year to cover. And the christenings of course. We often do a follow-up feature on the resulting babies of the happy events.'

'That must be nice to see. No wonder you like the events side.'

'And all good practice for our turn, eh babe?' Tim patted her on the head like an obedient Doberman and resumed scouring the wine list. 'Prices here are a bit steep aren't they? If I'd have known, I'd have had a drink before I left.'

'Was that before or after you moaned all the way here about not driving?' Emily said this through gritted teeth. Tim held firm.

'Well, I was just thinking of you. You've been so busy lately, what with work and the wedding …'

Sophie squeaked beside Calvin, making him jump.

'Of course, you guys are headed down the aisle aren't you! When's the big day?' Sophie was leaning in now, as though intent on listening to the date that Emily would utter.

'Oh, we don't have a date yet. It's been a bit of a long engagement … No rush and all that …' She went to rip off another chunk of bread, but Calvin was already tearing into it aggressively, his face a murderous scowl.

Tim cut in. 'Oh I wouldn't say there's no rush. We haven't got a date yet, but we have big plans. In fact, we were just talking about it on the way over here. Booking venues, you know the usual.'

Calvin choked on the water he was drinking. He wiped his mouth with his napkin, looking around for the waiter. 'Where is that bloody waiter when you need him? Anyone else need a drink?' He looked around at the table. Sophie, who seemed to be more interested in talking to Tim at this point, fluttered her eyelashes at him.

'I wouldn't say no to a glass of wine. Emily, what about you? What type of wine would you like?'

'A large one, in any colour.' Calvin stifled a laugh, and Sophie's face fell. Emily cringed, feeling guilty for taking out her bitchy mood on this poor woman coming into all this. She gave her a smile to smooth things over. 'Just pick your favourite, Sophie, that will do for me.'

Sophie was luckily easily placated and she leaned in close to the wine list and started discussing the various merits of the pink wines available. The waiter arrived, and they got to work ordering. Once the wine was poured and the food was ordered, the two couples started to make small talk once more.

'So, Calvin, what's it like living in Hebblestone?' Tim placed his arm across the back of Emily's chair, half-empty wine glass in his hand. 'Different from London I expect. I imagine it's a lot quieter and cleaner for one thing. Less pestilence.'

Without missing a beat Calvin said, 'Nah, mate, London has moved on a bit since Charles Dickens was knocking about. Much cleaner now, and the place is as quiet as you make it. I had some quiet times in London.' His rebuttal seemed to lose a bit of its power at the end. He'd gone somewhere, Emily could tell. Remembering something. Something he obviously didn't relish the memory of. 'Besides which, I was born and bred here. This was always home, not just London. I'm glad to be back here.' He looked across to Emily, and his gaze made her feel naked before him. Naked, with a hole drilled in the side of her head from Tim's annoyed glare. 'I always had a lot to come back to. This place has my heart.'

Over starters, things didn't get any better. Sophie was nice enough, but she obviously had no idea of the politics on the table. Calvin and Tim snarking at each other in little ways. The food was delicious as always, and Emily found herself concentrating on her food. There was low cheerful music playing in the background, and she almost found herself relaxing. If she ignored Tim, and the looks he was shooting Calvin's way. And vice versa. Other than that, it was quite good to be out enjoying herself, without the vouchers and the early bird specials.

'This is nice,' Calvin said, taking the thoughts right out of her head.

Tim looked around the room. 'It's not bad. I've eaten in nicer places. Lots of caffs in London, eh?'

'Lots of everything in London,' Calvin replied smoothly. 'Lots of choice, and open minds. You know, that liberal kind of thing.'

Tim looked confused, and Emily pinched her lips tight together. Sophie was looking bewildered, and she matched Calvin glug for glug of wine. Emily tried to steer the conversation around. After all, Calvin's date was just sitting there like a duck.

'So, what's it like being a radiologist?'

Sophie looked relieved to be asked a question, and she looked at Calvin as she answered. 'It's good. I like it.'

'I bet you have some funny stories.'

'Yes, I do.'

Sophie took another sip of her wine, her starter finished. The waiter took advantage of the awkward silence and cleared their plates away, replacing the water jug as he went. 'What's Isaac up to this evening?' Sophie turned her megawatt smile to Calvin again.

'He's with a baby-sitter, although he's hardly a baby. She'll have him cleaning his room and doing double algebra too. Our sitter is a bit of a professional.'

'He must be thrilled with the response though.' The waiter was bringing the main dishes out now, pasta and pizza, breads and salad. Emily wanted to tuck in, but she was too busy trying to listen in to their conversation. Tim started talking loudly to the server, drowning out Calvin's reply. Damn it.

'Getting on well aren't they?' Tim looked gleeful at the prospect. Emily looked at them, shrugging as she reached for the food again. 'Not bad for a first date. You might have something with this matchmaking malarkey.' Tim buried his face in the food, and she buried herself in the wine.

Before she knew it, they were scraping the mains dishes clean and asking about desserts. Calvin had been lovely to Sophie all evening, even with Tim inserting himself into the conversation with odd little stories. They chatted easily enough, and Emily felt herself feel worse and worse as the evening went on. She and Tim were just not on the same page, and the pressure of being in front of Calvin got to her pretty quickly. More wine was ordered, and Sophie was discussing the various merits of each dessert on the menu with the server, asking the bemused waiter about calorie counts.

'Come on, Calvin,' Sophie purred once their orders were in. 'Share some of the chocolate cake with me. I just can't eat it all!' She patted her flat stomach, and Emily groaned out loud. *Whoops.*

She was a little drunk. She caught Calvin throwing her an odd look, but she kept her eyes focused on anything else in the room.

'No thanks, I'm not really a dessert man. Emily, are you okay?'

He was still trying to catch her eye, but she just waved him off with a swish of her glass. 'Yeah, am fine.'

'Yeah?' Calvin's tone called bullshit. 'You're not normally this quiet.'

Sophie, hanging on Cal's every word, chimed in. 'Do you two know each other then – other than through the article?'

'Yes,' Calvin replied. 'We've been best friends since we were small. Ems, you sure you're okay?'

'I'm fine. Any more wine?'

Tim went to move the bottle away from her, but Calvin's hand was faster.

'Party poopers.' Emily giggled to herself.

'Best friends that long?' Oblivious Sophie struck again. 'You must know his secrets then, eh? Tell me something.' She looked around the room as if an Autocue full of questions was waiting for her. 'Oh, what shall we ask, eh Tim?' She looked at him conspiratorially. 'First kiss? Most embarrassing memory?'

'My first kiss?'

Emily's head snapped up at his words. His voice was different, and she realised he was tipsy too.

'Emily, you want to tell them?'

She looked from Cal, to Sophie, and finally to Tim. 'Oh God, I don't remember that …' She pretended to rack her brain.

'I do,' he said. 'It was you, Emily. My first kiss, our first kiss actually.' His eyes fell on Tim. 'Emily and I actually had our first kiss together.'

'It was spin the bottle though.' Emily giggled – just a tad too high-pitched. 'Just a game.'

'First kiss is a first kiss. Still counts.' Calvin's jaw flexed again. 'Next question.'

'I know.' Tim reached over and took the wine bottle, filling up his own glass slowly. Like a Bond villain. Emily felt the change in the air. 'Ask her if she knows who his first love was.'

'Tim!' Emily chided. 'Stop it.' She looked at Cal. 'I'm so sorry.'

'It's okay.' Calvin didn't look ruffled in the slightest. 'We all know that I lost Diane. Kind of obvious, given that we're on a double date from a video. I loved her. I will always love her, but she wasn't my first love.'

Sophie looked intrigued. Tim looked sick, and Emily wondered what the hell was going on.

'She wasn't?'

Calvin looked her straight in the eye, his smile broadening. 'Nope.'

Tim and Sophie's desserts arrived, the waiter clearing away more debris. Emily took the opportunity to head to the toilet. She hid in there as long as she could, checking her make-up, relieving her bladder of some of the alcohol she'd necked.

She finally came out of the toilet, and Calvin was standing out in the corridor.

'I came to see if you were okay, you were a while.'

'Too much wine I think. Took me a while to get back into my dress.'

'It is a nice dress.' He took steps toward her, and she looked past him down the corridor.

'The others finishing up?'

'Sophie's feeding half the restaurant her chocolate cake like a mother hen. She's nice, but not for me. Tell Isaac for me?'

'Ha.' She laughed. 'No thank you. Still, you could have dates any night of the week for months with the emails coming in.'

'Yeah, maybe.' He didn't look thrilled at the prospect. He was probably hoping they wouldn't be double dates, given the fractured nature of the evening. 'What's up with you and Tim?'

'Noth—'

'Don't say nothing. I can tell. You ignore my questions all the time. He's a bit of an ass, you know. I don't like him.'

'Calvin, I don't want to get into this now. He's not acting himself tonight.' She was feeling like she needed to get home and just pass out for the foreseeable. The first love thing was still playing in her head. Driving her mad, like a wasp in a helmet. 'How can you say Diane wasn't your first love?'

'She wasn't. That's why. Tim asked; I told him the truth.'

'It's a lie. I knew you my whole life, before uni. I never saw you fall in love with anyone. I don't get why you'd lie.'

'I didn't lie, Ems!' He laughed easily, his face going back to serious as he watched her. 'Bother you, does it?'

'The lying does, yes.' It made her feel sick in her stomach that he'd kept it from her. 'If I'd known, maybe things would have been a bit simpler.'

Cal's eyes widened. 'What do you mean?'

'Nothing,' she lied. *Shit. I need to go home. I can't keep my own thoughts from spilling out of my tired mouth.*

'Liar,' he retorted firmly.

As if. I would rather pull a pin from a grenade and just have done with it.

'Room to talk,' she fired back, putting the pin back into the bomb. 'You're the one who lied.'

'I didn't lie. I'm not lying now. I will never keep things from you again.'

She ignored his declaration. *What things? There was no girl. Was he secretly pining for someone all that time?* It shattered her to even think of it. *All that time, I was watching him, and he was watching her. He never really saw me. Not like I saw him. He was my favourite view.*

'Well, I still think I would have noticed. Maybe we weren't as close as I thought.' *Maybe I'm just a colossal idiot. She had a vision of him reading her letter and cringing at her words.* Her cheeks burned, and then she heard him laugh. He laughed hysterically. Slightly maniacally. The corridor was empty, and he slapped his hand on his knee. It rang out loud with his laughter. 'Oh, really? You think?'

206

'Yeah, of course! We were together the whole time. I would have known. You would have told me.'

'Yeah, well I didn't. I did what I always do. I folded it up and hid it away in the dark. I'm a chicken. OKAY!' He boomed the last words, his anger rising. His hair was taking the brunt as he ran his fingers through it. His eyes were hard to avoid, but she couldn't focus on them. Her own anger built, the frustrations and disappointments stabbing her in the back like hot knives as she faced him.

'WHAT THE HELL ARE YOU SHOUTING AT ME FOR?' She took a step closer.

'BECAUSE I THINK YOU'RE A BLOODY CHICKEN TOO!' He matched her step for step, his chest heaving. His eyes dropped to her lips, and she swallowed hard. 'EMILY, WE'RE BOTH CHICKENS? DON'T YOU GET THAT?'

'WHY DO YOU KEEP SAYING THAT! GOD, CAL, YOU'RE SO BLOODY CRYPTIC SOMETIMES!'

'That's the problem.' Cal sighed. 'That's always been the problem.' He took one more step closer, as if he didn't trust himself to walk any closer. His eyes were pleading. 'Please, Emily, tell me you get what I'm trying to say.'

'Emily?'

'WHAT!'

They both rounded on the intruder, and Sophie squeaked beside Tim.

'Sorry.' Tim's face was stony. 'Didn't mean to interrupt. Taxi's here. You ready?'

'Emily, we need to talk.' Calvin stood between her and Tim, his back to Tim's purpling face. 'Please. Five minutes.'

'Emily, the meter's running.'

Cal tutted loudly, looking at Emily one last time with his pleading eyes before turning to his date.

'I'm terribly sorry, Sophie, but I am going to have to say goodnight. Can I see you to a taxi? My friend and I are having a little disagreement.' Sophie, who had to be the nicest person on the planet, nodded agreeably. Emily went to follow but Tim stopped her.

'What was that all about, Emily? What's gotten into you lately?'

'What was that question about? His first love? You know he lost his wife, yeah? Why would you ask that?'

'Oh come on, Em! Of course I know he lost his wife; I'm not a total bastard. I feel like I know everything there is to know about bloody Calvin Albright. And his life. The whole town talks of nothing else. This first date is only the beginning, you know. I want to know what the hell's going on.'

'Nothing's going on.'

'Stop lying to me.' Tim leaned against the wall, his usually formal stance sagging against the surface. 'Tell me. You've been wanting to tell me something for a while. Just say it.'

'Oh, now you want to talk?' She felt a tear roll down her face, and she wanted to jump into it and disappear. 'I've been trying to talk to you for months! You pick now? What's wrong? No badminton on?'

She was shaking violently now, her nervous system feeling like it was going into overdrive as her mind tried to cope. 'I can't talk about this right now. I just want to go home.'

'Emily, say it.'

'I want to call off the engagement.'

Tim's face dropped, but she couldn't take it back. 'Call off the engagement, or us?'

Emily shut her eyes. Looking back at Tim, she pressed her lips together before answering. 'Us.'

'Because of him?' Tim jabbed his finger towards the door. 'Seriously? He's only been here a minute.'

'No, it's not about Calvin. It's about us! Tim, it's not working. We're too different.'

'I'm the same person I was when we met!'

'Yeah, well I'm not!' *Shit. Now she was screaming at another man outside the bathroom.* 'Tim, let's just go, okay?'

'Go where? You just dumped me outside a toilet! I'm not going anywhere with you until you stop lying to me.' Calvin came back into sight, and Tim glared at him.

'We're busy, Calvin.'

He turned back to Emily, reaching for her hand, but she took a step back. His whole body stiffened, and his next words were clipped. 'Make sure she gets home safe,' he spat in Calvin's direction.

At odds to the growl he'd just thrown Calvin's way, he turned back to Emily and his voice was softer.

'I'll get my stuff tomorrow, while you're at work. You know where I am when you want to talk.'

He strode out, leaving the two friends alone. Emily waited a minute, brushing her hot tears away and went to leave.

'Give him another minute – Sophie's only just got a taxi. It's busy tonight. You okay?'

'We broke up.'

'I gathered. I'm sorry.'

'No, you're not. You don't like him.'

'You're right, I'm not at all. The guy is a dick.'

'Oh, and Sophie is some prize is she?'

'Sophie was nice, sure. It was a date, not an engagement! You were engaged to that douchebag.'

'He's not a douchebag! He's just … mad.'

'He's not meant for you.'

'Well, since I just dumped him that's pretty obvious. I just want to go home, okay? I have to write some kind of article on tonight for Joanna tomorrow.'

'Why haven't you asked me who my first love was yet?' He walked over to her with purpose, and she couldn't tear her eyes away.

'I know who it was. You're being ridiculous.'

'Diane was not my first love.' His jaw clenched. 'I told you. I loved Diane, I really did. My first love was something very different to that.'

'Don't say it.'

'Why?' His brow furrowed, his teeth clenched tight. 'God, Emily! You twist me up! I need to say this. I wrote it in the damn castle walls!' He looked at her, his body tense and coiled. His hands were in his hair, ruffling it just how she liked. He was frustration personified. When he looked at her, she got her answers. She knew what it felt like to be devoured by a man's eyes. How his look could claim you for keeps, and flicker with lust? How would it feel to be loved by Calvin Albright?

'It was you. The prom night, all that weirdness with my friends?'

Emily thought back to a young Calvin, pulling his mates away that night, before everything happened.

'They were messing about.' Her mind was trying to make connections.

'They were teasing me, because I'd told them that night I was finally going to tell you how I felt.' He put his hands on her shoulders, pulling her closer to him. 'I'd had a crush on you since I was old enough to recognise what one was. I was all set to finally tell you when the meatheads decided to play their little trick. Since I've been back, I don't know. I guess I thought that tonight you were acting weird because you liked me, not because of the article. I've been feeling things … since we met again. I guess tonight I just thought …'

Emily didn't know what to say. She was far too drunk to connect everything, but she couldn't stop trying to fit the pieces together.

'Listen, I know that it's bad timing, and with Tim. I'm sorry, I guess I just wanted you to know. I'm tired of being a chicken.' He stroked one thumb along her cheek, and she shuddered at the touch. 'Aren't you? Do you feel this, any of this? Am I just drunk and seeing what I want to see? I don't think so, Emily. Tell me.'

'You wrote it in the castle walls?' she echoed. He nodded, his eyes focused intently on hers. She'd never seen him look like that before. He looked so flushed, so determined.

'I drew you. I wrote declarations of love all the time. Whenever you smiled at me, or wrote a story for us, I wrote you. Tucked every feeling and emotion I felt into those cracks. The castle is full of my love for you Emily. It's time the truth came out. I'm tired.'

She looked at him, taking in everything he was telling her. She'd wanted to hear it for so long once, but now it was such a mess. She thought of Isaac then, and him being at home waiting to see how his dad had got on with his first date.

'You have dates begging to take you out, and the article. And then there's Tim!' She pushed him away. 'I JUST broke up with Tim. I can't do this right now, Cal. I just can't.'

'And I can't do this anymore. I can't be that bloody teenage boy anymore. Not without you, anyway.' He looked stricken, and she wanted to run back to him. To take him into her arms and say screw it all. But she couldn't lose her job, and what would people think? What would the headline be? "Local wedding article writer steals local hunk, leaves bank manager fiancé devastated". She would be terrorised by every woman in Hebblestone. 'I don't want to date any of these women, Emily. The truth is, since I met you again I've not been able to think about much else but you. Damn it, I've always been thinking about you. And now you and Tim are not together.'

'Cal, I just broke up with him, like twenty seconds ago. Where is this coming from now?'

'It's been coming for years! I don't know, I didn't really feel the burning urge to tell you till tonight. I – I don't know … sitting there with Tim and Sophie, it just felt so wrong. Like we were doing this all wrong. Again. I thought I could get through it, but I can't do it again. I'm not strong enough.' He put a hand over his heart, and she felt hers skip a beat in time with the thud. 'We did it all wrong, Emily.' He searched her face, and she knew he was looking for a reaction. Her face felt frozen. His phone beeped in his pocket, and he looked down at it, his face sobering.

'Listen, I'd better go – the sitter will be waiting. I'll get you a taxi, but please just think about it, okay?'

'Just think about it?'

'Yeah.' He smiled. Leaning in close, he kissed her slowly on the cheek. She felt the stubble run along her skin, and shuddered. 'Just think about it. No pressure.'

Chapter 19

'No pressure,' Dennis repeated the next morning over breakfast. 'Blimey.'

'I know,' Emily moaned from under the duvet blanket she was wrapped in. She pulled another piece of toast from the rack and nibbled at it gingerly. She'd gone home to her flat last night and passed out promptly till morning. She'd woken at 5 a.m. with a terrible hangover and a sudden urge to drive to her parents' house and offload her relationship woes on them like a teenager.

'And then what happened?'

'He poured me into a taxi like the lush I am.'

'And …'

Emily moaned from beneath the covers. 'And I ended up crying over old photos, and then passing out. I woke up on the floor of the bathroom and came here. Knocked you out of bed. Dad, help me please. Tell me what to do.'

Dennis was sitting in his dressing gown at the table, tufts of hair sticking up at all angles. He'd left her mother sleeping in bed, and now the pair of them were watching the sun get higher in the sky as they dissected the night's events.

'So.' He glugged the last of the tea from his pot, and automatically clicked the kettle on for more. Dad always had his best

213

ideas when he was caffeinated. 'Tim just left? You ended things and he left?'

'Well he wasn't in the best of moods, Dad. He left, yeah. It's all a bit of a mess.'

'And did Tim hear what Calvin was saying?' Her dad had been peppering her with questions since the first sip of tea had hit his lips.

'I don't know, Dad; it was all a bit messed up.'

'But he wanted to talk to you, that night at the prom?' He spooned far too much sugar into his tea, but she didn't say anything. She had dragged him out of bed in the early hours, sobbing like an infant, stinking of booze and wrapped in a mascara-streaked duvet. To his credit, he had been amazing as always. 'I can't believe it. All these years, and you both wanted to say the same thing.'

'Yeah, but I did say those things. After the prom when he'd gone to uni. I wrote him a letter, and he never wrote back.'

'Well, did he mention it? How do you know he even got it? You should have told me! I would have bloody hand-delivered it.'

'I don't know! I was scared! He must have got it though! He met Diane around the same time. He made his choice then.' Her face paled. 'Oh God, he made his choice, and then Diane died. He came home, saw me. How can he know how he feels? Women are throwing themselves at him left, right and centre. He could have his pick.'

'Well, Calvin's never been the type of guy to do all that, has he? I never saw a girl other than you on his arm, ever. Till Diane.' He looked at her kindly, leaning over to pull down a patch of quilt that was obscuring her face. He winced. 'Why don't you just call him?'

'Oh yeah, I'll just call him shall I? Tell him everything! Why didn't I think of that? I just broke up with Tim yesterday. I just can't walk into another disaster.'

He huffed like a petulant teenager. Dennis wasn't having any of it. 'Emily Hendrickson, I could box your ears sometimes.'

214

Emily popped her head out of the fort she was camped in. 'What?'

'You know what.' Dennis looked at her sternly, and she suddenly felt guilty. Like she did the time she'd scraped his car going to the beach with Calvin, and Calvin had used marker pen to cover up the spoiled bumper. He didn't notice for weeks, but the look of reproach on his face now brought it all back. 'Cal's got a point, you know. You are a chicken. We had all this planned on prom night, and here we are, still talking about it. Don't you think it's about time you did something?' He pointed to a large photo on the wall. It was from her graduation. The local paper had done a piece on her return to Hebblestone. The new home-grown hot-shot reporter, ready to take on their little corner of the world. 'Where's that girl? That girl was so bloody brave. But she never told Calvin how she felt and look what happened.'

'Yeah, he fell in love and would have probably lived happily ever after. Then he lost her, and he had to survive that. Till he came here, and I messed everything up for him again. It's not just about Cal now, Dad. Isaac is a good kid, and I don't want to hurt him. He's been through enough.'

'The lad I have met before, and the lad in that video is one and the same, Emily. You didn't mess his family up. This isn't some kind of seedy affair. Your childhood sweetheart came back. Don't you think that means something? I mean come on, the last time the lad tried to tell you how he felt, he ended up in hospital. To say that to you, with Tim in the picture and a date at his side?' He shook his head, looking again at the smiling, confident girl in the photo on the wall. She was in her cap and gown, her face full of excitement for the future.

She remembered it a little differently. She'd been alone on the day, even with her parents. Calvin not being there didn't feel right, especially when she knew that somewhere else in the country, he'd be celebrating with Diane.

'The girl I know, my Emily, she's always thinking about others.

The girl in that photo—' he jabbed a slice of toast in her direction '—is not the woman in front of me now. I've watched you with Tim, get steadily unhappier year after year. I never said anything because you said you were happy, and I knew you'd come to me when the time was right. I think the Albrights coming home woke you up, my girl.' He came and pulled the quilt from her, ignoring her squeaks and loud protests. 'Now, come on. Get up. You have work to get to, and some men to speak to.'

Emily groaned but did as she was told. By the time Dad had waved her off home, and she'd resurrected herself in the bathroom, she almost felt normal. Tim hadn't been home; nothing had been moved. She looked at his sweater, lying on the bedroom floor. She picked it up, folded it and put it on the hall table. It felt weird touching the possessions of a man that she'd just ended a life with. After locking up, she headed to her car. The early morning chat and toast had soaked up some of the alcohol and anxiety, but she still felt decidedly shaky. Pulling out of her road, she dialled Cal's number. The ringing of the phone filled the car, and she held her breath till the line connected.

'Hi,' he said softly. 'I wasn't expecting a call this early.'

'Sorry. I've been up a while.'

'Me too,' he said, and she could hear the tiredness in his voice. 'Did you speak to Tim?'

'No. Not since last night. He's getting his stuff today.'

'Ah. Sorry. It must be hard.'

'It's been a long time coming. I don't really want to talk about it.'

'What did you call for?' he asked. She could hear Isaac in the background, the sound of a radio playing. 'Sorry, Isaac's just nipped back before practice. He's been a bit of a nightmare this morning, wanting to know how last night went.'

'With Sophie?'

'Yeah. I think he thought it was going to be like rescuing a dog or something. I think he half expected her to come bounding into the kitchen this morning like a cocker spaniel.'

Emily laughed, imagining the pretty Sophie sporting a little pink collar.

'If only it was that easy, eh?'

'I know. I might even get a dog and have done.' A silence descended. Emily kept driving, thinking of everything she wanted to say. It felt like a ball of words was lodged in her throat, making her chest feel tight. 'Did you think about what I said?'

Emily thought of Dad, and his metaphorical and literal kick up the arse this morning. She thought of Calvin last night, telling her everything she wanted to hear. And then she thought of Diane, and Isaac's worry about *his* dad. And then she came back to the letter. The letter she'd sent to him. The one he'd never replied to. That was their chance, she realised with a pang. *He didn't choose me.* Now everything was just so messy, so public. Beth had already emailed the stats of the videos to her that morning, crowing over how many replies they'd had. How happy Joanna was with the increase in readership and social media engagement. How was she going to ruin all that? Calvin was a great guy, and if it didn't work out, there was just so much to lose. Her dad was going to muller her when he found out.

'Listen, Calvin, I know what you said, but …'

'But what? I don't want to do this over the phone, Emily. Can we meet?'

'No,' she fired back, a little too fast. 'No sorry. I can't, Calvin. I know that things have been said, but …'

'Things have been said,' he said smoothly. 'Finally. I meant what I said. I can tell Isaac, put a stop to all of the other stuff.' His voice dipped, and the background noise dimmed. 'Listen, I have to see Isaac off but I really want to talk about this, please? I'm hiding in the bloody pantry at the minute.'

'That should tell you something, Cal.' She saw work loom into view and took a deep breath. 'Listen, I know that being back has been … strange for both of us, but I think we should just concentrate on the article.'

'What? No – Emily, listen to me. I don't want to date anyone else.'

'I know you think that.' Emily was crying now, trying not to let her emotion seep into her voice. 'I've been fighting with Tim for a while, and when you came back, I felt a little strange too.'

'About me?'

'Yeah, of course.' She took a deep breath, rubbing at her eyes one-handed as she pulled into the car park. 'You were my best friend. I missed you. We missed each other. I really think that's all this is.'

In her mind, her dad was yelling at her, making chicken noises and pretending to flap his chicken elbows. She shook her head, and her dad disappeared in a cloud of feathers.

Cal fell silent. She pulled into a vacant space, pulling on the handbrake and sinking back into her seat. The empty line hung between them, neither breaking the silence.

'Is that really how you feel?' he said finally. His voice was dull now, flat to her ears. The Calvin warmth was missing from his tone. 'That's it? It's all about the article, yeah?'

'Cal, I just broke off my engagement. I have this big work thing on, and you … you have Isaac, and your job. You have the chance of a shiny new life here. I want that for you.'

'You want the best for me, just not with you. That about right, bestie?'

'Cal, I … I …' Beth's name came up on her call waiting. 'I have to go. Work's calling.'

'Right. Work. Got it.' Calvin's voice shook when he spoke. 'I'll let you get on then.'

'Calvin—'

'It's fine, Emily. I asked; you answered. I'd better go.'

The line cut out, and Emily was left staring at the dashboard.

'Well,' she said to no one. 'That's that then.' She hauled her tired body out of the car and headed into the office with all the enthusiasm of a dog heading to the vet's to get his jewels taken off.

Chapter 20

Isaac, listening to his dad's phone call through the pantry door, dashed back into the kitchen area before his dad emerged.

'You nearly ready?' Calvin asked, and Isaac saw his face. *Oh my God, Dad's in love.* The thought struck him like a thunderbolt, and he thought back to the events of the last few weeks. Dad had been a different person since Emily had been back. Looking at him, and the house, Isaac could see how much had changed in such a short space of time.

'Yeah, nearly ready, Dad.'

Isaac's phone chirped on the kitchen countertop, and he reached for it. It was another email, another hopeful for the Calvin Albright auditions. He was about to delete it when he noticed something different about the email. This one had Emily's name on it. His eyes bulged as he read the content of the email. He couldn't believe what he was reading, but he knew he had to act if he was going to sort the grown-ups out.

'Dad, there's another letter from a woman. She wants to meet you.'

Calvin was already shaking his head. 'Not a chance, mate, I can't today. I have work to sort out for next week, and I think we need to discuss this whole dating lark a bit more. You're going to be late for practice.'

'But she sounds perfect, Dad. I really think you should meet her. She wants to meet at the c—'

'Isaac, I just can't today, okay. I'm not about to meet another stranger for another awkward date. I just can't today.'

'But, Dad, I really think you need to go.' He brandished his phone in his dad's direction. 'Just look at the letter she sent!'

'No, Isaac! No!' Calvin snapped, slamming the dishwasher door hard and giving it a little kick for good measure. 'Please, I just can't do this today. Owen's mum is waiting.'

Calvin stomped out of the kitchen, and Isaac saw he wasn't going to get anywhere. God, he knew he was a wimp sometimes, that he hadn't told Isobel he liked her yet, but he was a kid. His dad was old enough to speak his mind, and yet he was still acting like a child about the whole thing. He knew what he had to do. Mum would have been just the same. She was always the same with Dad; she didn't always get him all the time, but she knew when he needed a little push. She was always the pusher in the family. He looked at his phone screen, a photo of his mum smiling on the display. 'I know, Mum, he's being daft. Don't worry.' He stroked his mum's face on the screen. 'You taught me when to push. I've got this.'

Checking the door, he got to work. Quick as a flash, he clicked forward on the email, tapping ninety to the dozen on the keypad. He could see Calvin stomping around him, banging pans and muttering under his breath. He fired off a couple of messages to Isobel and Kai and shoved his phone in his blazer pocket. His dad was seemingly having a very angry fight with the dishwasher, which was apparently a big mechanical knobhead. His dad was losing his mind. He felt his pocket vibrate, and he galvanised himself. When he got back to school, he was going to finally get his dad a girlfriend. Being grounded for all eternity had better be worth it.

* * *

The minute his dad dropped him off at school the next Monday morning, Isobel and Kai were waiting.

They waved his miserable-looking dad off, and then turned to each other.

'What was he like yesterday?'

Isaac groaned. 'It was bad. He didn't say much at all. He put his sweatpants back on too. It was pretty grim. He ate squirty cream right out of the can at one point, and he watched *Die Hard* five times.'

Kai sucked his air in through his teeth.

'Damn. Sorry, Zac.'

'Right,' Isobel said. 'None of that. We are going to nail this. Here's the plan.'

Chapter 21

Emily shuffled flat-footed to her desk, slumping into her chair like a lump of marshmallow. Beth's desk was empty, and Joanna was nowhere to be seen either. Emily booted up her computer, picking up her coffee cup and giving herself a minute before wading back into emails from women who wanted the man she really wanted. Heading to the kitchen, she tuned out the noise of her co-workers, but she heard Cal's name mentioned.

'I hope this is the one. The letter is so cute! I mean, I feel like this could be the one, right?'

'Joanna seems to think so. She already tried to call Calvin, but no joy as yet.'

Naomi from accounting spotted Emily watching and beamed at her.

'You must be so excited! Are you going?'

'Going where?' Emily didn't have the brain hydration or the first clue what they were talking about. It was too early on a Monday for this crap.

'To the big meeting! Didn't you read the letter?'

'What letter?' Emily, who hadn't been listening, perked her ears up. Joanna had been excited this morning, but that was normal these days. She was constantly sounding off about the Cal project

222

like a tuning fork. Beth ran past the kitchen, ducking her head back in a second later and grabbing Emily by the arm. Her coffee sloshed down her hand, making her yell.

'Hey, Beth! That's bloody hot!' Beth took the cup from her hands and yanked her again. Right out of the kitchen and down the corridor. As usual, her colleagues looked up to see what the commotion was, and seeing the gruesome twosome acting like bickering siblings, they resumed staring at their screens with a shrug. 'Where are we going?'

'Our office,' Beth threw over her shoulder, and bundling them both into the lift, she hit the door-close button. Emily stared at her like a rabid dog would if it were a cornering stranger.

'Calvin got a new letter. Isaac saw it this over the weekend. He sent it to me.'

'Right.' Emily nodded. 'Okay. Good. Good stuff. Listen, Tim—'

'Tim called this morning,' she said matter-of-fact. 'He told me about Friday night. Why didn't you tell me you'd broken up?'

'Mate, a lot happened that night. I pickled my own liver and ended up crying on Dad's porch at six o'clock in the morning. It's just a big mess. I've been working and bloody hiding all weekend. Calvin told me he likes me.'

'Well, finally!' Beth stabbed the air with a sharp pointy finger. 'What did you say?'

'What do you mean, well finally?'

Beth huffed with impatience. 'Nothing. What did you say to Calvin?'

'What do you think I said? I told him that I had just broken off an engagement half a minute before, and it was tricky.'

'You bailed.'

'I did not bail.'

'You didn't tell him you liked him back though. You broke up with Tim; Calvin told you how he feels. How do you feel?'

'What does it matter what I feel? What about Isaac?'

Beth huffed, crossing her arms angrily. 'You mean the eleven-year-old boy who has more bloody brains and balls than the pair of you together? Isaac responded to the letter I was on about, Emily. There's a meeting set up for today. Isaac said yes, and Calvin will be there. What if this woman is the one?'

'Today? They're meeting today? Calvin never said anything.' *Not so soon, please. My heart can't take it. I'll leave, forever.*

'Calvin is not calling the shots. Isaac is dead set on this person, this meeting. Calvin will go – I know it. The question is, what the hell are you going to do about it?'

Emily opened and closed her mouth like a fish. Beth screamed through gritted teeth.

'*Jesus Christ, Emily!* Stop dicking around and start fighting for what you REALLY want. This is your life! Do you love him or what?'

'Of course I love him!' she screamed back. 'I always bloody have. I loved him as a boy; I love him now. I can't remember a fucking time when I didn't love him!' Fists clenched, she broke into wrenching sobs, Beth putting her arm around her, patting her back in slow circles. 'I told him once, and he didn't pick me. It's just too scary now! What if he doesn't really want me? What if I'm second best?'

'What, like Tim was you mean?'

She felt that one in the gut. 'That's not fair. He wasn't second best. Not on purpose. I didn't realise. I didn't see it. Tim's lovely; he's just not the one for me. My best friend was.' It was really clear now. The fact that she didn't miss Tim as much as she'd once thought she might. The relief that she'd ended it was evident. She felt lighter than she had in a long time. 'It wasn't that simple.'

'I know it's not, but it's true. Face it, the second Calvin walked into that coffee shop, you and Tim were done. You were already done! Calvin just bloody well woke you up! I can see it – why can't you? Do you love Calvin and want to be with him? Yes or no?'

'I do,' she said finally, her sobs giving way to a watery smile. 'I really do.'

She was right and sounding scarily similar to her own insistent father. Her annoying, pain-in-the-ass colleague and mate was right. As usual.

'Thank Christ for that!' She looked at her watch, clicking the lift doors open and grabbing for her phone. 'We still have time. The meeting's not till later.' She looked her mate up and down. 'Well, you could look better, but we don't have that much time.' She pulled a lip-gloss out of her cleavage and passed it to her.

'Here, slap this on, and you're good to go.' She pushed a folded piece of paper into Emily's hand. 'Details for the meeting.' Beth hugged her tight, dropping a motherly kiss on her forehead.

'Right, you go get ready. I'll deal with everything here, okay? I'll keep Joanna off your back.'

'Shit, Joanna! What the hell is she going to say if I ruin this date?'

Beth laughed. 'You really are too nice sometimes. And bloody clueless.' She hugged her friend to her again. 'Just go. Go get your bloody man. Don't cock this up, you hear me?' She wiped Emily's tears away, straightening her up. 'Dave has bet me one hundred pounds you won't fess up, and I don't back losers.'

Emily grinned at her, nodding. 'Okay. I'm ready.'

Beth winked at her before running off to cover the desk.

Emily knew exactly what she had to do now. She had to go home. She had to talk to Tim, and air out her secrets once and for all. She couldn't let Cal meet another letter writer without telling him how she felt. The time for chickening out was over.

* * *

She'd rang Tim over and over, but the line didn't connect. She left him a voicemail asking him to come to the flat urgently, trying not to sound like the horrible woman she felt. When she thought of Tim, she felt sick to her stomach, but she knew why. She wasn't sick about ending the relationship. She just didn't want to be the one hurting him. She never meant for any of this to happen. She needed to get the letter, get to Calvin, but she didn't want him hearing about all this from the Hebblestone gossip mill. He deserved better than that. She pushed down on the accelerator, pressing the call button one last time. It went to voicemail, and she gave up.

Bringing her car to a screech outside her building, Emily yanked up the handbrake and clicked the button on her key in the direction of the vehicle as she raced the other way towards the front door. She ran through the foyer and almost crashed into Mrs Everett from the ground floor. She'd been a good neighbour for many years, taking in parcels and the like. The woman never missed a trick. It wouldn't go down well if she took her neighbour out too. She was already worrying about the destruction she was about to wreak on Tim. She managed to swerve the woman at the last minute, but she copped her tartan shopping trolley right in the stomach.

'Sorry, Mrs Everett – oof! Jesus Christ, that hurt! Fu—! Sorry, I'm in a rush! You okay?'

Mrs Everett waved her off, heading to the doors with her shopping trolley intact and in tow. 'It's all right, dear. What's the rush!'

'Sorry! I have to rush, On a bit of a mission today!'

'Well.' The woman chuckled, surprised. 'Get on with it then, love.' Mrs Everett went to leave, her trolley wheel squeaking as she went. Just as she was nearly out of the main door, she turned.

'I remember you two, when you were little. My Mitch used to come and tell me when he'd seen you at the castle.' She looked wistful at the memory of her husband, and Emily had an image of a friendly man pop into her head. He used to work on the site, supervising the visitors to the castle and the visitor's centre next to it. He was always nice to her and Cal. He let them go into the grounds whenever they wanted, because he knew they loved the place just as much as he did.

'I remember your husband,' Emily replied with a warm smile. 'He was always nice to us.'

'He always thought you'd get together in the end. From what I've read, you might still have a chance. If that's what you want.' The woman nodded in the direction of Emily's flat. 'I hope you make the right choice.'

Emily turned to her, her shocked face displaying a rather accurate rendition of "The Scream" painting. Mrs Everett grinned at her, her spectacled eyes lighting up.

'I'm knocking on, love, I'm not dead. I've lived in Hebblestone all my life. I surf the net. I see things. It's about time you were happy.' She grinned at Emily, who was still looking at her slightly gobsmacked to say the least. 'Good luck.' The woman left with a last squeak of the wheel, and Emily's urgency reignited.

Tearing into her flat front door, she ran into the lounge and reached for the Calvin box of memories. She flicked through ticket stubs, pebbles and shells from their beach days, the many many photos of their lives together. It wasn't there. *It has to be here. Oh god, Tim might be on his way. Think Emily, think!*

She looked twice more, before getting desperate and tipping the whole lot onto the carpet. Still nothing. It wasn't there.

'Shit!' She slapped her hands hard, once against her cheeks, the sting of pain taking away her turmoil for a too-short second. She pulled out her phone to ring Tim again but the battery died as she hit the call button. "Shit!" She exclaimed.

'Emily, stop.'

A deep voice startled her. Standing there, in the doorway, was Tim. She jerked up, rubbing at her eyes, and trying to smile at him. 'I – I didn't know you were here. I thought you'd be at work. I've been calling you.' He raised the gym bag in his hand, lowering it to the ground. Behind him stood a carrier bag and the yucca plant from the bedroom.

227

'I turned it off,' he said softly. He didn't make a move to enter. 'I've already been here once, for my dumbbells. I didn't think *you'd* be here.' He frowned. 'Didn't you get my text?'

She scowled at her phone, now sitting dead on the couch after being left off charge all night and shook her head. 'My battery died.' It was then that she saw the yucca again, and she looked at him properly for the first time. He looked pale, uncomfortable in his own skin.

'Did you get everything? I can help. I called because I wanted to explain. About us, about how I've been feeling.'

Tim looked at her for a long moment, and then he reached for a box of tissues sitting on the coffee table and passed the box to her. She took it, not even realising she was crying again, and he gave her a sad smile.

'What were you looking for?' Gesturing to the boxes, he looked down at his entwined fingers. 'Don't answer that, I already know. I – I—' He tripped over his words, and she watched him as she wiped away her tears. After a long moment that felt like eternity, he sighed heavily and leaned against the doorframe. 'Just tell me. Please. I need to hear it. Why are you crying?'

'I'm so sorry Tim. I never meant for any of this to happen. I didn't know how I felt. I really care for you—'

Tim winced, and she stopped talking.

'Just tell me, Emily.'

Emily looked at the man she'd had in her life for so long, and sighed. No more playing chicken. 'I'm in love with Calvin Albright. And I hurt you, and made a big, huge mess.'

It came out of her in a breath, and her chest heaved with the effort of getting it out. She felt like she'd been swallowing those words for so long they had almost become stuck forever. 'I'm in love with him. I'm so sorry. I know I have no right to say anything, that I can't say anything, but—' She spied the clock on the wall and knew that time was fast ticking away. Calvin would be meeting her soon: the new love interest Isaac was excited about.

The date might not be the one, but the next one could be. The woman was getting ready out there, waiting to meet Calvin, and she couldn't bear the thought of letting history repeat itself. She couldn't stay silent one minute longer. Hang the consequences, she was blowing up her life to speak her truth. She just wished that there weren't going to be any casualties.

'I know.' He stopped her. 'I've known a while I think. I knew we were drifting apart, but I didn't really know how to stop it. I was pretty happy. I know I'm a bit set in my ways, but I did want to have a life with you. I think I was just too late.' He smiled ruefully, gesturing to the items around him. 'I came to get my things when you were working at the wedding, and I saw the memory box scattered everywhere.' He swallowed hard, like the next part physically hurt him. 'I read some of your stuff from when you were kids. I didn't realise you were such a good writer.'

He'd read her childhood stories. 'I'm really proud of you,' he said, his eyes a paler version of what I was used to seeing staring back at me. He looked washed out. 'I know you'll be amazing out there.' His smile is genuine. 'I found your letter too. The one you wrote when you were heading to uni. I sent your letter to the paper, Emily. I sent it to the email address, to Isaac.' He nodded to the box. 'You left the lid ajar the other night. I guess I knew on the double date that there was something there between you, and then I saw you'd been reminiscing. I knocked it by accident.' He tutted at himself. 'That's a lie. I guess I just wanted answers. I'm realising now I should have paid more attention before now. It's not all your fault, Emily. I messed up too. I wanted to make it right I guess. See what you did with the information.'

Emily covered her face with her hands, taking in everything he'd said. She couldn't just go now, to stop Cal. She would be the ultimate bitch if she just left him standing in her flat while she went to chase another man.

'I don't know what to say,' she started, but she knew he deserved better than that. 'I do actually.' She got to her feet, smoothing her hair back and looking Tim straight in the eye. 'I am sorry. I cheated on you. Not physically, but I did cheat. I never expected to feel like this. When he came back, I—'

One look at Tim told her that her words were cutting him, but he needed the truth. 'Before he came back even, I guess I wasn't happy, and that wasn't fair. I should have told you, but I guess that I just did what I've always done. I stayed quiet. I know it means nothing, but I really do mean it when I say I'm sorry. You deserve better.' She took off her engagement ring and held it out to him. He held out his palm after an eternity of silence, and she felt the relief once more as the ring left her possession. This was doing the right thing. She was always trying to do the right thing, but it was avoiding the pain she'd been struggling with.

Tim shook his head slowly, before finally dipping his chin and straightening up his already perfect suit. 'I can't lie and say that I've processed everything, but I sent that letter in because I think you need an answer to your question, and I know that I did. I sent it because then you'd know, and maybe then we'd, well … we'd all know.' He looked at the clock and then his watch, and back to her.

'Why are you here? Did you really not get my text?'

'What? No, my phone's dead, remember? Tim, I think we need to ta—'

'There's no time for this. I added something to the letter, a note when I sent it in. A meeting place and time.'

Emily's jaw dropped, and Tim nodded once. 'It's you he's going to meet, Emily.' He looked sad, and she wanted to cut her own heart out when everything clicked into place and she felt it leap. 'And you're late.' He walked over to the couch, grabbed her things, and put them into her hands. 'We can talk, later. I was hoping you just needed time, but … I want you to be happy, Emily. No matter what.'

He leaned in, and after kissing her on the forehead, he pulled away. 'Go, Emily, go and find out.'

Standing there in front of him, there were about a million things she wanted to say. She wanted to tell him everything right there and now, but when she opened her mouth to speak, she knew none of it really mattered right now. What would it change?

'Thank you, Tim,' she said, touching his cheek with the backs of her fingers. 'You really are a lovely man.'

He rolled his eyes but managed a smile as he stepped aside to let her leave.

'So, I've been told. I fear it will be the death of me.'

Emily squeezed his arm. 'Bye.'

'Bye. Good luck.' He gave her a weak thumbs up, and she left.

Closing her front door behind her, she sank against the door for a second. She felt the relief rush over her, as well as the guilt. She owed him a longer conversation one day. Bracing herself, she pushed all thoughts of break-ups behind her. She had a castle to get to, and another long conversation to get started.

Chapter 22

'What the hell were you thinking, running off like that? You know you and I don't work like that. If you have something to tell me, you say it. You scared the living crap out of me! The school were losing their minds! Who bolts a fence? You're not the cast of *Stranger Things* you know!'

'Dad, I had to come. She's going to be here! It's all part of the plan. I wish it could be inside though, it's bloody freezing up here!'

Isaac, wrapped in his black parka, grey bobble hat plonked on his dark head, shivered. He was evidently not happy about the cold.

'Language,' Calvin chided. 'It is bloody cold though. I don't remember it being this cold. Although, if you ever bunk off school again to come and meet a stranger, I want you to remember how bloody cold it is now. You should be in class, studying and being warm. And being a kid.' He rubbed at his arms again. It was a cold May day, and with the height he felt like the wind was licking at his very soul. 'I had to get my neighbours to drive me here. I was too bloody scared to drive!'

They were looking out over the ramparts, standing on the steel platform erected by the local preservation society to protect the ruins and enable visitor-friendly access. Down below, the car park was filling up fast, and from their lofty position they could see people walking up to the ruins. Some with dogs, others with banners. The Hebblestone community had seemingly come out in force to see their local YouTube celebrity finally get the girl.

She wasn't coming. Isaac was going to be crushed. He didn't want to think about what that meant for him. London and its anonymity held a certain appeal right now. He didn't even want to be here. He knew who he wanted, and she was never going to come. He just wasn't that lucky.

When school had called to say that Isaac had left the premises, his heart had stopped for a full minute. Alice and Jim had found him trying to open his car door with his phone and taken pity on him. Driving up to the school, he'd been taken to speak to Isobel and Kai. Isobel had given him nothing, but Kai folded like a cheap suit on interrogation.

Now he **was** here, reunited with his little runaway. He felt so mixed up, **but he** couldn't stop thinking about the letter, and the significance of the place. Was this real, or just some big prank? A publicity stunt perhaps? All sorts had crossed his mind, the most outlandish notion that this might be a comeback for the bobble hat streaker. Perhaps seeing a naked man's unmentionables run across the castle grounds would be preferable to being stood up in front of everyone. In front of his son, who was now doing star jumps to keep warm.

'If she doesn't come, I am going to blame you, you know, that right?' He eyeballed his son, and Isaac stopped jumping. 'When I'm stood up here alone, and the laughing stock of the media, I will blame you.'

'She'll come, Dad. Have faith.'

'Have faith! Huh!' He snorted so loudly Isaac laughed. 'It's not funny, Isaac,' he turned away from the crowds, keeping his stance relaxed so that everyone down below wouldn't realise that he was freaking out. He looked warily over the banister rail, wondering if he would make the evening news if he jumped off or vomited over the side. The fact that he was considering such options was lunacy. Plus, he had Isaac with him. He couldn't very well leave him standing there while he shimmied away. Even though it was the little turd's fault that he was here in the first place.

'What if it's not her, Isaac? This letter is old. It could be a huge mistake. Or a bad joke.' His face fell at the thought. It couldn't be though. That letter was like stepping back in time. He recognised her girlish scrawl on the pages. Letters forming words she'd never told him face to face.

'Emily will come, Dad. It's her. I know it. It's meant to be! She works at the paper! It's going to happen.'

'You really think so?'

Isaac looked at his dad as if he'd just sprouted up out of the ground. 'Definitely.'

'Really?'

'Daaa-ad! Yes! Be cool. You're sweating loads. It's getting a bit gross.'

Calvin tried to pull himself together, taking off his coat and laying it down by his feet. Leaning on the railing, he looked out over Hebblestone. The car park was full now, a small line of cars all indicating to join them. He could see a reporter down there too, speaking into a camera. He was about to show Isaac when he spotted a woman running through the crowd, pushing people out of her way as she headed towards them.

'Isaac? You see that?' He blinked like a tired toddler, trying to clear his vision and look again.

'Dad! It's her! Emily!' he shouted with cupped hands, and his dad didn't take his eyes off her. He walked alongside the railings, moving towards the walkway. Isaac fell into step alongside him, his phone coming out of his pocket, and he aimed towards the couple gravitating to each other.

They walked to the middle of the walkway step for step, neither one missing a step or blinking an eye. Calvin produced a piece of paper from inside his coat, and her heart stuttered. *The letter. My letter.*

There were ten short steps away from each other when he put his hand out to stop her. 'Wait.'

One shoe met the other as she came to an emergency stop.

'This letter … it's really from you?' He held the piece of paper aloft between them, and she nodded her head slowly.

'You know it is.'

'When?'

Her lips pursed. 'I wrote it after you left for university. I sent it to your dorm room.'

Calvin looked again at the letter, his face a mixture of awe and disbelief.

'I never got it. Emily, I never got this letter. If I'd got it, I would have replied. God, I would have replied. I'm so glad I got to see it.'

She smiled through watery eyes back at him. 'I gather that, now. It was Tim who sent it to the paper. I kept a copy, and he found it.'

Calvin's eyes widened. 'Tim?'

She nodded, looking behind her at the crowd, who were now chattering away and aiming smartphones in their direction. The news camera was pointing their way, the reporter looking straight at them. Their view couldn't beat the one she had right now. Her past, present and future standing in front of her with a look of astonishment and adoration across his features.

'Yep. Surprised me too. It's over between us. It had been for a while. I guess I just didn't face up to it. He's a good guy. I feel bad for hurting him. I needed to stop.'

'I think we're both a bit guilty of that. Hurting people. Getting it wrong.' He kept turning the letter over and over in his hands, but she could see the taut grasp in the whites of his fingers. 'I would have gotten in touch, you know, if I had gotten the letter. Why didn't you ever tell me? Ask me why I didn't reply?'

She looked back at the crowd and nodded in their direction.

'Believe it or not, I didn't want to embarrass myself.'

Calvin laughed, and she laughed along with him. 'I know, silly right? When you didn't mention the letter, I just thought you were sparing me from the embarrassment. And then you told me you'd met Diane, and that was it. I thought that was my answer, so I moved on.'

'You stopped writing as much.'

'It hurt too much.'

'I'm so sorry. I wish …'

'Stop. We're here now, right?'

'Here we are.' Those eyes again, claiming her for keeps. He took another step forward, and she matched him. 'So, you and Tim, it's really over?'

'It was over before you came to town, I guess I just didn't realise. Or I didn't want to. Things changed when you got back, Cal. I changed.'

'You seem just the same to me,' he uttered softly, taking two steps. She walked to match him till their shoes were inches apart. 'I don't think you changed that much. Still my Emily. I hid my love for you all over these walls.'

He tucked the letter into his pocket and reached for her cheek. As he cupped it in his hand, they could hear the crowd ripple with excitement. He glanced across at them, and then focused back on her features. She reached for his free hand and held it within her own.

'We have an audience; this lot aren't going to let this die down anytime soon. You're really sure you want all this? All of … us?'

She looked at the man she had loved since girlhood, his worried features roving hers for answers, and she found that she couldn't even hear the crowd anymore. It was just the pair of them, in this place that held so many precious memories. She lifted her hands to his cheeks, pulling him in and kissed him. Soft at first, but the minute her lips touched his, he reached for her and pulled her closer. The kiss said everything that she had

236

wanted to whisper to him for so long, but she didn't stop there. Dropping a kiss on his lips as she pulled away, she settled her hands on his shoulders.

'I love you, Calvin Albright. I've loved you since you were a geeky dork who loved to design skyscrapers instead of drinking in the park like the other boys. You're my best friend, Cal, and I will love you forever.'

Calvin beamed at her, grabbing her in his arms and lifting her off the ground. He twirled her around and then lowered her lips back to his. Kissing her tenderly as the crowd erupted into huge shouts of joy, a crescendo of clapping and whoops. Behind them, they heard a massive 'YEEEEEESSS! Finally!'

Pulling away reluctantly, Emily giggled as Isaac came bounding over, throwing his arms around the pair of them and wrapping them in parka-stuffed hugs.

'Hi, Isaac.' She ruffled his hair. 'So, what do you think of your plan?'

Isaac pulled his phone out and, after turning the screen to fit all three of them in, he hit record.

'Hi, guys! We did it!' He beamed into the camera, his dad and Emily at either shoulder. 'We got Dad a girlfriend! Woo-hoo!' He turned the screen round, heading off down the walkway to video the crowd. Calvin could see Alice and Jim calling to him, and he relaxed a little.

'Let him enjoy his moment; he's worked hard for this.'

'He's grown up a lot. I think we need to prepare for his teenage years.'

'Sounds like it will be a lot of fun. He's as stubborn as his dad too. Can't wait.'

Calvin tucked her into his shoulder, and they both headed back up to the top of the castle ramparts. Looking out over Hebblestone, everyone they knew and loved right below them was enjoying the excitement.

'I'm sorry about Tim,' he started, but she cut him off.

'You have nothing to be sorry for. He knew before I did, I think. I'm not proud of hurting him, but I couldn't shut up any longer.'

Taking her into his arms and kissing her senseless once more, he agreed heartily.

'Me neither. I love you.'

'I love you too. Kiss me again?'

His baby blue eyes locked on to hers. 'Never stop asking that question. It's sexy.'

Calvin kissed her, dropping a kiss onto her nose, and pulling her into his coat against the bite of the Yorkshire wind.

'Emily Hendrickson, I never plan to stop kissing you ever again.'

'Good.' She beamed. 'I didn't write that letter for nothing, and we have a lot of kisses to catch up on.'

'You're right there, bestie. Now, pucker up. We have an audience to say hello to.'

She sank into his arms as he reached for her again, the crowd cheering from below as the castle came to life under the ray from the bright blue Hebblestone skies.

Chapter 23

'Dennis, that's the second bacon sandwich you've had! Think of your cholesterol!'

Dennis, his mouth wrapped around a butty, still managed to roll his eyes at his daughter. Between chews, he beckoned to her.

'Emily, come over here and tell your mother to let me live! I only have bacon on a Sunday, and it's a football tradition now!'

Carole, who was unloading enough food to feed an army, brushed a crease out of her large tartan rug and tutted.

'Emily, you tell your father I made him Quorn bacon sandwiches, and I'll be telling the doctor about his "football supporting" on our next visit.' She turned to the pitch, where the boys were just coming back from their post-match coach talk. 'Isaac, I got you and the lads some snacks too.' She produced a large bag of sweets from her handbag, and Calvin groaned. Emily stroked the back of his head from her position next to him on their bench.

'Families eh?' She quipped, and he grinned, giving her a cheeky kiss before pulling her to her feet.

'The Albright and Hendrickson clan sure know how to rock the side of a pitch.' He looked across at Isaac, who was shovelling flying saucers down his throat. 'Easy on those, Zac. Your nana spoils you!'

That's what they were now: grandparents. Since Emily and Calvin had married, a year to the day after the castle, they were one big family. A growing family at that. Emily patted her growing stomach, laughing as Cal lowered his head instantly to talk to their unborn child. They'd found out the sex the second they could. They never wanted any secrets. Ever.

'She's going to spoil you too, little girl. Just you wait. This might be the last time you hear our voices. If Nana gets her way you'll both end up living with her. Isaac and his mates, and girlfriend Isobel, were always round there. Tinkering in the garage with Dennis, watching the football, getting spoiled by Carole. The last three years had been a whirlwind. Calvin's shopping centre project had been opened with great success, and Emily's career had taken off.

Since the fallout from the article, Joanna had given her the features writer position she'd longed for for so long. The local and national interest in their love story was immense, boosting the paper and Emily's work, and Emily found she couldn't *stop* writing. It was as though all of her insecurities had melted away. With Cal's encouragement, she'd even started writing her first book. A collection of short stories, all on the theme of love letters. It wasn't just that Cal returning had woken her up from her sleepy life, he'd reignited the girl she once was. With Cal and Isaac by her side, she felt ready to take on the world.

Isaac was a little YouTube celebrity now. MTV had been in touch to work with him, but Calvin and Isaac were happy to do things slowly till he'd got school done. He was a budding film-maker though, and Isobel and his friends were a solid little gang. They were always together, always up to antics. Isaac couldn't wait for his baby sister either. He was already planning her introduction to the world of cinema. He'd been planning what they would all do, and Cal's house, their forever house, was always full of life and colour, and noise. She couldn't wait to add their daughter to that.

It had been a rough first few weeks since the day at the castle.

240

The media frenzy was crazy, and they were fielding calls from agents and newspapers everywhere. It had launched Emily as a writer, and Cal was seen as the ultimate romantic hero. There were memes of him everywhere for weeks. Calvin was still bemused by the whole thing, but he was solid when it came to Emily. They were inseparable from that day on, Isaac making them the best little trio. They'd taken it slowly, been respectful to Tim and Isaac – although that was hard in itself, given the coverage.

Tim had been lovely. He could have sold his story, taken his heartbreak out on them, but that wasn't Tim. He was more hurt than she'd even known he'd be, and that was hard. She wished she'd found her voice sooner, spared him the pain.

Emily had sat down with him after the dust had settled and apologised again. And again. She'd felt awful; they both did. Calvin had insisted on going with her, to not let her face it alone. They'd thanked him for sending the note, and bringing them together, when it had cost him. Given that their lives were so separate financially, it wasn't a huge upheaval. They'd kept the money saved, and Tim had simply melted into the background. He'd refused to talk about anything to the press, only releasing a statement wishing them well, and stating that there were no bad feelings. It had made Emily feel guilty for a long time after, and Cal, but eventually, things had settled down in the town, and the sight of them together became natural. Just like it did had been when they were growing up.

It was amazing how things had changed. She'd blown her life apart, and now she had everything she'd ever wanted. She and Cal couldn't bear to be apart, him working from home when he could. He found that he loved his house now. It was full of life, and colour, and love. He didn't want to be anywhere else. The ex-wedding reporter and the widow were finally together, and neither one of them wanted to waste a second. They knew how precious life was, and how funny the twists and turns could be.

One of the last weddings she'd covered had been Tim's. Tim's and Pippa's. They lived just a few streets away from Calvin and her now, and she waved to them both when they passed in their cars. It felt like another life to them both now. She would always be grateful to Tim. He'd brought her closer to all this.

Looking around her, Calvin laughing with her parents, one hand on her knee. He always had to be near her, to touch her in some way, as though reminding himself that she was here. And his. She knew, because she did the same. She couldn't wait to bring their daughter into the world, and she loved Isaac so much. They had the best relationship, often ganging up on Calvin with hilarious results. She just knew her daughter would wrap both men around her little finger. It was going to be great.

Her dad came to sit next to her later, when her mother was laughing at Isaac and Calvin. They were having a game of goalie, and Calvin was not coming off well after the amount of food he'd just eaten. He shuffled close, wrapping his big arm around her.

'You did well, love. I love this.'

She felt him squeeze her shoulder and smiled at him. He gave her a wink, and they laughed together as Calvin took the ball on the forehead and hit the ground like a rag doll.

'I love it too, Dad. We've come a long way since prom.' Looking at Cal, blowing her a kiss before tackling Isaac to the ground and bellowing like a gorilla, Emily couldn't agree more. They'd come home to roost, but they weren't chickens anymore.

Acknowledgements

As ever, a huge thanks to my editor Belinda Toor, and the entire team at HQ Stories for their continued support, effort and hard work. You help make every book shine. Never change!

Huge thanks to my fellow writers at the Romantic Novelists' Association, and to all my amazing readers and blogger friends. You fill my days with laughs, I love you all.

As ever, love and thanks to my family and friends in Yorkshire, and to my local library service who are amazing.

With each book, I have a tribe of supportive people cheering me on, and the romance loving gang are the biggest cheerleaders going! Big mwah to you all.

And dear reader, thank you for taking adventures with me. I hope you enjoyed this one. I'm already excited about our next trip away from reality!

Keep reading for an excerpt from
The Second Chance Hotel …

RACHEL DOVE

The Second Chance Hotel

To You

If I was writing this letter under better circumstances, I could have written a much better opening. I'm sitting here on my bunk trying to think of what to say. I don't even know what to call you. I know we have to be careful. If I could, I would say your name over and over for the rest of my life. How lucky people who see you every day are, for they get to say it willy-nilly.

For you, nothing seems appropriate, or enough, so I decided that You will have to do. My You. My one and only You.

I have the shell you pressed into my hand that night, and I haven't stopped looking at it. It smells of you, of home, and it makes me feel like my recurring nightmare was just that, and that my real life is still there, at Shady Pines with you.

How long do we have left, till the letters have to stop? I fear the day, yet I know it must come. You must live your life, and I should at least try to start mine. Even with the huge You-shaped hole in my soul. Don't tell me, not till you have to. While you're free, let's pretend, just you and Me.

G

Chapter 1

April Statham sat as close to the steering wheel as she could get, nudging herself and her clapped-out brown Ford Escort along the road, turning slowly into the entrance to the chalet park. Unfortunately, a few seconds earlier, a horse rider had passed, and now his steed was going to the toilet in the middle of the road, leaving a huge steaming pile of horse plop right in the entranceway. April wasn't really one to believe in signs, but this was kind of hard to miss.

'Er …' She wound her window down. 'Excuse me?' The horse, and the rider, a thin man whose long features mirrored that of his thoroughbred, dipped their heads to look at her. 'Could you possibly move your horse? I need to pass.'

The horse snorted loudly. Or was it the rider? Both parties looked equally nonplussed, but the man nodded once and the horse trotted away, leaving his … offerings. April turned the car into the lane, avoiding the pile, and headed for the large wooden hut marked 'Reception'.

'Bloody great pile of steaming poo in the entrance, great advert for the place,' she muttered under her breath, her eyes flicking down to her petrol gauge, which was pointed straight at zero. Past zero, truth be told. She could feel the change in the engine, the car chugging along on petrol fumes. She pulled into the space marked 'Management' in between the reception hut and a small chalet. She yanked up the handbrake and turned the key in the ignition to off. She could swear that her car breathed a sigh of relief as the engine cut out. They had made it, her and her little car, all the way from Yorkshire to the tip of the Cornish coast. She sat back in her seat, her limbs and back stiff and wizened, as though she had been tied in a knot somewhere along the A38 and had driven bunched up like a pretzel ever since.

She was just easing the knots out of her neck when a sharp tap on her window made her jump. A woman stood there, her face pinched up tight, her dark hair tied into curling rollers on her head. She was wearing a pink dressing gown and dark green wellies, and looked more than a little crazy, even at 8 a.m. on a Monday morning. April wound her window down wearily, plastering a patient smile on her face.

'Are you lost?' the woman said pointedly, looking from inside the car to the boxes and suitcases strapped to a roof rack that April had nabbed from a Freecycle site. Her suitcases came from there too, with her not wanting to take the monogrammed luggage set she had been given as a wedding present. His and hers. She'd left it next to Duncan's in the detached garage. Camped out in her late mother's house. They'd looked so pathetic sitting there together, never to be used again, as they once were on honeymoon, and on their exotic holidays and horrifying business trips he'd dragged her along on.

'No,' said April. *Yes, I am a bit. I think I've made a big mistake.* 'I'm not lost.'

The woman looked again at the worldly belongings strapped to the roof and sighed, a small unsympathetic sigh that made April feel about an inch tall.

'Well—' the woman raised her eyebrows again '—you look lost. Can I call someone for you? We're expecting the hotshot new owner at some point today.'

'I'm the new owner,' April tried, her voice a faint whisper. 'I own this place.'

The woman, having caught the gist now, looked at her with wide eyes.

'You?' She leaned into the car window, her head floating there like a balloon. 'You—' punctuated by a jab of the finger in her direction '—actually bought this place?'

April nodded slowly. The woman began to laugh.

'Pull the other one, love, it's got bells on.' She guffawed, her face looming in April's window like an animal in a safari park now. A camel sprang to mind. Something that could spit at you from ten paces if it saw fit. Yanking her head back out, the woman tapped twice on the top of April's car and carried on her way, disappearing as quickly as she had appeared.

April was suddenly alone again, wondering what the hell she had gotten herself into. *Hotshot new owner? What had the camel … er … the woman heard?* April didn't want to ruffle any feathers here before she had even unpacked so much as a solitary toilet roll. Why did she think April was a hotshot? *Oh God.* She'd said 'we'. 'We have been waiting for the new owner.' Who were 'we'? The woman had obviously found her lacking, and once more, April's eyes turned to her phone, sitting there innocently in her handbag. It looked so normal, but April felt as though the damn thing was a ticking time bomb waiting to explode on her frazzled brain with an influx of messages. Posts on social media of 'you okay, hon?' People commenting on her life, strangers and people who didn't know her well at all. Not the real her, and nothing like the post-divorce her. Emails from old acquaintances. Purchase reminders for occasions she didn't need to be reminded of at all. Ever. It would all be in there, lurking.

It had been bad enough already, without her sudden departure from everything and everyone. Divorce was a great vehicle for gossip, her mum had told her. Boy, was she right, as ever. April had turned all her notifications off. If she didn't need to use the

251

damn thing to navigate, she would probably have pitched it into the nearest and deepest river she could find.

Soon, news of her escape would spread around her hometown, and the gossip would start again. *She couldn't have kids, you know. Tried for years, they did. Broke them apart. Still, his new girlfriend seems lovely. Child-bearing hips, that one. Shame about April, though. She never did quite fit in.* They chatted on social media as if they were in the hairdresser's or in the Post Office queue. *What was it that Gran used to tell me? Oh yeah. Loose lips sink ships. No wonder I feel like a crap second-hand dinghy with a Hello Kitty plaster holding in my deflated soul.*

They'd be feasting soon, beaks sharply stuck in everyone else's business. Just like the buzzards to return to a carcass in the hope they'd missed a piece of flesh, a strip of soft underbelly to rip from the bones of her failed life. She had failed as a wife, as a—

April stopped that train of thought by grabbing her phone and jabbing the off button hard, till the screen powered down. She didn't need her map app now, so why would she leave it on to tick away like a telltale heart? She felt instantly better. She was gone, out of their reach. She'd rather thought that being 'off grid' would make her feel a tad edgy or a bit hippyish, but instead, she just felt relief. Bone-deep relief. Un-contactable. Freeeeeeee! Relief that she wouldn't have to endure their pitying stares and sympathetic nods, complete with the 'little rub'. People thought that rubbing your arm or your shoulder was comforting, but it was just a bit too condescending for April. She hated it more than anything. She felt like a simpleton half the time after they had descended on her. What a joy life could be After Duncan. AD. Life after husband.

Zipping up her oversized handbag, she looked once more out of the window at the corner of the world she would now call home. It looked a little like how she felt: neglected, empty, peeling at the corners. Muted against the blue of the sky above. She pulled herself out of the car, her bones popping and cracking as her body unfurled itself. She could feel the shale beneath her feet, her black and white sneakers crunching as she looked around her. The Shady Pines Chalet Park was perched on a beautiful strip of land near Lizard Point, Kynance Cove a short distance away. From the park, April knew from memory that there was a direct walkway to the beach area, for the use of her guests. It had been there for many years and was one of the biggest selling points to her, the thought of waking up and having her toes in the water to start her day right.

Stretching her legs, she walked slowly to the reception hut, brand-new keys in hand. She'd picked them up from a key safe at the estate agent's that morning, and now here she was, about to start her new life. Taking a gulp of the sharp sea air deep into her lungs, she unlocked the door. The key slotted into the metal housing like a glove. There was a slight resistance, salt in the old locks making the mechanisms stick, but then she felt it turn, and the lock click open. It was times like this, right now, that April felt like she had done something right, for once. She'd done this; she was here. It was all hers, a new life for the taking. If she hadn't sworn off social media, she would have snapped a photo of the moment for Instagram with a witty hashtag like #divorcerules or #suckonthatduncanyouutterwan—

Maybe not. Not like she threw herself a divorce party, was it? She'd spent half the day crying, the rest feeling completely out of her depth. She obviously wasn't feeling #blessed quite yet, but she could fake it for now. This was her new life; it was time to get cracking. Pushing open the door, she took a step forward … and hit the deck with a very loud and dusty bang.

'Ouch! Broken boobs!' April shouted, or tried to shout. Since her face was smushed into the now broken wooden door, it came out as a muffled humming sound. Prising her lips off the peeling paint, she pushed herself up on her arms and inspected the damage. The whole door had collapsed, the hinges still attached to the door beneath her. Standing, she inspected the wooden frames and saw that the wood was old, brittle to the touch. It crumbled to dust and fell through her fingers.

'Great,' she grumbled under her breath. 'Better find a carpenter pretty sharpish, before the rest of my life turns into the bottom of a rabbit hutch.' She heaved up the door, resting it on her face at one point to get a better handle on the heavy wood. Placing it to one side of the room with a loud bang, she looked at the dust on her plain black T-shirt and old blue jeans and sighed. She brushed herself down, gingerly around the already bruising chest area.

'Well,' she said to the room, looking around. 'Cheers for the excellent welcome, new home. Be careful, or I will use the last of my money to have a wood chipper party, right here.' She pointed her finger to the centre of the floor and braced herself, but the ceiling didn't fall in. Phew.

The reception hut was deceptively large, a square room with a desk off to the left-hand side, complete with a counter in the same faded white-painted wood as the rest of the place. Off to the right, against the wall, were rows of shelving, all empty and filled with dust. The floor was the same white wood, giving the whole room a cube-like effect, and making April feel a bit hemmed in for a second.

There were windows behind the desk on the left, and on the back wall opposite the door was a large set of glass-panelled doors, leading out to a grassed area out of the back. The chalet park ran on the green grass like a horseshoe, twenty blue-and-white trimmed identical chalets, all with their own porches and back patio areas for dining out and sunbathing. Where the ends of the horseshoe met, on the left was the sign indicating the park, with a rack that must have once been used for bicycles alongside it. It was metal and had been painted cream at one point, with pretty shell details around the lettering. Currently, it looked a little worse for wear, the paint peeling and rust-coloured. There was a lone rubber tyre and a dented shopping basket using the facilities, and the sign was tilted to one side, looking as though it was hanging on with the one rusty protruding nail that was still attached. To the right of this was the reception, and on the other side of this, her chalet. It matched the others and looked just as dilapidated. Through the dusty doors, she could see the blue sky and the grass expanse beneath, leading off to the track to the beach. The beach where her mother had taken her, that first night here all that time ago.

It had nearly been dark, the sun setting slowly on their first long day in Cornwall. April had been tired. She remembered how cloudy her head had felt, how she'd moaned when her mother wanted them to see the sunset together.

'When are we going home?' She could hear her little voice now, remembered how her mother ignored her at first. Her back to her, facing the fading sun, head tilted up like a flower head. Her mother's fists clenched when she asked again, her voice whinier, higher. It sounded at odds to the crashing of the waves, the laugh-like call of the birds ahead.

The clenched fists were only there a second, but April thought of her father and shrank back. Her mother turned, but her face was kind.

'April, come here, petal.' April went to her mother, and she turned them back to face the chalet park. Other families were in the chalets, or out on their patios. Playing cards, having a glass of wine. Laughing as the kids played. They passed them on the way to the shore, and the happy noises of life filtered down to the beach.

Hands on her daughter's shoulders behind her, her mother spoke. Her voice sounded different. Louder, somehow.

'You hear that?' she asked, gentler now.

'The sea?'

'The people, April. You hear the people up there?'

April looked past the dunes, where the lights from the park could be seen. She could hear the sounds of people talking, laughing, kids screeching with joy as they played and ran about.

'Yes,' she said, her mouth curving into a smile.

'That's what life is supposed to be like, April. I want you to look around you, my girl, soak it in. I want this for you, all of this. We're not going home, April. It's just going to be me and you from now on, and we'll be just fine.' Her mother squeezed her shoulders, a loving gesture that warmed April through as the words washed over her like the waves behind her. 'This is our second chance hotel, sweetheart. New life starts right here.'

* * *

April's feet were moving, heading for the glass doors, key in hand, before she even registered the urge overtaking her body. This was what had been keeping her going, thinking of seeing that beach. Feeling the wind whip her shoulder-length brunette hair around her face, walking barefoot along the sand. She loved the beach, and always had – she thought back to the long summers she had enjoyed growing up. Crabbing off the docks, swimming in the clear blue waters, curling up with a fire and a hot chocolate on a dark night. After that summer at Shady Pines, the two of them had visited every beach they could find. She envied the child she had been, all innocent and full of hope. What did she have now? Besides wood rot, of course?

This, that's what.

As she pushed on the doors, they resisted at first, stuck fast with dirt and grime, but then she gave them a shove and she was outside, half running across the grass as she shoved her keys into her bra and picked up the pace. Walking out of those doors felt like stepping out onto the moon's surface. The grass led to a path cut out of the rocks and wild tufts, the thick carpet of green blades giving way to sandy dunes the closer she got. She kicked her shoes off, not giving a toss where they landed, and once her bare feet hit the wet sandy beach, she whooped with delight.

'I'm here, Shady Pines!' she yelled, her jean bottoms getting flicked with the sand she was casting off in her run to the sea. 'I'm really here!'

The sharp shock of the cold water took her breath away momentarily, and she squealed to herself. After a few gentle steps, she felt her whole body sigh with the pleasure of the sensations. This was her favourite place, by the sea. She loved it, had always loved it, and once more she found herself marvelling at the journey she had just undertaken. A year ago, she would have laughed in the face of anyone who told her the story. It would have seemed so unbelievable, so daring. Like a lifestyle piece in the magazines she used to read, once upon a time. Before they seemed to mock her, show her what she was missing. When your life didn't follow the usual expected path, where did that leave a modern woman? The knackers yard? Spinsterhood? She wasn't ready to start knitting a straitjacket just yet, thank you very much. She still felt twenty-one most days.

Not today though. Today she felt about eight years old, holding her mother's hand while she paddled in the sea, tiny toes wrinkling in the water. She felt brilliant. Right now, standing there in the sea, her old life miles away and out of reach, she felt amazing. This was day one of her new life. Peeling paint and broken doors be damned. Duncan seemed like a bad dream right now. Hoping the feeling would last once reality set in, she smiled to herself, turning to walk further along the shoreline, to leave her footprints in the sand, and make her own mark.

Dear Reader,

We hope you enjoyed reading this book. If you did, we'd be so appreciative if you left a review. It really helps us and the author to bring more books like this to you.

Here at HQ Digital we are dedicated to publishing fiction that will keep you turning the pages into the early hours. Don't want to miss a thing? To find out more about our books, promotions, discover exclusive content and enter competitions you can keep in touch in the following ways:

JOIN OUR COMMUNITY:

Sign up to our new email newsletter:
http://smarturl.it/SignUpHQ

Read our new blog www.hqstories.co.uk

🐦 https://twitter.com/HQStories

📘 www.facebook.com/HQStories

BUDDING WRITER?

We're also looking for authors to join the HQ Digital family!
Find out more here:

https://www.hqstories.co.uk/want-to-write-for-us/

Thanks for reading, from the HQ Digital team

If you enjoyed *The Forever House*, then why not try
another delightfully uplifting romance
from HQ Digital?